To Don,
Best Wishes
Jerome Court

Also by Jerome Arthur

*Antoine Farot and Swede*
*Life Could be a Dream, Sweetheart*
*One and Two Halves*
*The Muttering Retreats*
*The Journeyman and the Apprentice*
*The Death of Soc Smith*
*The Finale of Seem*
*Oh, Hard Tuesday*
*Got no Secrets to Conceal*
*Brushes with Fame*

# Down the Foggy Ruins of Time

A Novel

Jerome Arthur

*Down the Foggy Ruins of Time*
Revised Third Edition 2019

Published by Jerome Arthur
P.O. Box 818
Santa Cruz, California 95061
831-425-8818
www.JeromeArthurNovelist.com
Jerome@JeromeArthurNovelist.com

Dedicated to my mother

## Acknowledgments

I wish to acknowledge the invaluable editorial assistance of Morton Marcus, and special thanks to muralist John Ton for the cover art. I would also like to thank Kenny Mais for his help with the some of the research.

# One

For thirteen of the first fifteen years of my life I was confused about my cultural identity. I met George Nieto when I was two and a half years old, and I got it into my head that I was a Mexican, not the American-Franco/German that I, in fact, was. My fair complexion, and brown hair and eyes betrayed me throughout life. I wasn't ashamed of my heritage, and I did indeed love my parents and grandparents. In fact, the French part was actually pretty cool because I saw it as my hereditary link to Latin culture, and the same goes for the Catholic religion I'd been baptized into, but those two things didn't alter the genetic reality of my situation. And the fact that my childhood screen heroes were guys like Leo Carrillo, Anthony Quinn and Jay Silverheals didn't make me either a Mexican or a native north American, no matter how much I wanted it to be so. My problem was that I lived in a light beige skin, surrounded by family, friends and neighbors of a similar shade, but mentally, I was a Mexicano, or at the very least, an American-Mexican.

*Jerome Arthur*

I was lucky to be born in Minneapolis, Minnesota. Lucky, that is, because Minneapolis was then and still is a town that's steeped in Native American culture and myth. The birth took place in the front room of my grandparents' house seven and a half months before Japanese warplanes made their attack on Pearl Harbor. I've always felt fortunate to be born in the house because it stood on land that was farmed and hunted on by tribesmen of the Sioux nation long before my European ancestors even knew it existed.

It was an auspicious and interesting beginning. According to my mother, my actual birth had been an easy one. It was just a long time coming; I was almost a month overdue. It happened on a Monday afternoon as the springtime bloomed. Grandma was waiting at the bus stop as my mom and my big brother, Frank, got off the bus. Grandma pulled Frank and her youngest daughter, my Aunt Jessie, back to her house in a red wagon. My mom walked the one block down to her doctor's office on the corner of Queen Avenue and Lowry Avenue.

I've always carried a picture in my mind's eye of Francesca on that day, bracing her lower back, palms flat on her high rump, elbows akimbo, toes pointing slightly outward, as she waddled off down the street. I don't doubt she felt bad about her dumpy appearance that afternoon, but I'm sure she also had a strong sense of the bloom that pregnancy

## Down the Foggy Ruins of Time

bestows on a woman. When she wasn't pregnant, which is the only way I ever saw her, she was really beautiful—an absolute knockout. She was five feet four inches tall, and she weighed around a hundred and ten pounds. Her light brown hair, medium-length with a permanent wave, soft brown eyes, and creamy-smooth skin all highlighted her Judy Garland smile.

After the exam and the doctor's reassurance that everything was fine, even though she was in her tenth month, she left his office, cut through the Cleveland school playground, and walked the other half block to my grandma's house. I must've heard this story a half dozen times from as many points of view when I was a little kid. Mom told it to me first, having experienced it from beginning to end. Grandma, Antoine (that's my dad), and Grandpa each added his or her own twist to the tale. They were there, too.

"When I got to the top of the steps, I pulled open the screen door, and my water broke right when I turned the doorknob," Francesca said in her Minnesota/Great Lakes accent. "I pushed the door open and called out to Ma. She was fixin' dinner. Frank and Jessie were out in the backyard with Pa and all my brothers and sisters, except Helen. They were all there, you know? Ma came out of the kitchen on the run to help me get to the couch. Then she hurried out to the front porch and called out to Mrs.

Rungren, next door. She had a telephone, so she called the doctor."

Grandma came back into the house just in time to be my mom's midwife. By the time Mrs. Rungren arrived on the scene, I was already born. She also had an anecdote about that day. When I was eight years old, we were back in Minneapolis for my Uncle Danny's ordination into the priesthood. At a party at Grandma's house, Mrs. Rungren told a gathering in the living room all about it.

"We were lucky the doctor didn't leave his office yet," Mrs. Rungren said. "When I phoned him, he said he'd get an ambulance out here, and he'd come right over for an emergency house call. I hung up and rushed over here, but I was too late because you were already born. You gave me a bit of a scare. When I first saw you, it looked like your umbilical cord was around your neck, but it wasn't, and you were fine. Such a big baby. You were crying. You wanted to be fed."

"Jeekers!" Grandma said. "You were a fat little baby, and you were hungry from the start. I was in the kitchen gettin' dinner ready. Danny was right there at the dining room table doing his homework. All the other kids were in the backyard with Conrad. Just as soon as I got Frannie settled on the davenport, your little head popped out, and the next thing I knew, I was holdin' you in my arms."

## Down the Foggy Ruins of Time

Since it was a late Monday afternoon, so close to the dinner hour, all but one of my mom's siblings were around the house. Helen, the next in age to Francesca, missed it because she was a University of Minnesota coed and lived on campus. Danny, who was graduating from high school in June and going to seminary in September, was the second person after Grandma to see me. Maddy (short for Madeleine), Luke, Casey and Edith, tenth grade, eighth grade, fifth grade and second grade respectively all came in to stare in wonder and awe at the goings-on on the living room davenport. Jesse and Frank were there, too, but they were only two years old, so who knows how much they knew about what was going on?

The doctor showed up ten minutes later. He immediately cut and tied off my umbilical cord. Then he did all of his checking with the stethoscope, and Grandma and Mrs. Rungren cleaned up the afterbirth with the water Grandma had heated on the stove while she was waiting for him to show.

I wasn't fifteen minutes old and already suckling when Dad showed up. He was a pressman's feeder at a big printing company in downtown Minneapolis named Brown and Bigelow, trying, without much success, to break into the lithographers union. Minneapolis was a union town, and the only way you could get anywhere in the printer's union in those days was if you were related to someone in the

11

hierarchy. Needless to say, Antoine didn't have relatives, or friends for that matter, anywhere in the hierarchy, but he did know a couple of guys in the rank and file.

He knew how to run a press and he should have been an apprentice pressman like his buddies in the union, but since he couldn't gain membership, he was stuck as a feeder. The feeder was the guy who oiled the press first thing in the morning, and then he kept paper-loaded skids fed into it for an eight-hour shift. When the paper came out all printed up at the other end, the feeder then unloaded it and muscled it over to the bindery. When I was in high school, I got a job as a feeder in one of the print shops where Antoine worked, so I know, first hand, how hard the work is. For him it was back-breaking labor that barely paid a subsistence wage, but he considered himself lucky to even have a job, because, as far as he was concerned, the Depression was still going on, and he had no idea then that it would end in just seven and a half months.

The first time I heard the story of my father's arrival at my birth, I tried to imagine how he looked that day. Antoine was a wiry little guy who bore a strong resemblance to James Cagney in facial features, stature and attitude. His thinning, black hair was parted on the left and combed straight back on the sides and top, and it was such a contrast to his white skin that it made his cobalt blue eyes really

## Down the Foggy Ruins of Time

stand out. I'm sure he was hunched and hobbled that afternoon after eight hours on the job. I picture him straightening up and coming alive at the sight of his newborn son as he came into a house that hummed with women, children and childbirth.

"I got there before the ambulance," Antoine said at Danny's ordination gathering in Grandma's living room. "What a little roly poly you was! Prit'near tipped the scales at twelve pounds!" My dad always liked to exaggerate. "The cord just bare-ly cut, and already you was suckin' on your ma's tit. Your curled-up little fingers were on each side of your head, tryin' to get a-hold a' that tit. I stuck my baby finger into one of your hands, and you just grabbed onto it and squeezed to beat hell. Then you pulled your face away from that tit and hauled off and gave me a big grin, and not a tooth in your head."

Grandpa—his name was Conrad Konig—had been home from work since three-thirty. He was out in the backyard with the kids when all the ex-citement started. He was also a little guy, but he was stockier than my dad and he had a potbelly. He had about an inch and a half of wispy, gray hair that wrapped around the back of his head from one tem-ple to the other. He and Grandma both had soft brown eyes, framed by rimless wire bifocals. They both also had false teeth from a young age. Grandpa and Grandma—her name was Gretchen—were both

13

a couple of inches taller than Mom, and Grandma probably weighed more than Grandpa. He looked like a cross between Elmer Fudd and Mister Magoo. Grandma, on the other hand, could've doubled for Marjorie Main in her role as Ma Kettle.

"I be jiggered if you wasn't a picture of contentment, nursin' the way you was," Grandpa said. "And so alert, too. Seemed like you knew what was goin' on around you from the first day on."

At ten to six an ambulance pulled up at the curb. The attendants wheeled Mom and me out to it on a gurney. The doctor walked alongside the gurney and got in the back of the ambulance with us. After he made arrangements with Grandma and Grandpa to leave Frank with them, Dad followed us to the hospital in the car. Mom got settled in her room, and I was taken to the nursery where I was weighed (eleven pounds two ounces) and measured (twenty-two inches). Dad took care of the paperwork for the birth certificate. I was named after him: Jerôme Antoine Farot (his name was Antoine Georges Farot, and he was proud of his French heritage, thus the circumflex over the O in my name).

I was the healthiest of the three babies my mom had. My older brother Frank was born five weeks premature, spent a month and a half in the incubator, and, according to Antoine, was still small enough to fit into a shoe box when they brought him home from the hospital. My younger brother André

## Down the Foggy Ruins of Time

was born with one lung and died when he was only six months old. Mom was in hard labor for hours with my two brothers and only a few minutes with me.

Frank's full name was Franklin Paul Farot. He was named after President Roosevelt, who was Antoine's idol. Dad rode the rails from Minneapolis to Seal Beach, California when he was fifteen years old. He left Seal Beach a year later and went up into the Owens Valley to work in a C.C.C. camp. He told the story many times over the years of how he once shook hands with Roosevelt when he came touring the camp. He thought the guy was great, or as he put it himself countless times through the years, "Franklin Delano Roosevelt was one hell of a swell fella'." Frank's middle name came from Paul Konig, who was Mom's cousin and Dad's best friend.

I don't remember too much about those early years in Minneapolis. Because I've always been such a warm-weather person, I find it ironic that the only two memories that remain are snow memories. It was probably our last winter living there. I was freezing, and I didn't like it one bit. My Latin blood was rebelling. One night right after a fresh snowfall, a pregnant Francesca with Frank and me in tow got off of a city bus. As it pulled away from the corner, the reek of acrid diesel wafted in the air and clashed with the crisp, fresh smell of the new fallen snow. Every time I've ever been in the snow and smelled its fresh scent, I'm reminded of that night those many years ago.

The only other memory I have from that time is of one snow-covered day when we were at Grandma's house. As Mom and Grandma sat over steaming coffee mugs at the dining room table, Frank, Jessie and I wrestled Uncle Casey's skis up the basement steps. The coal furnace roared on that cold winter day, emitting the smell of coal gas, heating the dank, musty basement as well as the house above. That day must have been a coal delivery day because the stuff was piled almost to the lip of the coal chute. When we got the skis out the back door at the top of the basement steps, the freezing cold took my breath away. It didn't even seem to faze Jessie and Frank. We took the skis around front and tried to use them like toboggans to go down the five-foot embankment from Grandma's front yard to the sidewalk. We weren't too successful as the skis were probably at least six feet long. Frank and Jessie were having a great time, but I was miserable from the cold. I yearned for the desert, yet I knew nothing about it.

I don't remember a thing about my little brother André. He was named after our other grandpa André Farot. His middle name was Georges, after Dad, and he was born twenty-two months after me. He only lived for six months. One-night Mom went in to check on him in his crib, and he lay dead, the

## Down the Foggy Ruins of Time

result of complications from having just one lung. That was a defining moment in my mother's life and the event that finally convinced her and my dad to leave Minneapolis and head for Southern California. America was fully engaged in the wars in Europe and the Pacific, and Antoine had heard that there were good job opportunities at the naval shipyard in Long Beach. His job at Brown and Bigelow was more than ever a dead end, and Mom just wanted to get out of Minneapolis and get shut of the reminders of her late infant son.

So, they packed as much as they could get into the thirty-six Packard Dad was driving at the time, tied a loaded steamer trunk to the rear bumper, and one morning in late September the four of us headed west and south. I don't remember anything about that trip, but Mom later told me that when we crossed over the Rocky Mountains, I was getting some pretty bad nose bleeds which scared her a couple of times. We were otherwise lucky, driving away from winter, and actually winning the race with the weather, making it to warm and sunny Long Beach by the middle of the first week of October with no car trouble, not even a flat tire.

# Two

For my parents our two years in Long Beach were prosperous and successful, and for me a lot of fun. Some of my happiest childhood memories are from that time. It was when I met George Nieto. For the first time in my life I had a playmate other than my brother Frank or my aunt Jessie. My parents rented a California bungalow on Cota Avenue on the westside, not far from the shipyard at Terminal Island. George lived in the house next door. He was born in Long Beach, but both of his parents were born in México. His dad came to California from San Luís Potosí when he was two years old, and he grew up in Long Beach with his uncle's family. His mother was twenty-one when she came up from Guaymas. They were about the same age as my parents, mid-twenties. George was their only child.

He and I were the same age—two and a half when my family moved into the neighborhood and four when we left and the Nietos stayed. We took to each other right away. The fence between the two houses had some pickets broken out, so we both had easy access to each other's backyard. We mostly just

## Down the Foggy Ruins of Time

hung out at his place. When we played cowboys and
Indians, we'd trade roles so that he was the cowboy
and I got to be the Indian. It was cool! As the
months passed, we'd venture out front to the sidewalk and go to the little grocery store a block down
on the corner of Anaheim Street and buy some
Flears bubble gum or penny Tootsie Rolls.

By Christmas, only two months after we'd
moved there, George and I had become constant
playmates. It seemed like throughout the two years
that we lived next door to each other, I was spending
more time at his house than he was at mine (I really
felt comfortable there more in my own element), so I
was getting exposed to all kinds of cool stuff, like
the kid-size burritos Señora Nieto served us for
lunch. She made the beans from scratch, simmering
a bag of pinto beans in water on the stove. As we
ate, I'd watch her through the kitchen door, grinding
corn in a stone molcajete with frontera music playing in the background on a Mexican radio station out
of Los Angeles. We'd have some pan dulce after we
finished our burritos.

I spent the morning of Christmas day with
my family. We opened our presents, and then we got
dressed and went to Mass at Saint Lucy's. After
Mass Frank and I fooled around with the presents
we'd gotten from Mom and Dad. Around noon I
went next door, but before George and I could get
out to the backyard, Señora Nieto made us sit down
in the breakfast nook in the kitchen, and she served

us some delicious tamales she'd made the night before.

"Take some salsa, mijito," she said to me, as she helped both of us peel the cornhusks off of our tamales. "It's rreeally gooodt."

At the same time, I was hanging out with George, Frank was hanging around with a bully who lived halfway between us and the corner grocery. The guy was a real jerk. He was a big kid for his age, very intimidating with Norse blond hair and eyes as cold and blue as frozen ponds. One day when George and I were on our way down to the store, Frank and his pal tried to stop us from going through on the sidewalk. It was our last summer in Long Beach, two weeks before the Enola Gay delivered her payload. Frank and his buddy were hanging around on the guy's front porch, and as we approached, they ran out to the sidewalk and blocked our way. If we wanted to get around them, we'd have to go out into the street, and our mothers had told us to stay out of the street. As we were dodging around trying to get past this six-year-old punk and my brother, the punk says,

"Hey, Frank. How's come your little brother hangs around with beaners all'a time? Wha', is he a beaner, too?"

"I don't know," Frank said, playing dumb.

Then George and I split up and managed to get around them without going into the street. They didn't bother to chase after us; they didn't have that long of an attention span. When we left the store, we

## Down the Foggy Ruins of Time

went around the block to get back home. That way we didn't have to mess with them again. But what a jerk that guy was for calling George a beaner. I'd never heard that word before, so I didn't know what it meant, but by the way the guy snarled when he spoke it, I knew it wasn't good. I hated him for barking his ugly word at us, but at the same time, I was proud to be included with George in its use. If that's what George was, then that's what I was, too. And Frank just stood by and listened to that kind of talk and didn't say anything against it. This incident was my first realization of who my true brother was.

"Hey, George. What's a beaner?" I asked.

"Don' know," he said and smiled.

His white teeth and pink gums were a sharp contrast to his brown skin, black hair and dark eyes. I remember thinking how lucky he was to look like that. I wished I could look just like him, so for many years after that, I worked diligently on my tan, which turned out to be a mistake because I got malignant melanoma when I reached middle age.

Antoine had steady work at the shipyard for twenty-two months, and there was a lot of overtime too, so he seemed to have plenty of money through that whole period. Mom was busy being a housewife and mother and doing a hell of a good job of it. Unfortunately, Dad wasn't saving anything against the day when the war ended and he'd lose his job, so when that day came, we were suddenly just as poor as we'd been back in Minneapolis when he was a pressman's gopher. Between all the good times I was having with George and the year-round, warm, sunny days of Southern California, I really didn't notice our slip back into poverty. It just wasn't something that I was paying a whole lot of attention to. I did notice little things here and there that informed me that life was going to be different than it had been the past two years, like Mom adding water to an almost-empty quart bottle of milk so that Frank and I would have enough for our Wheaties.

If Antoine had been able to get work there, we might never have left Long Beach, but with the closing of the shipyard, there were suddenly hundreds of guys looking for work, and there weren't enough jobs to go around. The situation was a little better in Los Angeles, but not much. After a couple weeks of being out of work, Dad finally landed a job as a milkman. His route was in Beverly Hills. We loaded the Packard with all of our suitcases and boxes, the steamer trunk tied to the rear bumper, and went thirty miles up the road to Los Angeles. I hung out at George's house all day long the day before we pulled out. His mom made us some delicious chicken tacos for lunch. That would be the last homemade Mexican food I'd have for a long time.

We moved to a bungalow court in the Echo Park district of Los Angeles. Dad had a five-mile drive to get to his job in Hollywood, and then he had to drive a milk truck another couple miles to get to Beverly Hills. Echo Park was about as close as someone in our economic straits and social class could get to that little movie-star enclave. Every-

## Down the Foggy Ruins of Time

thing in between was a long way out of our price range. The court consisted of five cottages on three sides of a small rectangle of unkempt, dried-out Bermuda grass. We moved into one of the bungalows that was closest to the street. It was a miserable, run-down place, a definite step down from what we'd left in Long Beach. The other four families, Mexicanos or American-Mexicans every one, were poor just like we were, and they all had kids, so I had a lot of playmates, but our stay there was short, and I never really got to know any of them. I forgot their names the day we drove away for the last time.

Christmas in the bungalow was pretty stark. That was probably the lowest point yet for the Farot family. We were never poorer than we were right at that moment. Because there were so many of them, and they were only one rung up from us on the cash ladder, Francesca's parents and siblings drew names out of a hat so that each family member only had to buy one present for the person whose name he drew. The only presents under our small tree were the ones from the people who drew our names, and the ones Mom and Dad gave each other. They gave Frank and me one present, a red Radio Flyer wagon.

What I remember most about that Christmas was the feeling of loneliness, the feeling of being cut off from the family that had been present at my birth. The loneliness was compounded by the recent separation from my best friend, the only friend I ever had up till then, my Mexicano brother, George Nieto. Now that I'm older and have a better understanding of such things, I can see that poverty was the cause of it all. It must have been the same feeling Antoine experienced when he was a teenager riding the rails during the Depression.

Dad delivered milk to Jimmy Stewart, Bob Hope and others, famous and not so famous, for less than six months. In the end the job was just plain boring, and it really didn't pay enough for Antoine to support us all. He and Francesca finally decided to give up on staying in California, go back to Minneapolis, take their chances there one more time. Once again all of our possessions were loaded into the Packard, and on the first day of Spring, Mom and Dad, with great reluctance, set out on the road back to Minnesota.

"Hey, let's stop in Glendale, tell Carolyn and Baxter what we're doing," Mom said as we were pulling away from the bungalow.

Francesca had really gotten to like the year-round warmth. She dreaded going back to freezing winters and muggy, mosquito-infested summers. So, it seemed that her suggestion to stop in Glendale on the way out of town was simply an attempt to postpone the inevitable. Maybe she was hoping that Carolyn and Baxter would come up with an idea that would keep us in California. Little did she or any of us know that's exactly what would happen.

"Let's go," Antoine said. "It's on the way."

We took Glendale Boulevard straight out through Atwater to Glendale. Frank and I had our feet propped up on the boxes that were on the floor-

## Down the Foggy Ruins of Time

board in the back seat. It was a beautiful, warm day; the sun was shining; not a cloud was in the sky. It was so clear that the crags and crevices, the scrub oaks and eucalyptus on the side of the mountain in front of us stood out in bold relief. Palm trees lined both sides of the street. You could smell the flowered perfume of spring in the air. As we passed the Glendale city limits sign, I started to get depressed, thinking how we would soon be leaving it all behind. And I just knew that there wouldn't be as many Mexicanos or American-Mexicans in Minneapolis as there were in Los Angeles, so all I could think about was how culturally deprived I'd be when I got there. The others were pretty down too.

"Goddamn!" Antoine said. "What a beautiful day! This is damn nice weather, and I hate like hell to leave it. This whole deal of goin' home is makin' me feel like a real quitter. And how can you not make it in California? Damn place is booming."

"Oh, I know exactly how you feel, dear," Francesca said. "I don't wan'a go into that deep-freeze back home either, but I just don't know what else we can do."

As she was talking, she was looking at Dad, and I was watching her profile. She looked like she was about ready to cry. I was too young to appreciate it then, but now I can see that Antoine was really feeling like he'd failed himself and his family, so I'm sure he was even more depressed than I was.

Carolyn and Baxter Woodman were a young married couple from Minneapolis. Mom and Carolyn had grown up together in the neighborhood, had graduated from high school together, and had remained friends ever since. When we were living in Long Beach, Francesca took Frank and me on the Pacific Electric Redcar up to their house a couple of times on weekdays, when Dad was working, to visit with Carolyn. A couple of other times on the weekends when Antoine got a day off, we drove up and the two families hung out together for the day. They were a childless couple who owned their own house. Baxter had a steady job in a bank and Carolyn was a sales clerk at Eastern-Columbia, Broadway at Ninth, downtown Los Angeles.

We pulled into their driveway at eight-thirty in the morning, and they came out onto their front porch to greet us. Inside the house, Frank and I were left to play on the carpet-less concrete floor of their living room while the adults gathered around the dining room table for coffee. They were in the last stages of remodeling, and the carpet was all that remained to be done. I've thought about that concrete living room floor often, how the sun was shining directly on it through the front window, and it wasn't cold. Within the next five minutes my parents would act on a suggestion by Baxter that would change their fortunes and our lives for good, and I think that warm, sun-drenched concrete floor was an omen.

"You ever think about getting back into printing?" Baxter asked Antoine after he'd heard the

## Down the Foggy Ruins of Time

explanation of why we were going back to Minne-apolis.

"Jesus Christ! Yuh know, it never occurred to me to look for anything in that line," Antoine said. "Just never even thought about it."

Baxter went into the kitchen and came back out with a newspaper, which he plopped down in front of Dad.

"Check the want-ads in the Times there. Maybe something there for printers."

Dad found the want-ad section and rifled the pages. When he found the two pages of the help-wanted ads, he went down the columns with his index finger and stopped, asking Baxter for a pencil. He circled several of the ads.

"Well, I be go-to-hell!" he said. "Five ads for pressmen. I'm go'n'a find out about these."

After a short discussion, they decided that Dad would take the Packard and go check on the jobs while Mom, Frank and I stayed with Carolyn and Baxter. They had a telephone, so Dad wrote the number down and went out to the car. That scene is still one of my most vivid childhood memories: Antoine, with his Panama fedora cocked rakishly to one side, a smoking Camel dangling from the corner of his mouth, his swagger making him look a good three inches taller than his actual height of five-seven. He stepped up onto the running board and climbed into that dusty old car loaded down with everything we owned. He was back out the door before he could push the starter button. He'd remembered that he had to take the steamer trunk off the rear bumper. When he finished that job, he lit up another Camel, and with the same flair he'd shown five minutes earlier, he stepped up onto the running board, climbed in behind the wheel and drove off.

Frank and I hung around in the backyard. Baxter got dressed and ready to go to work. Carolyn drove him there and came back with their car. It was her day off, so she said she'd hang with us until we found out what was happening with Antoine. About an hour after he'd left, the phone rang and Frank and I went running back to the house. Carolyn handed the receiver over to Mom. Dad was calling from the job, a place called Dillon Lithograph, a non-union shop on Grand Avenue near Eighth Street right in the center of downtown Los Angeles. He was getting paid eighty dollars a week to run a thirty-six-inch Rutherford offset press. He told Francesca to see if she could find us a place to live.

"Antoine got a job," Mom said to Carolyn as she placed the receiver back in its cradle. "He's already workin'. I could hear the presses running while I was talking to him. Wants me to find us a place to live. Think you can help me out with that."

"Absolutely," Carolyn replied. "I took Baxter to work so I'd have the car if you needed to go anywhere. Here, let's look at these want ads. See what's available for rent."

The newspaper was still on the dining room table. Antoine had ripped out the one page with the job ads, but the page with the furnished houses for

## Down the Foggy Ruins of Time

rent was intact. Mom started to go through the ads, and after she circled a couple, we finished our lunch, piled into Carolyn's Plymouth and went to check them out. We were about a mile from the closest one in Eagle Rock, a district in the city of Los Angeles, like Echo Park. It was a one-room cabin in a trailer court called Eagle Rock Springs Tourist Court.

The court had five one-room cottages, five with two rooms, and twenty or so trailers in the upper and lower courts. Mom looked at the cabin she'd found in the paper, and decided to rent it, but it took a little coaxing to convince the court manager to rent such a small space to two adults and two little kids. She pleaded with the guy, and in the end she talked him into giving her the key. She used up all the money she had on her and borrowed ten dollars more from Carolyn.

The little cottage that would be our home for the next year and a half had just the one room, which served as a living room, bedroom and kitchen. Along one wall were a kitchen sink, an oak icebox (every other day the iceman delivered a block of ice with his heavy steel tongs) and a very small three-burner gas stove with an oven down below. The only furnishings were a double bed and a davenport that folded out into a bed. There was also a small table and two chairs in one corner. The wall opposite the kitchen had a six-foot alcove bumped out about four feet. On his first day off, Antoine built a wood bunk bed set for Frank and me that fit right in the alcove.

29

A toilet/shower facility was located in the center of the lower court.

After Mom paid the rent and got the key, we went back over to Carolyn's house to pass the afternoon and wait for Dad. He only worked six hours the first day because he hadn't started until ten o'clock that morning. He got back to the Woodman's about the same time that Baxter got home from his job. We stayed and had dinner with them, and then went to our own place. We got most of the stuff out of the car and were in bed by nine o'clock our first night in the cabin. It took us a few days to settle in after that.

# Three

It must have been the luck of the draw for Antoine and Francesca to end up in Eagle Rock; it had to be the luck of the draw for me to have been raised there. They certainly didn't settle there because it reminded them of home. Ensconced as it was in the foothills of the San Gabriel Mountains, it was about as opposed to the lush greenness, the rolling and watery flatness of Minneapolis as any place could be. It lay in a desert whose terrain consisted of three ridges and two valleys running east and west.

The Eagle Rock, the big dome outcropping after which the town got its name, stood like a sentinel at the eastern end of the larger valley a couple blocks down the hill on Colorado Boulevard from the Pasadena line. Its western face near the top was eroded in a way that made it look like an eagle in flight when the descending sun cast shadows upon it. Down toward the bottom, maybe twenty feet up from the sloping ground were two shallow caves.

Colorado Boulevard, the main drag in town, was the old Route 66 in those days. It came out of

Pasadena in the east and made a three and a half mile run through Eagle Rock and continued on into Glendale in the west. It climbed a half-mile grade from Figueroa to Linda Rosa Avenue. From that summit the western descent was a gradual one for about a mile and a half to Eagle Rock Boulevard at the bottom of the valley. Locals called that intersection the Center. It was the main commercial area in town, and it was the end of the line for the two Los Angeles Transit Lines streetcars that came to town. Westward from the Center, Colorado went up another gently sloping hill to Glendale. You could see how the Center was the watershed for this little section of the mountain. Eagle Rock Boulevard was probably once a streambed stretching downhill from the Center to where it turns into Cypress Avenue on the eastern bank of the Los Angeles River.

The other main east/west thoroughfare in town was Yosemite Drive, which meandered like an asphalt stream downhill through the narrower south canyon from Figueroa to Eagle Rock Boulevard. Whereas Colorado and Eagle Rock were the town's two main commercial streets, Yosemite was mostly a neighborhood street lined with California bungalows and flat roof stucco houses. Yosemite Village at the corner of Townsend Avenue and the intersection at Eagle Rock and Yosemite were the only commercial locations on that street. Yosemite playground and Eagle Rock High School occupied a

## Down the Foggy Ruins of Time

four-block stretch in the middle of the street's mile and a half run. All of the streets intersecting Colorado and Yosemite were the avenues that made up most of the residential neighborhoods in town. It was all residential on those same streets north of Colorado up to Hill Drive. Hill Drive was the classy street in town, strictly upper middle class.

Eagle Rock Springs Tourist Court, almost exactly in the middle of this grid, was our little neighborhood in the larger community of Eagle Rock, which was only one of the many districts in the city of Los Angeles. The court occupied a couple acres of land on Argus Drive and Chickasaw Avenue one short block off Colorado Boulevard. The northern boundary of the upper court was the alley that ran behind the Safeway grocery store and came to a dead-end at the Ford dealer next door. Directly behind Safeway on the corner of the alley, a neon sign glowed on top of a fifteen-foot iron pole. It identified the park and advertised trailers for sale and rent. When we moved in, there were two rows of one- and two-room cabins, one right in the center, the other separating the upper and lower courts. A running spring shaded by a spreading pepper tree and replete with goldfish and night-croaking frogs bordered the western edge of the park. The backyards of the houses that fronted on Hermosa Avenue were on the other side of the spring.

The trailers and cabins were packed tightly into that small space. There were other kids all over the place, but not one of them was a Mexicano or an American-Mexican, and they were all older than I was, so I didn't get friendly with any of them. I wanted there to be another George Nieto, but that just wasn't going to happen. In fact, I wasn't seeing any brown faces anywhere in Eagle Rock, and I was really feeling out of place among all the white ones, even though mine was one of them.

Mom and Dad started a friendship with a couple who lived in a big trailer in the upper court. They also had two sons. Gregy Forest was three years older than his little brother Bobby who was the same age as Frank. The parents, Greg and Louise, became friends with Mom and Dad, and within two months the four of them and another couple, Pat and Sherry Banks, Louise's sister and brother-in-law, had a poker game on Saturday nights.

That Antoine and Francesca could afford to play in a weekly poker game was one indication of how well he was doing on his new job, and there were other signs that our fortunes were once again on the rise. After Dad's first paycheck, Mom quit stretching out the last of the milk by adding water to it. When the bottle got low, she'd simply go up to Colorado to Forcette's market or the Safeway store and buy a fresh quart. We also had money enough to go to a movie at the Eagle or Sierra Theater every

## Down the Foggy Ruins of Time

once in a while. The folks pulled Frank and me
down to the show and back home in the Radio Flyer
wagon we got for Christmas. We never made it to
the end of the picture, and we'd end up half asleep,
half-awake jouncing along in the wagon all the way
back to the trailer court.

The cabin was small, but we were warm and
cozy in it, and when the rains started to fall after
Christmas, we stayed dry. We were living in close
quarters, though, and there wasn't much privacy.
Mom and Dad slept in the double bed. Frank and I
only had to sleep on the foldout couch the first two
nights. We moved in on Thursday, and Dad got his
first paycheck at the end of the day on Friday. First
thing Saturday morning, he bought the necessary
tools and materials at a lumberyard and had the bunk
beds all put together by afternoon. He strung a rope
across the alcove opening and hung a curtain that we
closed at night when we slept, giving us the illusion
of being in a room with a closed door. It really was
only an illusion. I always wondered when my parents ever made love in those days. The curtain didn't
block out any sound, and all I ever heard in the night
from their side was the slow, stertorous breathing of
two people sleeping.

Mornings at the breakfast table, Antoine
tuned the radio to Dick Haynes, a country music
deejay who disguised his voice for the different
characters he did between platters. Gravel-voiced

35

Gumdrop Gus, who was pure corn pone, and Wilhelmina Mildew, the nagging old woman with the shrill voice, were followed by some corn ball laugh track, "Ah, he, aho, aha, hahahahaha." He'd say stuff like, "we've got yucca bean and yucca stew," and he did his own quaint little promos during station breaks, "This is Haynes at the reins, with records on the roam, and old folks at home." He played some good music, groups like Bob Wills and his Texas Playboys doing "Roly Poly." I heard "Cool Water" by the Sons of the Pioneers and "Blue Tail Fly" by Burl Ives on Haynes's show. He also played stuff like "Smoke, Smoke, Smoke that Cigarette," "Ol' Buttermilk Sky," and "The Big Rock Candy Mountain."

Frank and I followed Mom out the door when the Helms Man sounded his multi-tone pitch pipe as he drove his truck through the court. We'd pick out stuff we wanted her to buy, but it was okay with me just to stand next to the Helms Man and smell all those warm aromas as he pulled out a drawer filled with freshly baked pastries.

After breakfast Dad was off to work, and Mom got Frank outfitted in his school uniform. We walked with him and Bobby on their first day of school. Frank went to Saint Dominic's, and Bobby went to Eagle Rock Elementary. It was also my first day of kindergarten, so after we got Frank settled at Saint Dominic's, we went over to Eagle Rock Ele-

## Down the Foggy Ruins of Time

mentary. Saint Dominic's didn't have kindergarten. The two schools were one block away from each other on Maywood on either side of where Chickasaw ended.

Mom came back to the school at noon when kindergarten got out and walked me back home. Then she got busy with her housework. I went over to the spring, and that's when I met Ramón Sandoval. He was sitting in a folding chair on the little patio next to his front door smoking a cigarette. I guessed he was at least as old as my grandparents, maybe even a couple of years older. He was a small, thin guy, with a light complexion, medium brown hair that was going gray at the temples, and hazel eyes. He was wearing khaki trousers, black oxfords and a short sleeve, striped sport shirt. He put out his cigarette and came over and squatted on his haunches next to where I was sitting on the roots of the pepper tree.

"How yuh doin', kid?" he said, keeping his eyes on the spring, not looking at me.

"Pretty good. Just sittin' here watchin' the goldfish 'n' pollywogs."

"Yeah, they're fun to watch, all right."

"No kiddin'."

"My name's Ramón. What's yours?"

He pronounced his name with a perfect Spanish accent like George's mom had, so I figured

I couldn't go wrong if I went ahead and gave him the name that Señora Nieto used to call me.

"Mine's Jerónimo."

"Great accent! You a muchacho mexicano?"

"Nah, but I wish I was," I said. "My best friend is, though. His name's George Nieto. He lives in Long Beach. His mom taught me about my name bein' Jerónimo. It's really Jerôme."

"Yeah, well, I'm a Mexicano myself, and you could've fooled me," he wheezed. "Some of George must've rubbed off on you, 'cause, except for your güero complexion, you sure do act and talk a lot like a Mexican. My wife Mildred's like that. She's a gavacha, but she migh's well be a Mexicana. She sure does talk like one. Cooks like one too, eh."

"I sure miss those lunches George's mom used to fix for me and him."

We talked like that for almost an hour, and then he went into his trailer to take a nap. That was a nice compliment he paid me when he said I talked and acted like a Mexican. I didn't realize that I did. For the rest of the spring semester, while all the other kids in the court were in school, I hung around with Ramón and learned all kinds of cool stuff.

"You're better off being a gavacho," he told me by the end of the first week of our acquaintance, when I mentioned a second time that I wished I was a Mexican. "That way you don't get harassed all the time."

## Down the Foggy Ruins of Time

"What's a cavacho, Ramón?" I asked.

"It's gavacho," he said, putting stress on the hard G and gesturing with his hands, "and it means paddy or white guy."

"I thought that was gringo."

"It is, but gringo don't have a good sound to it. It's more of a put down word."

"Wha'da yuh mean about gettin' hassled?"

"Oh, man. Mexicanos been getting hassled in this town since day one. I knew a guy once, Leopoldo Limas, who got deported to México back in the twenties when he was just a twenty-two-year-old kid. He was born and he grew up right here in Los Angeles, but the migra, they didn't care about that. They rounded him up with a bunch of other people they thought were undocumented. It took him a couple years to make it back, eh."

"Wow!" I said. "Sounds like he got a raw deal."

"He did, hombre. And just because he was a Mexican. And you know, three years ago when the war was still going on, some of Uncle Sam's soldiers and sailors jumped some vatos who weren't doing nothing but strolling with their rucas in downtown Los Angeles. Those gringo pendejos in uniform didn't like the way the vatos were dressed, so they stripped 'em of their clothes." His breathing was becoming labored and he was wheezing heavily. "And then they gang-raped their girlfriends. No, Je-

39

rónimo, you don't wan'a be a Mexicano. Es muy peligroso. And you know the only reason I'm living in this part a' town is 'cause my wife's a gavacha. They'd never let me in here on my own even though I don't look a lot like I'm un Mexicano. I'm probably passing for white."

Ramón had tuberculosis and was on Social Security disability; his wife did secretarial work at City Hall. They didn't have any kids or grandkids and probably for good reason. He didn't have a lot of stamina; two hours was his limit. In the hour or so that I hung with him every day, I learned a lot about my adopted culture; he was an oasis in the middle of the trailer court wasteland that we lived in. He always used the correct Spanish pronunciation for the Spanish words, and he always said, "Los Angeles" in Spanish, never the two initials that became the standard years later. I met Mildred on the first Saturday that I went over there, and she really was a gavacha, a natural red head with green eyes, slightly overweight.

I hadn't made friends with any of the other kids in the trailer court, mostly because nobody was my age. Frank had two good buddies, Bobby Forest and another guy from the upper court named Jim Darrow. The three of them were inseparable through our first summer in the court, going most days to Yosemite playground. I never could figure why Frank hung around with Darrow. He was a jerk and

## Down the Foggy Ruins of Time

a bully who made fun of our last name, and besides
that, he was a racist punk like that other fool my
brother hung around with in Long Beach.

"Hey, Farthole, come here!" he'd say con-
temptuously when beckoning Frank.

He was the first person I ever heard ridicule
our last name, and it pissed me off so much when he
did it, but there was nothing I could do about it. I
was just a little shit who couldn't take anybody my
own size let alone someone who could probably take
my big brother. And besides, I never was a fighter,
unlike my dad. I told Antoine about the jerk's abuse,
and he said it'd happened to him all the time when
he was a kid, but he'd just kick the guy's ass. He
also said fighting was a bad deal all the way around,
because "whether you win or lose, you still get hurt.
'Sides you guys are smarter'n I was, so I think
you're handling it better'n I ever did as a kid."

One day when I was hanging with Ramón,
Frank and his two buddies were walking by the front
of the trailer, and as they passed, they looked in our
direction.

"How's come your little brother's always
hanging around with that ol' greaser?" Darrow said
to Frank, but by the time he responded, they were
out of earshot so we didn't hear the response.

"Pendejo!" Ramón muttered under his
breath.

"What'd he say?" I asked.

41

*Jerome Arthur*

"Called me a 'greaser.' That's a bad thing to call a Mexicano. Like calling a black man 'nigger.'"

"Another one of my brother's friends in Long Beach called George a 'beaner' once," I said, "but I didn't know what he was talking about then either. All I know is it sounded like an insult."

"Yeah, that's another one the pinchi gringos like to use to put us down."

I was glad that Darrow didn't hang around long. Before school started in September, he and his family moved out of the court and I never saw him again.

Living in the trailer court was a lot like being a second-class citizen in a segregated neighborhood. The court had different social strata, the upper court representing the upper class, the lower court representing the middle class, the cabin dwellers representing the lowest class of all, and the pecking order prevailed. But I always thought these divisions were really ridiculous, because when all was said and done, it was still a trailer court, and let's face it; there are some who'd say that people who live in such places are all "trailer trash." I figured out early on that everybody in the court must've known that Ramón was a Mexicano because nobody tried to be friendly to him and Mildred.

# Four

Mom checked me into kindergarten at Eagle Rock Elementary School and was I ever ready for it. It had been a six months since I'd had someone my own age to hang around with. When I got into the classroom, I was right in the middle of twenty-five other five-year-olds. It was cool, but the bad part was that I got home at about the same time Ramón took his nap, so I wasn't able to hang around with him as much as before.

My first school chum was the only boy in the class who was smaller than I was. We were first drawn together by our size. Some of the girls were bigger than we were. When we did the Pledge of Allegiance, Miss Hartley had the class form two rows facing the flag with the smaller kids in the front row. He and I stood side by side from the beginning. His name was Emile Gervais, and that was the second thing that drew me to him. He had French heritage just like me, and he had French features like Antoine—dark hair, blue eyes and a pale complex-ion.

But that was all. That he was of French heritage didn't really matter to him one way or the other.

He went by the nickname, Melo. He hated his given name because it was so different from everybody else's name. My feelings were exactly the opposite; I liked my name for the same reason he disliked his. His parents had started calling him Melo almost as soon as they'd named him Emile after his father. I'm sure Emile senior knew what a drag it was to be strapped with such a name; after all, he was the one who thought of the nickname. And Melo used it right on into adulthood. When I was in my late twenties, I met a guy our age who had grown up in Eagle Rock and still lived there. When I asked him if he knew Emile Gervais, he said he didn't, but when I said, "how about 'Melo' Gervais?" he copped to it and said he knew him.

On the first day of school, Mom came down to meet me at noon when class let out. Melo's mom came for him that day, but he was left on his own to get home any way he could on the second day, and since it was on his way, he walked with us back to the trailer court. He'd walked to school in the morning with his two sisters. They were first and second graders. As we approached our cabin, he asked Mom if I could go over to his house. He only lived a block away from us on Argus Drive across Colorado.

"Golly, I don't know," she said. She was naturally hesitant since no adult had come to meet him after school. "Is your mother or another adult at home?"

"Yeah, she's home," Melo said. "Pro'bly makin' cookies. Said she was go'n'a make me some for when I get home. I got lots a' neato stuff to play with in my backyard."

That was enough reassurance for Francesca, so she walked us up to the stop light on Colorado and crossed with us. There was a vacant lot on that corner and Melo lived in the house just the other side of it. Francesca walked with us up to the house. She stayed on the sidewalk, but Melo and I cut through the lot and climbed the embankment to his driveway. We mounted the steps to the front porch. The door wasn't locked, and Melo pushed it open and went in. Mom and I followed.

Melo's place was a big old two-story Craftsman with a large, gabled dormer notched into the front slope of the roof. A porch spanned the full breadth of the front of the house with the entry door set dead center at the top of four wooden steps. A glider in a rusty metal frame sat to the right of the door; a water-stained couch was on the left. On the right side of the house, an exterior stairway climbed to a separate apartment that Melo's mom tried to keep rented out. She and Melo's dad were divorced, and he was seldom around Eagle Rock, but a couple of times over the years, when the apartment was vacant, he showed up on the scene, and he and his girlfriend would move in and stay for a couple of months.

Like us, the Gervaises had come to California from another state, in their case Vermont. I think Melo's dad moved back there after the divorce. Like his son, he was a little guy, probably under five-five. If he hadn't had a wooden leg and a gimpy way of walking, Emile senior could easily have passed for a jockey. In fact, as Melo and I got to be better friends and he started hanging around our place, Antoine would suggest to him from time to time that he'd make a good jockey when he grew up.

Melo and his mom and two sisters lived in the whole downstairs of the house. Compared to where I lived, it was a mansion. The living room and dining room were paneled with mahogany wainscoting. The five-foot-wide doorway between the two rooms had heavy mahogany sliding doors that disappeared into the wall on either side. There were three bedrooms and a bathroom along the left side of the house, and the kitchen and walk-in pantry were at the rear on the same side as the living room and dining room. His mother came out of the kitchen wiping her hands with a dishtowel and trailing the aroma of fresh baked peanut butter and oatmeal cookies. She had dark auburn hair, blue eyes and a pale complexion.

## Down the Foggy Ruins of Time

"Meeloo," she said in a high-pitched voice. "Did you just get home from school? Ooo, and you've brought a friend, and his mother."

She looked at Mom and said,

"Hi, I'm Harriet."

"How do you do?" Mom said offering her hand.

"How do you do? Would you like a cup of coffee?

Harriet reminded Melo that he had to take his medicine, so we went off to his room, and Harriet and Francesca went to the kitchen. He placed a little chunk of something in an ashtray and struck a match to it. As it smoldered, he leaned over it and breathed the smoke in.

"What're yuh doin'?" I asked.

"I got asthma, and this helps me breathe better. Got'a do it every day."

After the little chunk burned out, we went back into the kitchen where Harriet and Francesca were finishing a cup of coffee.

"I'll come back in a couple hours," Francesca said as she went out the front door. "That should give you boys plenty of time to play."

Harriet had set out two glasses of milk and a plate of the cookies I'd smelled earlier. They were warm from the oven and they tasted great with the cold milk. The snack was Harriet's way of celebrating Melo's first week of school. She didn't otherwise do a whole lot of parenting because she was a single working mother at a time when that phrase wasn't even a part of the American vocabulary. I never knew what Melo's dad contributed to the household, but obviously it wasn't enough for Harriet to stay home and be a full-time mother. She worked as a waitress at Henry's Rite Spot on Colorado just across the Pasadena line, and having the job meant that Melo and his two sisters, Anita and Phyllis, spent a lot of time unsupervised. Even when she was around and prepared to supervise them and be in charge, the three kids, Melo more than the two girls, walked all over her.

When we finished our little snack, we went out to the backyard to play on his tire swing. There was definitely plenty of yard for a couple of five-year-olds to explore. We took his rabbit out of its hutch and petted it and played with it. Then we went into the backyard next door, and he showed me a secret tunnel that was formed by some hedges and ivy gone wild alongside of an old abandoned barn on the back property line. It was a very neat little open-ended cave and we hid out there for a few minutes. After a while when we could see that no one was coming to look for us, we came out into the daylight and went back through the yard to the house.

When we got back to the kitchen, Melo's sister Phyllie and her friend were there. She was the first grader, and like her mother and brother, she had

## Down the Foggy Ruins of Time

a light complexion with dark hair and blue eyes. She was as skinny as a rail and about my height. We had some more milk and cookies with them, and then they left to go to the girlfriend's house. Anita, the second grader, who also looked like her mother and siblings, but with a darker shade of blue eyes, and a scattering of freckles across her nose and cheeks, got home at a little after three. That was when Harriet started to get ready for work. I went home at about three-thirty. Anita and Melo walked me down to the corner and waited as I crossed the Boulevard. I went back to our little cabin, which now seemed like nothing more than a shack after where I'd just come from.

The next day, Melo and his sisters stopped by my house in the morning. The girls went ahead and Melo and I trailed along not far behind. Frank and Bobby had already gone to school ahead of us. Francesca didn't walk with us, nor did she come down to meet us at noon. When we got back to the cabin that day, we went over to the spring, and Ramón was out on his patio having a smoke. I introduced Melo to him, and the three of us watched the goldfish and talked, but I had the feeling that Melo made Ramón uncomfortable. He didn't talk about any of the Mexican stuff he'd talked about when it was just the two of us. In fact, he didn't talk much about anything while Melo was around. We only

49

hung with him for a few minutes, and then we cut out and went to Melo's house again.

The friendship between us grew, but sometimes my patience was put to the test. I found out early on that he was a prankster, and he didn't waste any time playing his first dirty trick on me. We hadn't even been friends a month. One day after school when we got back to the trailer court, I checked in with Mom in the cabin, and then Melo and I headed over to the spring to climb in the pepper tree. As we were passing the toilet and shower building, we saw a hole in the ground a little over three feet deep. It was kind of like a posthole, but about two feet in diameter. Naturally curious to see what was down there, Melo and I sidled up close and peered down into the hole. I saw an exposed four-inch cast iron pipe with two chalk marks about a foot apart. It looked like it was all prepped and ready for someone to start doing some plumbing.

As I was looking in the hole, I wasn't paying attention to what Melo was doing, so I didn't notice it when he backed away a step. From that vantage he pushed me from my butt, and I fell head first into the hole. Luckily, I got my arms up in time so that when I hit bottom, I landed on my hands and not my head. I screamed and yelled for help, and not a half-minute passed before some adult hands had me by the ankles and were pulling me up out of that dark hole. It

## Down the Foggy Ruins of Time

was a guy in bib overalls and a blue Brooklyn Dodgers baseball cap.

After he got me back onto my own two feet, he picked up a chain snapper and went to work on the pipe. Melo was still there, but he had a sheepish, embarrassed look on his face. He knew he'd screwed up, but I never squealed on him, so nobody but the two of us knew what he'd done. The cabin was only about thirty feet away, and Mom showed up on the scene just as the plumber was setting me down. She whisked me up into her arms and brushed my tears away all in one motion. Melo and I never made it to the spring that day. Mom took me back to the cabin and she sent him on his way home. I never told her that he'd pushed me, but I always thought she figured it out herself.

He was a sneaky little bastard all right, and it took me a long time to get wise to it. Sometimes he'd even broadcast his bad intentions, and I still wouldn't get it. His mother certainly knew, and she'd take precautions against it. One Saturday as we were hanging around in his backyard, Harriet came out and asked us to go with her to The Feed and Fuel down on Caspar to get some rabbit pellets. As we entered the store, she told both of us to put our hands in our pockets and to keep them there until we left. She went about her business while Melo and I, hands in pockets, browsed around. I asked him why we had to keep our hands in our pockets, and he said it was the only way she could be sure we wouldn't steal something.

# Five

    By Thanksgiving Antoine had been working for Dillon for ten months. Since she could easily afford it by now, Francesca bought a twelve-pound turkey for the holiday. It was quite a turnaround from just ten months ago and Echo Park when we didn't have a pot to piss in or a window to throw it out of, to quote something Antoine said all the time. This Thanksgiving we sat down to a lavish turkey dinner with all the trimmings, and as Antoine carved thick slices of white meat from the breast, he told us the story of his last Thanksgiving dinner at home when he was fifteen years old.

    "You kids got it made," he said. "When I was a kid, I had this asshole of a stepdad took all the good stuff for himself and left the rest of us with what you wouldn't even give a dog. So, on Thanksgiving of '31, my ma went out and bought a ham with the loot we made on doughnuts. Ma and Sis made 'em and I'd go out and peddle 'em. My stepdad didn't do naughtin', just sat on his ass and pissed and moaned all day long. There was a depression goin' on and we were damn lucky to even get a ham that year. The Polack bastard cut off all the fat and gave it to us, and he took the lean for himself. I got so pissed off I clubbed the son of a bitch with a ball bat and ran away from home that same day."

He'd put prime cuts of turkey breast on each of our plates, and then he sat down and started passing the trimmings around. I hadn't noticed that he'd cut off a piece of gristle with a greasy chunk of skin hanging from it, and after all our plates were full, he stabbed it with his fork and tossed it into his mouth. He didn't actually eat it; he just whirled it around and spat it out.

"I ain't eatin' it now 'cause I don't have ta, but boy when you're hungry, it's pretty amazing what you'll eat. I'd put syrup on it, anything to make it taste better."

That Thanksgiving feast was just the beginning. Dad went all out for us on Christmas. We all went together to the lot on the corner next door to Melo's house and got a tree, and on Christmas day there were a bunch of presents under it. We each had a present from the Konig relatives in Minneapolis who drew our names, and Mom and Dad got Frank and me complete cowboy outfits: cap gun six-shooters and holsters, cowboy hats, leather vests, chaps, and spurs. All that leather sure smelled good. The only thing missing was boots, so we had to put the spurs on our oxfords. It looked okay. Dad got

## Down the Foggy Ruins of Time

Mom a really neat coat, and she got him a fur felt Royal Stetson fedora with a satin lining.

My biggest worry that Christmas was how Santa Claus was going to come down the sewer vent pipe of the kitchen sink. That was the only thing we had that resembled a chimney, and I just couldn't picture him fitting through it. That must've been about the time when I quit believing in Santa Claus, but imagine me reaching a point in my life when something that inconsequential was my biggest concern. It was the first time that I felt like we were something other than a poor, penniless migrant family. Suddenly, I was feeling like there was a future again, and maybe soon we were going to break through.

In February, Mom's brother, Luke dropped in on us for a few days on his way home after being discharged from the Navy. He'd been in and out of trouble throughout his three and a half years in high school, mostly for getting into fights, and before he started the second half of his senior year, he quit to join the Navy. The war ended shortly after he got out of boot camp, so he didn't see any action, but instead spent the next year and a half on a destroyer doing cleanup and peace-keeping in the war's aftermath in the Philippines and Singapore. He was still in uniform when we picked him up at Union Station, and he stayed in uniform the whole time he was with us. He said he'd keep on wearing it until he got back to

Minneapolis because he wanted to take advantage of the good treatment servicemen usually got in those days in bars and restaurants and on the train. He'd come in from San Diego where he'd mustered out.

He was a wild young guy, looking for a good time. I guess he found it that first night when he and Antoine got drunker than skunks. They sat at the little kitchen table and quaffed down a half of a fifth of Early Times, and then they passed out.

The next morning Frank and I woke up before anybody else, so we went outside and kept out of the way while Dad and Luke slept off their hangovers. We went over to the spring and climbed in the pepper tree. There were a few other kids out there too; their parents were probably also sleeping off hangovers. When it was okay to go back to the house, Frank and I went in and had some breakfast. Luke and Antoine were both looking pretty pale and peaked as they sat at the table drinking black coffee. Francesca was in better shape than the two men because she knew her limits when it came to booze, so she went to bed after only a couple sips from Antoine's first drink. She was cooking up some eggs and sausage and toast.

After breakfast Antoine went to the glove compartment of the car and got a map of the city. Luke had a buddy who lived out in Van Nuys, and he wanted to go visit him. They spread the map out

## Down the Foggy Ruins of Time

on the table, checked the street location in the index and found it on the map.

We stopped at a car dealer in Glendale because Luke wanted to look at a forty-one Plymouth businessman's coupe he'd seen in the want ads. He wasn't serious about buying a car, so we really didn't need to make that stop, but Frank and I were glad we did because the dealer had a big sale going on, and they were giving away helium balloons. We each got one.

On our way out to the valley, we drove past West Glendale on San Fernando Road. I was surprised to see that most of the people over on San Fernando Road West on the other side of the railroad tracks were Mexicanos. A couple of the stores had signs in the display windows that said, "Se habla Español." I didn't realize until that day that there was this barrio so close to Eagle Rock. I knew about Cypress Park three miles south of us, because we'd go through it when Mom took Dad to work on days when she needed the car, but that was the first time I'd ever seen West Glendale.

"Boy, this here looks like the Mex district! And right next to a nice, clean neighborhood, too. How do yuh like that?" Luke said in a derogatory tone that probably sounded worse than it actually was because of his harsh, tough-sounding voice.

I shudder now when I think about what he might have had on his mind. I'd already decided to keep Ramón to myself and not introduce him to any of my family members. Luke's remarks only reinforced that decision. However, right at that moment, Francesca made me proud that she was my mom.

"You know, Luke," she said evenly. "You should be a little more charitable. I can't see that you or I or any of us, for that matter, are better than any of them."

She was in the back seat with Frank and me. Luke was riding shotgun next to Antoine, and all he did was give Dad a wink and a grin. Antoine glanced over at Luke and rolled his eyes ever so slightly.

"Don't mess with my little woman 'cause she'll put yuh in ye'r place," he said.

"You betcha," Luke said, still smiling but now looking out the right-side window into the manicured neighborhoods of Glendale.

Luke's buddy lived in a flat-roof stucco and red tile bungalow court off Victory Boulevard. At that time Van Nuys was still a small valley town way out in the country. It was surrounded by horse ranches and open space, but you could see housing developments starting to sprout up all around. I never dreamed then that one day it would be all built out and engulfed by the city.

On the trip back home, Luke raved about California, the weather in general, and his friend's situation in particular. He said he wanted to move to the Golden State. He planned to go back to Minne-

## Down the Foggy Ruins of Time

apolis only to see Grandma and Grandpa, and then turn right around and come back and settle near us. He stayed with us for a couple more days, and then we took him to the Naval Air Station down in Los Alamitos where he got on a plane that took him to Wold Chamberlin Naval Air Station near Minneapolis. Two months later, we got a letter from him telling us how he got a job as a butcher at National T, a Minneapolis grocery chain. He also wrote that he was going to get married the next month. And we never heard anything more about him moving to California.

# Six

I visited Ramón when I could during spring semester. Most days after school Melo and I went by the cabin and checked in with Francesca before crossing the Boulevard to his house. When I got home from Melo's, I'd go over to the spring and try to catch Ramón. If he was out on his patio having a smoke after his nap, I'd hang with him until Mildred got home. During those sessions, he was always teaching me something new about México and Mexican culture and history. Even though I wasn't reading yet, he gave me a pocket edition of the University of Chicago, Spanish/English-English/Spanish Dictionary. The things I learned from him I never learned in school, or if I did learn them in school, Ramón said the teacher's point of view would be so skewed that I wouldn't be getting the straight story. He told a very different story than the one I got from the American history books I read. Indeed, those books didn't even make reference to the things I learned from Ramón. On one of those kindergarten afternoons he told me about the Mexican War which resulted in México's loss of most of the Southwest, including all of California, to the United States.

"Es verdad, Jerónimo," he said, his breathing labored, his pronunciation of the Spanish words perfect as usual. "The pinchi gringos stole all that territory from México and kicked the Mexicanos off their land. It was almost exactly a hundred years ago right now, January 1847. They fought the last battle of California just five miles east of here in San Gabriel. Two gringos named Stockton and Kearny defeated the Mexicanos, and that was the end of the war and we lost the state to the Americanos."

"Wow!" I said. "How'd you find out about all this stuff?"

He said, "I been studying up on it ever since I quit working. I'm just passing it along to you 'cause you think you're a Mexicano, and I want you to get the straight story before you start learning it wrong from the gavachas who teach in the schools."

I said, "W'll, tell me some more."

"Another clear case of Yankee military power over a smaller, weaker country, hombre. Los Americanos invaded México, and they even occupied the capital, el Distrito Federal, or what the Americanos call México City. It was an act of aggression against a sovereign state. It was a bad scene, eh."

He started coughing and his breathing became labored to the point that he had to quit telling me. That day I went back to the cabin before Mildred got home, but first I helped him into his trailer so that he could lie down. Later when I was sitting down to dinner with the family, an ambulance pulled up next to Ramón's place. The driver had turned his

## Down the Foggy Ruins of Time

siren off, but the whole time they were stopped in front of his trailer, the gumball machine rotated on the ambulance roof, casting alternating red and blue light in the window of our cabin. I excused myself from the dinner table to go out and look. Half of the people in the lower court were out in front of their trailers and cabins gawking at the activity around Ramón's trailer. I stood next to our door and watched from the shadows as they wheeled him out on a gurney and put him in the back of the ambulance. Mildred climbed in behind him. The siren went on as soon as they left the court. A couple of hours later Mildred got out of a forty Lincoln in front of her trailer.

The next afternoon when I split from Melo, I went over to the spring and waited until Mildred got home from work. As she approached her front door, I got up off the roots of the pepper tree and went up to her.

"What happened to Ramón?" I asked.

She said, "He had a real bad T.B. attack. They took him to Glendale Sanitarium and put him in an oxygen tent. I'm on my way over there right now."

I said, "When you see him, tell him hi for me, and I'm go'n'a check again tomorrow to see how he's doin', okay?"

"You're so sweet, Jerónimo," she said. Her Spanish pronunciation was perfect. He was right when he said she might as well be a Mexicana. "Maybe you'd like to go with me on the bus tomorrow night when I visit him? The Asbury'll pick us up right here at the corner and drop us off a block from the hospital. Ask your mother."

"Gee, that'd be real keen," I said. "I'll ask her."

But I didn't mention it to Francesca because I knew she'd never let me go. I'd spent quite a lot of time hanging around with Ramón and Mildred, but my parents had never met them or talked to them, and I was still only six years old. I did want to see Mildred before she went to visit Ramón again, so the next evening I went over there to try to catch her on her way to the hospital. I got to the pepper tree at a little before six and waited until seven-thirty, but she didn't come home. I finally went back to the cabin where I hung around by our door watching for the lights to go on in Ramón's trailer, but that night they never did.

When Melo and I got home from school the next day, Mildred was coming out of her trailer with a man who wore a brown, pinstripe, double-breasted suit and matching brown fedora. You could see from his graying temples and neckline taper that his hair was red, and he looked a lot like Mildred. I hurried ahead of Melo and got to her just as she was getting into the shotgun seat of the forty Lincoln I'd seen dropping her off the night they took Ramón away.

## Down the Foggy Ruins of Time

"Oh, Jerónimo!" she said. Her eyes were red from crying, and as soon as she saw me, she started in again, and her sadness so overwhelmed me that I started to cry too. "Ramón passed away yesterday afternoon. I was with him when he passed."

Through our tears she introduced me to the driver of the Lincoln. He was her younger brother, Tom. She said she'd stayed the night at his house, which wasn't far from the hospital, but I could barely concentrate on what she was saying. I was so distracted and I suddenly felt empty. Ramón just didn't seem in that bad of shape when I saw him only two days ago. I'd since learned that he'd actually lived a long time for the condition he had. He was fifty-four years old, and Francesca had an uncle who'd died from the same disease before he even reached forty-five.

I didn't make it to Ramón's funeral; I didn't even find out when or where it was. Francesca wouldn't have let me go anyway, and with good reason. I was already a basket case just getting past his death; I couldn't stop crying. If I'd gone to the funeral, I probably would've been traumatized. I couldn't get over the fact that the Mexicans in my life kept disappearing. First George and now Ramón, whose death left a huge void. I'd been well acquainted with him for almost a year. He treated me like I was a Mexicano. I really missed him and the feeling continued through the summer. I missed the stories he told and his insights into Mexican history and culture. He really made me feel like it was my culture. He showed me that there were more similarities than differences between us.

We took our first trip back to Minneapolis that summer. We hung out for one day at Grandma's house on Russell Avenue North, and one day at Aunt Megan's on Logan Avenue South. On the third day, we drove out to Cosmos to visit Uncle Elmer's farm. He was Grandma's brother, and he'd taken over the family farm when his father died. Elmer tried to show Frank, Jessie and me how to milk a cow, and when we couldn't do it, he squirted us in the face with milk warm from the utter. I found out from those few days on the farm just how much of a city kid I was. Of all the farm things I did, I'd have to say the best was tasting ice-cold well water that they pumped into an oaken bucket next to the back door. The rest of it was all warm milk and a stinky outhouse. I wanted to get back to Minneapolis, so that we could leave for home. That's where I really wanted to be.

And when we did get home, we were greeted with the news that Mildred wanted to move out of her trailer. Antoine and Francesca jumped at the opportunity to rent it. She moved downtown to an apartment in the Oviatt Building on Olive Street. Before I went into first grade, we moved out of the cabin and into Ramón's old place, keeping the connection between him and me alive.

Even though it wasn't any bigger than the cabin, the trailer was partitioned off into sections, so we could at least get away from each other if we had to. The rear section was an enclosed sleeping loft with a window view of the spring. This was where Ramón and Mildred had slept, and it became our parents' bedroom. Frank and I slept on the foldout davenport that also served as the living room couch. There was a dining nook with a window at the very front of the trailer that looked out onto the rest of the court. Every time we sat down to a meal, we had a view of our old cabin. A small counter next to a butane powered stove and refrigerator (no more iceman) separated the nook from the living area.

We weren't in the trailer a month before Frank almost set the place on fire. One night after all the rest of us had gone to sleep, he stayed awake listening to "The Shadow" with the volume turned down. He was too scared to listen to it in the dark, so he left the light on, and he threw his red and white cowboy bandanna over the lampshade. The show couldn't have been too scary because he fell asleep before it was over. The radio and light were still on at a little before eleven o'clock when I woke up coughing and choking on the smoke that filled our confined little space. The bandanna was smoldering, just on the verge of catching fire when I pulled it off

67

the lampshade, tossed it into the sink and doused it with water. Frank awoke when I opened the front door to air the place out, and then I woke up Mom and Dad. Everybody was okay. Actually, my parents had the door to their loft closed so there was no smoke in there at all. We opened all the windows and waited for the smoke to clear out. Then we all went back to sleep, and I was feeling like a hero for having saved my family.

# Seven

I went into first grade at Saint Dominic's a couple of weeks after we moved into the trailer. On the first day of school, Mom accompanied Melo and me down Chickasaw. He split from us at Maywood, and Francesca walked with me to the Saint Dominic's schoolyard. She joined some other mothers who were gathered along the fence to watch us march into class. The bell rang and all the classes started to line up. The routine was to assemble in neat lines and then recite out loud: "The Apostle's Creed," one "Our Father," three "Hail Mary's," a "Glory be...," and "The Pledge of Allegiance" (this was a few years before they added the phrase "under God"). When all the recitation was finished, we'd sing "The Star-Spangled Banner." Then the students filed into class to the scratchy tune of "Stars and Stripes Forever," or some other John Philip Souza march played on a Victrola sitting inside the open window of the second-grade classroom.

My first day didn't work out that way at all. When the bell rang, seven of the eight classes lined

up neatly, boys in one line, girls in the other, small
kids in front, tall kids in back, standing at attention.
The first-grade class was the only exception to this
neat, orderly assembly. Those kids were forming one
line, girls and boys in a jumble, pushing and shov-
ing. At first I went to the end of that line, but after
looking the situation over, I figured I was in the
wrong place, so I made what I thought was the next
logical move. I jumped to a line that was all boys
about my size, but it was the line for the second-
grade boys. The kid in front of me turned around and
said,

"You ain't no second grader."

If that wasn't enough to scare me, then sure-
ly the nun, all dressed in white with a stern look on
her face, coming right at me did the trick. I scurried
straight across the schoolyard to where the parents
were standing and clung to my mother's skirts.
Francesca was so embarrassed that she hurried me
out the gate and down to the corner where the school
building stood between us and all those kids and
adults in the schoolyard. Father McNaughton, our
pastor, came out of the rectory and was looking at us
from his front porch. He came across the street,
walked up to Francesca and said,

"We having some trouble here?"

Mom said, "Little Jerôme here doesn't seem
to want to go to school today. I don't understand it.

## Down the Foggy Ruins of Time

He didn't act like this last year when he went to kindergarten."

He came up to me, crouched down and spent the next ten minutes trying to convince me that the nuns weren't boogiemen, and that I should join my first-grade class. I sat on the retaining wall, my arms folded across my chest, my head down, my lower lip sticking out. Then I really blew it big time and got the priest thoroughly pissed off at Francesca and me. It had been about fifteen minutes since the entire student body had marched into class, and I wasn't moving. I guess the priest thought he'd gotten me convinced, so he put his hand out to me and tried to coax me out of my shell and into the building. I misinterpreted the gesture as an aggressive move and started flailing about. I was acting so stupidly. One of my kicks landed and left a black smudge on his white cassock (it was actually yellow with age). He glared at Francesca and hissed something like,

"Get your kid under control," and huffed off to the rectory.

It fairly broke my heart the way he'd spoken to Mom. His words hurt so badly that I marched straight into my classroom out of sympathy for her. I was the one who provoked him in the first place, and he shouldn't have taken it out on her. I think a lot of my insecurity that day came from the fact that Melo wasn't there with me. I was sure he was in a classroom filled with the kids from our kindergarten class. I didn't recognize anybody from kindergarten among these kids, and Sister Grace's habit was a lot scarier than Miss Hartley's skirt and blouse, but that was no excuse. I'd seen plenty of the nuns at Sunday Mass. I knew there was nothing to be afraid of.

Sister Grace told me to take the only empty desk left in the room over next to the row of windows that looked out onto the schoolyard. I surveyed the room as I moved to my desk. It had a crucifix in the center of the front wall just above the blackboard. The American flag flew in the corner above the door. The desks, each with an inkwell hole bored into the upper right-hand corner, were made of wood and attached by a scrollwork iron frame to wooden runners on the floor; the wooden fold-down seat of the desk in front was attached to the desk behind it.

She seated us alphabetically. Ronald Day sat in the desk in front of me, Lucille Ferrante behind me. Ronald was the first kid in the class to talk to me. The first chance he got, he turned around and asked me my name and told me his, and he said he understood about my being scared. He was scared, too. That little bit of kindness drew me right to him, but the fact that he had dark Latin features and looked like a taller version of George Nieto also played a big role in our burgeoning friendship. His father's heritage was Black Irish and his mother's American-Mexican, with the emphasis on American. He had blue-black hair (like both of his parents),

## Down the Foggy Ruins of Time

dark eyes (with long, thick lashes), and an olive complexion (from his mother). However, his Mexican heritage only manifested itself in his looks. Ronald was otherwise a gavacho through and through.

After school he invited me to his house on Mount Royal Drive, two streets over from the trailer court. It was a two-story house with a flat roof, built on a fairly steep, terraced slope above a two-car garage. You had to climb some steps next to the garage to get to it. The first door you came to on the lower level opened into the service porch. The kitchen, dining room and family room were also on that level. There was another set of steps that went up the left side of the house to the front door. The living room and three bedrooms were up a staircase on the upper level.

We entered the service porch door and went through to the kitchen where Ronald's mother was fixing us an after-school snack. She was really beautiful, a Mexicana in appearance and genes only. She was a gavacha in all other respects. She spoke no Spanish, had no Mexican accent. Her cooking was strictly meat and potatoes, no tamales at Christmas or frijoles refritos and flour tortillas warmed over the open flame of the gas burner for lunch. Mildred Sandoval was more of a Mexicana than Rita Day.

Ronald's little sister Margie came down from upstairs and sat at the table with us. She was a kindergartner, cute as a bug's ear. I could tell, even at that early age, that she would grow up to be a beautiful woman like her mother. I was smitten! And I was at an age when I didn't even like girls. It must have been the brown skin, the dark eyes, the black hair.

Rita fixed us each a slice of toasted Weber's bread with Skippy peanut butter spread across it, and a glass of milk. As we ate, Ronald's older brother Richie came in. He was in Frank's class at school, and like his mother and siblings, he looked like a Mexican. Mister Day's pale Irish complexion was the lightest in the whole family.

When we finished our toast and milk, Ronald and I went down his street to where it came to a dead end. A path went through some bushes and came out on a bluff overlooking Yosemite Drive and the high school football field. We sat up there and looked up and down the valley. The Eagle Rock High football team was working out under the letters E.R. that were limed into the side of the hill beyond the other end zone. Somebody was building a house on stilts along the ridge on the other side of the valley.

When our six-year-old attention spans ran out of things to hold them, we cut back through the bushes to Ronald's place. We hung around his tire swing for a while, and then it was time for me to go home. Ronald walked down La Roda with me to as

## Down the Foggy Ruins of Time

far as the alley. I cut through it and the Pueblo Motel to get back to the trailer court. After such a shaky start, my first day of school turned out okay in the end. And I could see that Ronald was going to be a hell of a lot better friend than Melo.

In fact, I lost touch with Melo the whole first week of school. He'd told me when we split up on the morning of the first day that he'd meet me on the corner after school, but Ronald and I waited there for ten minutes and he never showed up. I didn't see him again until Tuesday of the second week when he came by the trailer after I'd just gotten home from Ronald's house. We fooled around at the spring, but it was already late in the afternoon so he went home a short time after he'd arrived. Through the remainder of the semester, I'd do stuff with Ronald and Melo individually, but not with both of them at the same time. They didn't meet until Halloween when the three of us went trick-or-treating together.

My brother Frank was in the schoolyard along with everybody else that first morning, and he also saw me make a fool of myself. I think his response to that incident marked the beginning of his abusive treatment of me. I guess the embarrassment was just too much for him, and, so that he could feel better about himself, he started to put me down, and he continued to scorn me until well into adulthood. The teasing and taunting actually began two days after Halloween when Frank came down with the measles and the next day I had them, too. We were confined to the trailer for a week with the shades all pulled and drawn because Francesca was trying to limit our exposure to the sunlight. It was a boring week, and Frank's boredom turned to acrimony. I suddenly became the focus of his rage.

"What a big crybaby," he said for probably the tenth time during our confinement together. "Pretty stupid runnin' to Mom cryin' 'cause you're scared to go to school. You ain't nothing but a scaredy cat!"

And on it went until the end of the week. By Saturday I was able to escape his heckling because Francesca finally let us go outside, but that wasn't the end of it. Indeed, it was just the beginning.

# Eight

Frank and I got bikes that Christmas, brand new Columbias, mine a red twenty-four inch, his a blue twenty-six inch. He climbed right onto his, made some kind of disparaging remark about how I didn't "even know how to ride a two-wheeler," and rode off down Chickasaw with Bobby Forest who got a new Schwinn. He was right; I didn't know how to ride it, so Antoine spent a good part of the morning trying to teach me. He'd jog alongside holding me up by the seat springs while I pedaled. Forty-five minutes later, he was worn out and I was still falling over as soon as he'd let go. Then at around noon Gregy Forest showed up with Greg and Louise, who'd come by for a Christmas drink with Antoine and Francesca. After Gregy spent about five minutes with me, I was riding by myself. He held the seat springs just as Dad had done and trotted alongside balancing me. On the second try, I stayed up on my own when he let go. I panicked when I realized he wasn't still there with me, and I fell over, but I didn't get hurt, and I got right back up and rode it without any help.

Ronald got a new bike too, a twenty-six-inch Hawthorne, but Melo didn't get one, so when he and I were hanging around together, I'd buck him on my crossbar. On those few occasions when the three of us got together, Melo would ride on Ronald's buddy rack. Ronald didn't like hanging around with Melo because of his pranks. I suppose I should have followed his lead and stayed away too, but I had hopes, false hopes, that he'd change his ways and one day be a nicer person. I waited in vain for that day; in the meantime I just put up with him.

Two weeks before Easter, Melo and I went to see a double feature, *Hopalong Cassidy: The Dead Don't Dream* and *Abbott and Costello Meet Frankenstein* at a Saturday noon matinee at the Sierra Theater. During the intermission, we got in the line at the candy counter behind Bart Pendagast. Bart was a grown adult with Down Syndrome, and I saw him around town all the time. He was a regular at Sunday Mass and Communion at Saint Dominic's. I remember being in the church one Saturday afternoon when he was in the confessional unburdening himself so loudly that his sins echoed through the nave for all present to hear. He was a harmless soul who'd never hurt anybody, especially not Melo, so there was no call for what came next.

## Down the Foggy Ruins of Time

I was standing between him and Melo in the line, trying to give Bart as much room as he needed. I was talking face-to-face to Melo with my back to Bart, and every so often I'd turn to see how the line was moving and move with it. One of those times Melo gave me a good shove, and I went crashing face first into Bart's back. You'd think I would've learned by then not to turn my back on him when we were so close together, but I hadn't figured that out yet. Of course, Bart thought I was either attacking or teasing him, so he got pissed off. He turned on me and gave me an ear-ringing slap across the face that left a red handprint on my cheek, and I didn't blame him. There wouldn't have been any point in trying to explain what really happened, so I just faded away from him and the stares of all the other kids in the crowded lobby (I was embarrassed) and gave Melo the dirtiest look I could put on. Then I just kept it cool until after the second feature.

By the time we got to Chic's liquors on Colorado, almost halfway home, I couldn't keep my cool any longer, and that's when I slugged him (a Sunday punch) in the chest. I never could punch anybody in the mouth or nose or even upside the head. He lost his balance and back-pedaled a couple steps before going down on his butt. He got right back up, but he didn't come after me. He knew better. I was a little bigger than he was, and he knew I could over-power him, even though I wasn't much of a fighter,

*Jerome Arthur*

and I usually chickened out of any fight with somebody my own size or bigger.

"Hey, wise guy! The hell you think you're doin'?" he asked, as if he didn't know.

"I've had it with your bullshit and I ain't takin' it no more. That was for pushin' me into Bart. Quit messin' with me, man."

"Oh, yeah? Well, fuck you!"

He stalked off and I walked back to the trailer alone. The two movies were short (two and a half hours including intermission), and when I got home at ten to three, the afternoon was still young, so I got my bike out and pedaled up to Ronald's house. I caught him just as he was leaving to go to the soda fountain in the drugstore at Yosemite Village, so I went with him. When he finished his cherry Coke and I my chocolate root beer, we pedaled down Yosemite to the playground rec. room and played some caroms. When I got home at five o'clock, I judged it to have been a pretty good day after all. The little hassle I had with Melo proved to be only a ripple on the otherwise smooth surface of the afternoon. The movies were cool, and those last couple of hours hanging with Ronald were really cool.

Melo didn't stay away long. The next morning after we got home from ten o'clock Mass, he was knocking on the door of the trailer wanting to go for a bike ride. As usual, he didn't apologize for

## Down the Foggy Ruins of Time

what he'd done; he didn't even mention it, like it never happened. But I made up with him and took him out riding. My slugging him must have made some kind of an impression though, because he didn't play any dirty tricks on me for a couple of months after that. I always thought Melo's size had a lot to do with his being such a jerk. People tended to overlook him, which wasn't hard to do, so he'd do something stupid to get attention. Unfortunately, and all too often, I was the one who suffered the consequences of his actions.

On the following Monday, Ronald and I got permission to leave the school grounds and go with Darrell Hall to his house for lunch. Darrell was a skinny little kid who lived on Maywood Avenue just the other side of Colorado Boulevard from the school. It was close enough for him to go home for lunch every day; he carried his Roy Rogers lunch box to school on rainy days only.

His mother was really a neat lady, and the day Ronald and I showed up with Darrell, she treated us great. He introduced her to us by her first name, Hildie, and there was no disrespect in that at all. On the contrary, she liked it that way, and you could tell that Darrell loved her, and for him, calling her by her first name was a sign of respect. It was so different from the way Melo treated Harriet. He also called her by her first name without disrespect, but he called her every other name in the book you could think of, too. Whenever he got upset or pissed off at something, he'd take it out on her, cussing her up one side and down the other. The first time I saw that happen, I was stunned, and I knew that if I ever talked like that to my mother, I'd have to deal with Antoine. It would never enter Darrell's mind to talk to Hildie that way.

Thus, I found his relationship with his mother refreshing, and I really liked both of them. Nevertheless, Darrell and I never became close friends. We were just too different. When it came right down to it, in my early years, I was attracted more to the likes of Melo than Darrell. Whereas Melo was a sneaky little tough guy, Darrell was a quiet, sensitive little boy with good manners. And Darrell didn't play practical jokes on anybody. Their size was about the only thing I could see that they had in common.

As we ate our lunches, Hildie and two other ladies entertained us with a rehearsal of a dance number they were doing for a fund-raising event that the Saint Dominic's Mother's Club was putting on. Ronald and I were on the couch and Darrell sat in his dad's easy chair. We watched as they danced in unison, chorus line-fashion, to a scratchy seventy-eight of "By the Sea, by the Beautiful Sea" played on a mahogany Victrola. It was fantastic. When we got back to school, I was so exhilarated that I had

## Down the Foggy Ruins of Time

extra energy for Dick and Jane and the Baltimore Catechism.

I couldn't see it at the time, but getting a Catholic education was probably one of the best things that could have happened to me. The key to the whole system was discipline, and I'm not just talking about cracking knuckles with a wooden ruler. In fact, I never actually witnessed any knuckle cracking in eight years of elementary school, so I don't know, first hand, if that kind of thing ever really happened. Indeed, whether it did or not is irrelevant. All I needed was to hear other people say they saw it happen, and that was enough to keep me in line.

Discipline was the main component in the hour's worth of homework they expected you to do every night. My doing homework in grammar school was the foundation for the good study habits I developed later when I went to college. I had homework for the entire twelve years that I was in Catholic school. Melo, on the other hand, never had any homework, at least not through grade school. It was also for discipline that we wore uniforms and lined up every morning and marched into class.

And all of that discipline was handed down by the people who perhaps knew it best of all. The Dominican nuns had to have it to live the kind of life they lived. They wore wrist- and ankle-length white habits with a wimple and veil that completely cov-

*Jerome Arthur*

ered their hair, forehead, ears and neck. Their high-top black shoes were the same kind my grandma wore. The only skin showing was their hands, and their faces from chin to eyebrows. I don't think I even realized that they were women until fourth grade (no matter that we called them "sister" and all but two of them had women's names).

One of the hardest things to deal with was the religious part of the process, the guilt and church dogma, saying "Our Fathers" and "Hail Marys" at different times throughout the day. From the pulpit the priests were alternately spouting hellfire and brimstone (Father McNaughton, our pastor) or simply paraphrasing and quoting scripture (Father Mahon). Father Segretti was somewhere in between the two. He gave a better sermon than Father Mahon, but he couldn't touch Father McNaughton's seething rhetoric.

"Father Mick," as he was known affectionately among his parishioners, was a big, burly San Francisco-reared American-Irishman whose pudgy face flamed red as he described the horrors of hell–odious, burning gases in some dark, labyrinthine cave stinking of sulfur and scorched human flesh. This, he said, is what we had to look forward to if we died with mortal sin on our souls. It scared the shit out of me! Especially when I found out what kind of a minor infraction constituted a mortal sin,

84

## Down the Foggy Ruins of Time

stuff like missing Mass on Sunday or eating meat on Friday.

Father Mick rode a fancy ten-speed Italian racing bike that he left unlocked in an enclosed, covered patio behind the rectory. He was an avid cyclist, and there were a few eighth graders and Saint Dominic's alumni with similar bikes who went with him on long distance rides. They had all the necessary equipment: helmets, jerseys, shorts and special shoes. The priest had a policy for students who wanted to park their bikes with his in the patio. He only allowed ten-speed bikes similar to his and his riding buddies'. Frank and I didn't get to park ours there, but that was okay, because one of Father Mick's buddies got his stolen from the patio when he followed the priest's example and didn't lock it up.

Father McNaughton was the guy Antoine credited with converting him to Catholicism. It's true that before he could marry Mom, who was baptized Catholic at birth and raised in the faith, he had to take instructions in the Church and promise to raise his kids Catholic. He probably even got baptized then too, but the story he always told was that he didn't believe in any of it until he met Father Mick. On Palm Sunday as the four of us were leaving nine o'clock Mass, the priest waylaid Dad and asked him if he could speak to him in his office. As Antoine followed him off to the rectory, Mom and

Frank and I started the trek up Chickasaw back to the trailer court.

Dad came home an hour later, saying he was a changed man. I don't know what Father Mick said to him, but after their little chat, Antoine turned into a stronger Catholic, even more orthodox and devout, than Francesca. He started to go to Confession and Communion often and regularly. It was typical behavior for a convert. And he really grew to love Father Mick's fiery sermons, oftentimes quoting him from the one he'd just heard that day.

"I'm goin' to Magloon's Saloon, have a couple beers," Antoine said, referring to McGuire's Inn, one of his favorite beer joints. It was the Sunday after Easter, just two weeks since he'd spoken to Father Mick. "'Sinners repent, lest ye' suffer eternal damnation in hell,'" he said, his right index finger, which was amputated at the second knuckle, pointed heavenward. Then he turned and headed out the door.

The first anniversary of Ramón's death was coming up. I was going to the 8:15 Mass every day and saying a complete rosary for him. I missed him so much. True, I was having a good time hanging around with Ronald. I always liked seeing Margie when I went to his house. It was cool that they had Mexican blood running through their veins, but they just couldn't fill my Latin well like Ramón used to do.

## Down the Foggy Ruins of Time

The first day of summer vacation, Ronald and I got in line to go swimming at the Yosemite pool. They charged a dime for kids under twelve and fifteen cents for everybody else. It was larger than an Olympic-size pool, a shallow three feet at both ends and six feet deep in the middle with a low springboard in that section. Neither of us knew how to swim when we first went in, so we had to stay in one of the shallow ends for a few minutes. You had to be able to swim back and forth across the width of the pool before they let you go on the deep side of the ropes. Ronald was a natural athlete, so it only took him about fifteen minutes to get good enough to pass the test, and I was about fifteen minutes behind him. We spent the rest of the afternoon swimming in the deep part and learning some dives too, and after that first time, we swam an average of four days a week all through the summer.

# Nine

I started the second-grade school year by joining Cub Scouts, and I ended it with First Confession and Communion. I really got into Cubs, and by Christmas I'd earned my lion and wolf badges and a half dozen gold and silver arrows. By Easter I got the bear badge and one more gold and three more silver arrows. I got so many arrows that they disappeared below my belt when I tucked my shirttail in. We had ten kids in our den, all of them in my class at Saint Dominic's. Hildie was our den mother, and we had some pretty cool meetings at her house. Jack Meador's mom was assistant den mother, and she'd bring the refreshments, which was always the best part of the meetings.

By spring semester Cubs was a welcome diversion from the intense indoctrination that Sister Elizabeth subjected us to in the classroom, preparing us for First Communion at the end of April. We learned how to go to Confession ("Bless me father for I have sinned…"). We had extra catechism classes ("Who made me? God made me. Why did God

## Down the Foggy Ruins of Time

make me? God made me to know, love and serve Him in this world, and to be happy with Him in the next."). It was intensive drill on the one topic, and I think some of our other classroom subjects took a beating as a result. First Communion was on the Sunday following Easter, and we studied for it exclusively during the two weeks before Easter Sunday.

Thursday before the big weekend was my eighth birthday, and Francesca had a party for me out on the patio where Ramón used to sit and smoke. Ronald and I waited for Melo, who was a Catholic and making his First Communion too, to get out of the catechism class he had every day after school at Saint Dominic's. The three of us pedaled up to the party together. All the guys from my den showed up. Melo was the only one from another den. My mom had baked a chocolate cake, and she'd bought a half-gallon of Neapolitan ice cream. I blew out all the candles on the first try. We had cake and ice cream, bobbed for apples, tried to pin the tail on the donkey, played "Musical Chairs" and "Mother May I."

Mom had thrown me a very cool party, and the next day I broke her heart and paid her back with stupidity. When I was riding home to the party, my rear tire had picked up an upholstery tack, so I didn't take the bike to school on Friday. Instead, Melo and I walked together down Chickasaw in the morning and back up Colorado in the afternoon. On the way home, we cut through the vacant lot at the corner of Hermosa and Colorado. Melo just barely missed stepping in a fresh pile of dog shit on the beaten path.

When we came out on the other side, we were on the sidewalk in front of the bungalow court on Hermosa across the street from, and a little behind the service exit of the Ford dealer. A black lawn jockey, holding a steel ring in his outstretched hand, stood on a pedestal out on the front lawn of the court. You could almost see Melo's brain working, putting together a scheme that was going to get us (read that, me) into trouble. I followed him over to the row of thirty-gallon trashcans behind the Ford dealer, and he picked out a slightly dirty, discarded blue paper towel. Then we went back across the street to the lot and, using the paper towel, he picked up the dog shit he'd almost stepped in a little while ago. He took the steaming turd and smudged it in the jockey's face.

From behind the slatted blinds of her bungalow, the court manager watched Melo do the deed as I stood by. Then she opened her screen door and stepped out onto her front porch to get a closer, unobstructed look at us. I was a dead giveaway in my school uniform. I knew I was busted as soon as she saw me. We took off across the street, ran through the vacant lot behind the Ford dealer and climbed over the fence and into the trailer court.

## Down the Foggy Ruins of Time

Francesca wasn't home when we got to the trailer, so I just dumped my books, and we cut through the court to Argus Drive and crossed the Boulevard to Melo's house. We didn't hang around there long; we went up to Robert Munson's house on Hermosa near Las Flores. As we got down off the bluff at the back of Melo's property, I glanced across Colorado and saw Francesca on the sidewalk in front of the Ford dealer. When she saw me, she waved and I waved back, but my heart sank under the weight of embarrassment and guilt over what we'd done to the lady's statue. Mom didn't know about it yet, so she was smiling and carefree, but she was going to find out very soon (the lady in the bungalow court shopped at Forcette's and knew her).

I got home from Robert's house at about five-thirty, and Francesca was unpacking the groceries she'd just bought at Forcette's. When I entered the trailer, she abruptly stopped what she was doing and glared at me.

"Boy, you sure do know how to break a mother's heart," she said. "How smart was it to do that to the lady's statue, I ask you. I'm so mad I could crown you."

"I didn't do it," I said. "Melo did it. I just watched."

"I know that! Don't you remember? I saw you with him right after you did it. Besides, that only makes it worse for you. You shouldn't have let

91

him do it, or if you couldn't stop him, you should've left when you figured out what he was up to."

That one stung me. She and I both knew I could've stopped him from doing it if I'd used my head, but like a fool, I just stood by and did nothing. To the bungalow court manager, Melo was just another one of the many little kids running around Eagle Rock dressed in blue jeans and a T-shirt. She didn't even know who he was, but Francesca knew, and she didn't put the finger on him to Harriet because she knew how futile that would've been. How would Harriet have punished him? She wouldn't have, indeed, couldn't have done anything to him. She didn't have any control over him.

I never was quite sure whether I was supposed to confess the incident or not. Ultimately I didn't, because I didn't quite know how. I mean, what the hell was I supposed to say? The words "feces" and "excrement" weren't even in my vocabulary yet, and if I'd used "shit" or "crap," I would've been guilty of the sin of using "impure language," a fact that, I was pretty sure, made those words unacceptable in the confessional. I guess I could've used "poop," but the more I thought about it, the more ridiculous I felt about my part in it. I was embarrassed, and I just wanted to forget about it, so I skipped it at my First Confession. I felt a hell of a lot more guilty about the deed itself than I ever did about not confessing it, but I have no doubt that if I

## Down the Foggy Ruins of Time

burn in hell for anything I did that afternoon or didn't do the next day in the confessional, it'll be for the omission, not for the sin.

The day I received First Holy Communion was fantastic. For one thing it was one of those spectacular Southern California spring days, bathed in sunshine and blue sky. The rugged San Gabriel foothills were a landscape painter's dream. I wore the standard uniform that all the other boys wore to the ceremony: matching white trousers, shirt, shoes and socks. The belt was just like the one Uncle Luke wore with his dress whites, the brass buckle the only thing on me that wasn't white. I was never a more devout Catholic than I was right then. Something about going to Communion instilled the faith in me, but I think my being scared shitless of going to hell had a lot to do with it, too.

After Mass we went home and Mom took some pictures of me next to our trailer with the spring as a backdrop, and then we went inside and had a big Sunday breakfast. I'd been fasting since eight o'clock the night before when I had milk and cookies, and the little thin wafer of unleavened bread that the priest had placed on my tongue at Communion had done nothing to satisfy my appetite.

The school term ended a month and a half after First Communion. We only had class until noon on the last day. Ronald and I got together with Jack Meador, and we pedaled over to Jack's house.

He lived on the western edge of town right near the Glendale city limits.

"My front yard's in Eagle Rock and my backyard's in Glendale," he said as we approached the house on Eagledale Avenue. Then he said, "We just crossed over the line," when we passed the kitchen window coasting down his driveway.

He'd dug an underground fort in his backyard. It was an oblong hole about four feet deep; the roof was a four by eight sheet of three-quarter-inch plywood lying across four-by-four redwood joists. He'd shoveled some of the dirt from the hole onto the top of the plywood so that the fort was under a smooth grassy mound that blended with the surrounding landscape. It was actually a roomy space considering how big both Ronald and Jack were, so we hung out down there for quite a while. We got out when a potato bug scurried across the dirt floor. When we came up, we went into the house where Jack's mother served us milk and chocolate chip cookies, the same homemade recipe she'd been preparing all year long and bringing to den meetings.

# Ten

That summer we took our second trip back to Minneapolis. The oldest boy of my mother's siblings, Danny, had completed his course of study at the seminary in Saint Paul, and was taking his vows in June, so we were going back to attend the ceremony. He'd been recruited by the Church in Utah and was riding with us to as far as Salt Lake City on our return trip. We were pulling in on a Wednesday. The ordination, which was the main reason we were making the pilgrimage, was on the following Sunday.

For the second year in a row, Ronald and I made it to the first day of swimming at the Yosemite pool. We swam until four o'clock, and then I went home to get ready for the trip. On Sunday morning we went to eight o'clock Mass, which put us on the road by nine-fifteen. Dad had traded the Packard in on a '38 Chrysler Airflow at a used car lot in Glendale. The Airflow had a fancy two-tone paint job: navy blue over the roof, trunk and hood, and creamy off-white on the door panels and fenders. It wasn't quite as big as the Packard, but it was a lot more stylish and deluxe than the angular, sharp-edged, black dinosaur that had brought us to California. End-to-end the Packard was about the same size as the trailer, and the Airflow was about six inches shorter than both. The Airflow's lines were rounded, smooth and aerodynamic. It would be the last car we'd own with running boards. The back seat had suicide doors. Antoine rented an air-conditioning cylinder that mounted on the outside of the car, rolled up in one of the rear-door windows. It was a feeble, and ultimately failed attempt to beat the scorching temperatures of the Mojave Desert. He also bought a canvas water bag with a rope handle that he looped over one of the front bumper guards.

On the trip Frank and I were horsing around so much in the back seat that we drove our parents to distraction before we even got to San Bernardino. In Las Vegas Antoine got drunk and lost at the tables, but after he came back to the room and passed out, Francesca went down to the casino and won it all back. There were golden sunrises on the desert and high plains leaving Las Vegas, Rock Springs, Wyoming and Pierre (locals pronounced it pier), South Dakota, and we saw Burma Shave signs in every state. When we crossed the Minnesota line at Lake Benton, Antoine sat taller in his seat, got a fresh grip on the wheel and said,

"Well, Ma, there she is.  Home at last."

## Down the Foggy Ruins of Time

From as far away as Lake Minnetonka you could see the Minneapolis skyline and the Foshay Tower, a phallic obelisk that stood taller than any other building in town. I immediately thought of the City Hall building in downtown Los Angeles, but the closer we got, the less apropos the comparison seemed. Whereas the City Hall building was white and clean looking, the Foshay Tower looked like a soot-covered, symmetrical, gray stalagmite.

The excitement mounted in me as we got onto the Beltline on the outskirts of town. As we got closer to my grandparents' house, I felt a special draw to the place, an awareness of my connection to it. Maybe, too, I was getting caught up in Antoine's and Francesca's exhilaration over their return home. Especially Antoine. He was really something to watch from the time we crossed the state line until we headed home eight days later. He could only be described as excited, animated and stoked from being in familiar digs with a host of memories, both pleasant and unpleasant.

We drove down maple-canopied Russell Avenue North and pulled up in front of my grandparents' house at around one-twenty. The house looked like an under-sized circus big top or a large wigwam with its steeply pitched hip-roof design. The neighborhood was quiet, and the place looked deserted, but it wasn't. Grandma and Jessie came to the front door as we were getting out of the car.

97

*Jerome Arthur*

What a cool time we had in Minnesota! It seemed like one continuous party from the time we got out of the car and stretched our legs until we piled back in with Uncle Danny and headed west. It was my first real meeting with Francesca's family. True, I had met them all two years earlier, but our stay was shorter then than it was this time, and it didn't seem like I had much time to get acquainted with them. And of course, they all had been present at my birth, and I'd had regular contact with them through my first two years, but I was so young when we moved that I had little memory of any of them. We were greeted first by Grandma and my aunt Jessie, Mom's youngest sister, who was only seven days older than Frank. She was really more like a cousin than an aunt. As they descended the steps to the sidewalk, Mom's seventeen and fourteen-year-old siblings, Casey and Edith, came out the front door and followed them down. Grandpa was at work and wouldn't be home till about three-thirty.

We all went into the house, but it was pretty hot in there, so we just walked on through and out the kitchen door to the backyard. We gathered around a wooden picnic table set up under a huge maple tree. Grandma and Mom went back into the house and returned with a pitcher of ice-cold lemonade and glasses for everyone. The adults sat down to chat, and that included Casey, who talked mostly to Antoine about fishing while Mom and Grandma had

## Down the Foggy Ruins of Time

their own conversation. Edith, Jessie, Frank and I drank our lemonade down pretty quickly, and then we went over to the playground at Cleveland school. We were hanging around by the swings when Antoine and Casey came out of the alley, and Dad called out to us,

"Hey, kids, we're goin' over to Penn Avenue, surprise Pa, take a ride on his streetcar. Wan'a come?"

Frank and I said, "Sure."

Edith and Jessie said, "You betcha."

Grandpa was a conductor on the Penn and Lowry line, which ran down Penn Avenue, just two blocks over from the house. As we stood on the safety zone, I was looking across the street at the marquee of the Alhambra Theater. A Hoppy double feature was playing: *False Paradise* and *Silent Conflict*. Then we saw the single, round headlamp on Grandpa's streetcar and felt the murmur of the steel wheels on the tracks as it approached. Just before the air breaks hissed and the car glided to a stop, you could smell the hot electricity as sparks flashed off the trolley where it made contact with the overhead wire.

Grandpa was a simple, uncomplicated man, so when we boarded his streetcar, he played it straight and refused to show any surprise at our arrival, sticking strictly to business, making sure Antoine had paid the nickel fare for each of us. He wasn't about to let anybody ride free, no matter that we were relatives, especially that we were relatives. He was a model of professionalism in his sharply pressed gray uniform with shiny black stripes down the out seams of the trousers, and hat to match with its glossy black beak and black and gray checked band. The official way he dispensed pennies, nickels, dimes and quarters from the changer on his belt was very impressive. We went to the end of the line, came back and got off in front of the Alhambra. As we stepped down onto the safety zone, Grandpa told my dad he was on his last run, and that he'd be home in about an hour.

And so ended our first afternoon in Minneapolis. That night we mostly just kicked back and relaxed around Grandpa's house. Uncle Luke lived only a mile away in a new subdivision off Osseo Road on the other side of the switching yard north of town. His neighborhood was the last development at that end of the city. The next time you saw any civilization after you left his neighborhood was the little town of Anoka, thirty miles north. That night he brought his family over to Grandpa's house, so we got to meet his pregnant wife, Jessica, and their one-year-old son, Danny.

Antoine and Luke made a party out of the evening. They polished off a pint of Canadian Club. Grandpa didn't approve of such behavior, and he told Luke so, but he didn't say a word to Dad be-

## Down the Foggy Ruins of Time

cause in his eyes Antoine could do no wrong. We all hit the sack soon after Luke took his family home. When I passed my grandparents' bedroom on my way to the bathroom to brush my teeth, I glanced in through the half-open door and could see both of them on their knees next to their bed praying together.

We spent the next three days getting ready for Uncle Dan's ordination and the attendant parties. Grandma did most of the preparation, but she was never so busy that she couldn't find time to listen, as she worked, to "Ma Perkins" on the radio every day. The first full day in Minneapolis, we kids went swimming at Twin Lakes in the afternoon, and we saw Ma and Pa Kettle at the Twin Theater, which was a brand-new movie house, in Robbinsdale, that night. We Farots spent Friday at the Bergmans', Antoine's older sister Aunt Megan and her spouse Uncle Luke. Their son, Kenny, was Frank's age.

It was mostly out of a sense of duty that Antoine took the time to visit Aunt Megan. It's true that he liked Luke (he affectionately called him Swede; he called every Swedish guy he'd ever known by that nickname). He also wanted to see Frank and me get to know Kenny, and that's pretty much what brought him around. He probably wouldn't have gone out of his way to be with his sister, otherwise. They'd been pissed off at each other ever since they were teenagers when he'd clubbed their stepfather,

Wiktor Sadlo with a Louisville Slugger. After he did the deed, he ran away from home and rode the rails with his best friend at the time, a kid named Helge Nelson, whom Antoine called, Swede. As mean as Wiktor was to Antoine, he was just that nice to Megan, so she'd stick up for him, and I always got the impression that she held Antoine responsible for their mother's death when he hit Wiktor with the bat. I'm sure Antoine thought she did.

As far as getting Frank and me together with Kenny, for my part, he could have skipped it. Frank and Kenny were the same age just like Frank and Bobby Forest, and every time we were in that kind of a situation, I always wound up being odd kid out. I wish I'd stayed at Grandma's house that day, gone to Twin Lakes again with Jessie, or maybe gone to see the two Hoppy movies at the Alhambra. The first thing Frank and Kenny did was ditch me, so I wound up hanging around with the adults.

Two good things did happen as a result of the visit. One was that Aunt Megan made a batch of the famous doughnuts she and my grandma used to make and Dad used to peddle. The other cool thing was the ride down to their place. Antoine turned off Lyndale at Twenty-sixth Avenue North and as we were passing Washington Avenue, he pointed out Grandpa's car barn on that corner. It was a four-story brick building two blocks from the river. When we got to Second Street North, Dad took a right. As

## Down the Foggy Ruins of Time

we passed Plymouth Avenue on Second, he pointed at a railroad yard down below the river bridge and said,

"That switching yard's where I spent my first night on the road back in thirty-one. A goddamn cold Thanksgiving night it was, too."

All of Mom's siblings were on hand for Dan's ordination. Those who were married brought their spouses and families along. My great-grandpa, Martin Konig, who was in his nineties, came up from the farm in Waseca. Francesca's oldest sister, Aunt Helen, my godmother, and her husband Bill, an internal medicine doctor by trade, were up from Knoxville, Tennessee with their three kids. The kids had southern accents, but Helen and Bill talked like the educated Minnesotans that they were. Maddy, the twenty-three-year-old sister between Uncle Danny and Uncle Luke, was there with her husband Josh, the forty-year-old pharmacist, and their baby daughter Juanita. They lived down on the Minnehaha Parkway in south Minneapolis. Since Luke and his family, Casey, Edith and Jessie were already in town, they were at the ordination as well. On Saturday afternoon the whole family gathered for a party at Grandma's. She was grilling some chicken and some walleyed and northern pike that Luke and Casey had caught at Hanging Kettle Lake the previous weekend.

*Jerome Arthur*

I gravitated right to Donald Wahlstrom. He was Aunt Helen's oldest kid, one year younger than I. He was a big kid like Ronald. I liked the southern drawl he and his sister Beverly and little brother Billy had, because it was so much different than the Minnesota/Great Lakes accent everybody else had. Donald and I ducked out of the party and took our gloves over to the schoolyard to play catch. Then we went to the drugstore soda fountain on the corner of Penn and Lowry for root beer floats. When we left the drugstore, we walked down Lowry to Memorial Drive. We went out into the huge lawn parkway and looked at some of the markers they had that memorialized the guys from Minneapolis who'd died in the First World War. We played some more catch, using one of the markers for home plate. We cut back across the lawn and went up Thirty-fourth to Russell and back to Grandma's.

Antoine, Maddy, and Luke were doing some hard drinking, and were being castigated and preached to by Helen and Grandpa. Helen gave all three of them a bad time, but Grandpa only came down on Maddy and Luke. He didn't say anything to Antoine, nor would he ever. Danny had no comment because he would never rebuke anybody, and certainly not Antoine or any of his own siblings for drinking too much, even though he was a teetotaler himself. The only alcohol he ever drank throughout his life was altar wine.

104

## Down the Foggy Ruins of Time

The party really got going after dark. Mom started to tell the story of my birth, and Grandma, Mrs. Rungren, Antoine and Grandpa, each with his or her own anecdote, followed her. After they finished that story, Dad took over the conversation and told stories about his experiences riding the rails in the Depression. The whole party gathered around him, and he went on and on, living up to his reputation among Francesca's family that, "he could talk to anybody."

Sunday morning Grandma lit some votive candles that she'd gotten blessed by her pastor at Saint Anne's, and put them in every room in the house, this she explained to us kids, to purge it of evil spirits. I hung out with Jessie that morning. We went up in the attic and rummaged around in a couple of musty old steamer trunks filled with photo albums and religious artifacts—crucifixes, rosaries and small statues of Jesus, Mary and Joseph. The pictures were old, faded black and white photographs and sepia daguerreotypes of various of my grandparents' parents, siblings, aunts, uncles and cousins in a farm setting, probably Waseca and Cosmos. I didn't know who anybody was, but Jessie knew some of them, and she showed me some pictures of Grandma and Grandpa when they were so young that I didn't even recognize them. There was one picture of Grandpa from when he was in the

Army. He looked as spiffy in that uniform as he did in his streetcar conductor's uniform.

Although it was only nine o'clock in the morning, it was starting to get warm up there, so we decided to go to the opposite temperature extreme in the house, and we headed down into the basement which was as cool as a wine cellar. The coal burning furnace had been replaced with a gas one, and the coal chute was gone, as was the smell of coal gas, which had been replaced by a damp, musty odor. Grandpa had a grindstone about thirty inches in diameter that was set up on a framework with a bicycle seat and pedals. Casey still stored his skis there, only now he had a couple pairs instead of only one. On a shelf next to the skis was a pair of hockey skates. A wringer washer was in one corner and clotheslines were strung across the room.

Finding that stuff decidedly less interesting than the pictures in the attic, Jessie and I were soon bored, and we ran up the steps and out to the backyard where we joined Frank and Edith who were just leaving to go to the school playground.

The ordination at noon was a huge spectacle. About fifty seminarians took their vows that day. There were cardinals and bishops everywhere. The archbishop said a Solemn High Mass, and the guys getting ordained had to lie on the floor in a prone position throughout most of the ceremony. Afterwards, there was a huge reception in an auditorium

## Down the Foggy Ruins of Time

across the quad from the cathedral. Everybody who was at Grandma's party was there for Uncle Danny. And the families of the other seminarians were there for them, too.

On Monday the Wahlstroms left for Knoxville. They took my great-grandpa with them and dropped him off in Waseca. Those of us who were left filled two cars and went up to Gull Lake. Luke had gotten some vacation time so he crammed Grandma, Grandpa, and Edith, as well as his own family, into his forty-one Olds. Danny, Casey and Jessie rode with us. Maddy and her family didn't go because Josh couldn't get the time off from work. We got a couple cabins with docks right on the lake. Each dock had a rowboat pulled up on the beach next to it. There was also a canoe turned up-side-down at the side of one of the cabins. While the adults moved our stuff in, Frank and Jessie and I pulled one of the rowboats down off the beach and into the lake. We rowed out twenty feet or so from the end of the dock. Frank was rowing and Jessie and I were sitting in the stern. I looked over my shoulder at the dock and saw Mom standing out on the end taking a picture of us with her black box camera.

After they got set up in the cabins, Antoine, Luke and Casey went to a bait shop down the road and rented an outboard motor, and they went out fishing that first afternoon. They had good luck and we had plenty to eat for dinner that night. The next morning Antoine and Luke left Casey behind when they took off to go fishing. They didn't do it on purpose. He was sleeping and they just forgot to wake him up, but his feelings were hurt plenty. When he woke up and realized that they were already gone, he made a futile attempt to go after them in the canoe. He didn't even know which way they'd gone, so he didn't get far before he paddled back. He wound up spending the rest of the morning moping around at the end of the dock and sulking in the cabin. They came back in for lunch, and he got to go out with them in the afternoon.

Danny spent his time at the lake saying his daily prayers and walking in the woods along the lakefront. The other adults who didn't go fishing spent most of their time playing my grandparents' favorite card game, thirty-one, and we kids rowed around the lake in the other boat and went swimming. We drove back to the Twin Cities on Wednesday morning after breakfast. Wednesday afternoon and evening we packed and got ready so that we could pull out early the next day.

We took the same route home that we'd taken to get there. The first day on the road we made it to Mount Rushmore. Antoine and Francesca took pictures of each other with Danny, Frank and me lined up along a wooden rail fence with the presidents' heads above us in the background. We made

## Down the Foggy Ruins of Time

Salt Lake City the second night out and Las Vegas the third night. At Stateline we started singing, "California here I come, right back where I started from...." We crossed the Suicide Bridge out of Pasadena into Eagle Rock at one-thirty. Five minutes later we turned off Colorado Boulevard onto Argus Drive and into the trailer court.

It didn't look like anything had changed much in the two weeks that we'd been gone, but it looked a lot different than where we'd just come from. Eagle Rock, even though it had its share of trees and greenery, looked denuded compared to lush, green Minneapolis. We'd experienced rain, lightning and thunder a couple times while we were there. The last rain we'd had in Southern California had been at the start of spring. We were home, and though it wasn't like Minnesota, it was great to be back. Of the four of us, I think only Antoine missed Minneapolis enough to actually still want to be there.

# Eleven

The next day after we got home from the trip, I went over to Yosemite and got on the Eagles' roster. The Eagles was a sandlot baseball team. Neither Ronald nor Melo had any interest in baseball, so they didn't go out. Thus, absent my two best friends on the sandlot, I started a new friendship with the pitcher on our team. Steven Gómez was a fifth-grade classmate of Frank's at Saint Dominic's. He and his family were the only American-Mexicans in Eagle Rock, a fact that naturally attracted me to him. I think he liked me because my accent (the one I first picked up from George Nieto and his mother and has stuck with me to this day) was similar to his. Same thing that attracted Ramón's attention. My friendship with Steven was the first in which a buddy and a contemporary of my brother's actually became better friends with me than Frank after he got to know us. The scene would repeat itself over the years, and each time it happened, Frank became infuriated and carried on his sibling grudge with a vengeance.

## Down the Foggy Ruins of Time

I was the second baseman on our team. I had a good glove and arm, but I couldn't hit, and I was slow on the base paths when I was lucky enough to get walked. Despite those weaknesses, however, by the end of summer, I wanted to be a major leaguer when I grew up, wanted to play for the Cleveland Indians like my favorite big-league player at the time, Bob Feller, the great, ninety-five-mile-an-hour fastball pitcher.

Steven and I had a great pick-off strategy with a runner on second. When the guy was leading off, I'd stand on the bag. Steven was a southpaw, and the way he checked the runner was so deceptive. I was the only one who could tell if he was going to the plate, or if he was going to try to pick the guy off. If he went to the plate, I was quick enough off the bag to fill the hole if the batter tried to hit into it. I had my moments, but never enough of them to overcome my weaknesses at the plate and on the base paths.

Besides playing in the sandlot, I also got into going out to the ballpark with Antoine and his buddies to watch our two Triple-A Pacific Coast League teams, the Los Angeles Angels and the Hollywood Stars. The Angels played at Wrigley Field down near Vernon in South Central Los Angeles, and the Stars played their home games at rickety, old, wooden Gilmore Field on the corner of Beverly and Fairfax opposite Farmer's Market. Every big

113

city on the west coast from San Diego to Seattle had a team that played the Angels and the Stars, but we mostly went to games where they played each other. That way we could see both teams, which accommodated my brother and me at the same time. Antoine and I were Angels fans and Frank was a Stars fan. Dad's friend, and our frequent companion to games, an old drunkard named Andy Anderson (his real first name was Art, but Dad called him Swede even though everybody else called him Andy), pulled for the Stars. Later in the season, we went to a couple of Seattle Rainiers games, one at Wrigley and one at Gilmore. Another one of Antoine's buddies, a guy from work named Gilbert, born and raised in Vancouver, British Columbia, went with us to those games and rooted for the Rainiers. He'd been a Rainiers fan ever since he'd emigrated from Canada to Seattle, and he stayed a fan after he moved to Los Angeles.

When we went to games at Wrigley Field, we usually got seats in the right field bleachers. It was a fun place to sit because you were close enough to watch Max West in right and Cecil Garriott in center bantering with the fans and each other as they warmed up before the first pitch. Antoine and Andy made bets on different plays throughout the game as they got drunker'n skunks quaffing down East-side beer ("What'll yuh bet Gene Baker gets a hit next time he goes to the plate?" "A half-buck says he

## Down the Foggy Ruins of Time

don't…"). Sometimes Dad was so wasted by the end of the game that we were lucky we made it home without getting into a car wreck or him getting busted for drunk driving.

At that stage of his life, he was still a happy, benevolent boozer, and the baseball games were probably more fun because he got so drunk. Over the next few years he'd go through a metamorphosis. Before long he'd start to experience extreme personality changes, and his benevolence turned to hostility. As each year passed, it took fewer drinks to get him stoned so that by the time I was in high school, he'd get mean and nasty after only two shots.

But I have to admit, no matter how mean he got, he wouldn't ever take his hostility out, in any physical way, on any of the rest of us in the family. That's the one thing I can say about Antoine as a father: he never got rough with either Frank or me. He always remembered the beatings he'd taken from his evil stepdad, and he made sure that Frank and I didn't suffer the same fate. From time to time over the years, he'd tell us,

"By God, I never laid a hand on either of yuhs. Learned real good from that Polack son of a bitch, Wiktor Sadlo. After I took the ball bat to the bastard and ran away from home, I swore that if I ever had kids of my own, I'd never touch 'em. And I ain't never."

Mom told a different story for herself. Many years later, when I was an adult, I told her how I remembered Dad making that statement.

"Well, that sure don't apply to me," she said. "I'd take the belt to the both a' yuh, if I thought yuh deserved it."

"I'm sure you did and I'm sure we did," was my only reply.

And so, I spent most of my summer weekdays in the sandlot picking off base runners with Steven, and weekends at Wrigley or Gilmore watching Coast League games (Sunday doubleheaders, mostly) with Antoine and his buddies and Frank. I also hooked up with Ronald or Melo a couple days a week for swimming.

As the summer was ending and I was getting ready to go into Sister Ruth's third grade class, Antoine and Francesca found a house to rent on the corner of Colorado and Wiota, and we moved. It was about a mile and a half from the trailer court, only a couple of long blocks from Figueroa Street.

On move-in day we got some help from a kid who lived a couple doors up Wiota. His name was Dicky Fears and he was in Frank's fifth grade class at school. After we'd been moving stuff for a while, his parents, Henry and Lila, came down with a couple of their other kids, Jean and Joan, and introduced themselves. They were a big Catholic family, five kids in all. Jean, the third oldest, was in my

## Down the Foggy Ruins of Time

class. She was a nice girl and I liked her a lot. I always thought she got a raw deal when she got polio and was left with a pigeon-toed limp.

Within less than a month after we moved in, Mom and Dad became good friends with Henry and Lila, and by Thanksgiving the Fearses were in on the Saturday night poker game with the Forests and Bankses. They were an odd addition to the group. Greg Forest was such a fastidious, self-important snob, and they were nothing but down-home, big-family Catholics, a little on the sloppy side. Years later I found out that Greg did indeed despise Henry. In the end he and Louise quit the weekly game in disgust.

The move to Wiota turned out to be only temporary, which I was glad of because I didn't like the neighborhood or the house. The only good part of it was the last tenant was William Boyd, the actor who played Hopalong Cassidy, and when he moved, he left a couple things in the garage that I think were movie props. One was a bearskin rug. Probably the worst thing about living there was its location right on Colorado Boulevard, a street on which some of the heaviest, noisiest traffic in town rumbled by. Mom wouldn't let us ride our bikes to school because the only way to get there was down busy Colorado. We had to walk, which meant that we needed to leave a half-hour earlier in the morning, and we got home that much later every afternoon.

Since Frank and Dicky didn't want me tagging along with them and I wasn't about to walk with Jean and Joan, I had to go it alone to as far as Argus Drive where I met up with Melo. On the very first day of school, we saw some exciting action when we got to the light at Highland View Avenue. The Twenty-five streetcar jumped off the tracks a half block up in front of us. It shrieked on its steel wheels across two lanes of eastbound traffic and came to a stop in the parking lot in front of Psenner Poff auto body and paint shop. Amazingly, nobody was hurt, neither the passengers on the streetcar, nor any pedestrians on the sidewalk. Melo and I were the closest pedestrians to the accident, and we were a good half block away. The scores left by the wheels remained in the street for another two years after the derailing, which was when they pulled up the tracks, resurfaced the street and replaced the streetcars on that line with buses. That left the Five car as the only streetcar to come to Eagle Rock. In five years buses would replace the streetcars on that line, too, when the conversion would take place citywide.

Spending Christmas in a house was a nice change, but the pad was so weird that it took a lot of the spirit out of the holiday. The traffic noise on the Boulevard was really bad, and that was only the half of it. The place was spooky and the furniture rundown. The lampshades were made of some kind of ghostly material that glowed in the dark and scared

118

## Down the Foggy Ruins of Time

the shit out of me more than once in the middle of the night. The house was also not in good shape. Later, when they built the Foothill freeway on the side of the mountain above Hill Drive, they bull-dozed it and about four or five other houses to make room for an off ramp.

I was not an unhappy kid when Mom and Dad announced, right after Easter, that they'd bought a trailer in the upper court back at Eagle Rock Springs. There was only about a month and a half left of school when we moved, and Ronald and I rode our bikes down Chickasaw Avenue and back every one of those days. What a difference only tak-ing five minutes to get there by bike, versus forty-five minutes walking.

We moved into the Forests' trailer. Greg and Louise had bought a two-bedroom house on Mount Royal Drive north of the Boulevard. Our new trailer was laid out similar to the old one, except all the rooms were bigger and the space it sat on was big-ger, and the fenced, concrete patio with a metal awn-ing was also bigger. On warm summer evenings, Mom set up the dinner table out there. Construction on the new upper court toilet/shower facility had been completed just before we moved in.

During the time we'd been living in the house, there seemed to be a marked increase in the anti-Communist fervor that was sweeping the coun-try. When the paranoia came to Eagle Rock and

Saint Dominic's, we started having air raid drills to prepare for an A-bomb attack. A few Congressmen and Senators (I think there were more fools in those two chambers during that era than at any other time in the history of the country) had Americans duped into thinking Russia was going to attack us with nuclear weapons. I wonder how many of those people were around to witness the performance (or lack thereof) of Russian-made missiles in Iraq in the early nineteen-nineties. The people at the firehouse on the corner of Colorado and Maywood started doing twice-weekly civil defense drills. At random times during the week, they'd sound the firehouse siren, and the nuns had us diving under our desks and staying there until it stopped. Sometimes it seemed like it lasted forever. I was so young and gullible that I got taken in by the ridiculous contemporary rhetoric and started wishing we had a bomb shelter instead of a covered patio next to our trailer.

My third-grade teacher, Sister Ruth, was of the same mind as the fools in the government, and she was always getting on her high horse about "the godless red menace in Russia," and now most recently in China. She was a tough old gal, which prompted her students to call her "Sister Ruthless," and a staunch anti-Communist who introduced the expression "iron curtain" into my vocabulary. I had a hard time trying to imagine what it meant the first time I heard it. Then I started hearing it from news

## Down the Foggy Ruins of Time

commentators on the radio, and Lamont Cranston even used it a couple times on episodes of "The Shadow." Over the next couple years, the phrase insinuated itself into the American vernacular. By the end of the school year, I felt like I'd been through the mill of fear. I'd had three years of hearing about the apocalypse in the Bible; since First Communion I was scared shitless of mortal sin and going to hell; and no sooner was I instilled with those fears than they threw in the Communists and the atomic bomb to really scare the hell out of me. Sometimes I thought I'd be lucky if I made it to my next birthday.

One thing you could do to redeem yourself from the tortures of hell or purgatory, I thought, was to be an altar boy. I wanted to start serving Mass as soon as possible, start working off some of the purgatory time that was building for my venial sins. You were supposed to be at least in fourth grade to go on the altar, but I wanted to try out while I was still only in third. I was too anxious to wait, so I sat down and memorized by rote from beginning to end all of the Latin parts required of the server. I had the sequence down, but that's all I had down, so if anybody pulled a quote out of the middle and asked me for the appropriate response, I couldn't give it, and that's exactly what Father Mick did when I applied in the springtime.

"What do you say when I say, 'Sursum corda'?" he asked.

The correct answer was, "Habémus ad Dóminum," but those phrases were from the middle of the Mass, and I didn't know them out of sequence, so, with what looked to me like a gleam of delight in his eye, he sent me on my way, telling me to come back again next year when I was old enough to qualify.

I think he was still pissed off at me for the way I'd acted two and a half years ago on the first day of school. Needless to say, after he rejected me, I was more than ever intimidated by him, and I think I resisted his attempts thereafter to make a true believer out of me as he'd done with Antoine. The incident almost made me not want to be an altar boy at all, but I was determined not to be defeated so easily, so I tried again eight months later when I was in fourth grade and I made it. I got a lot of encouragement and help from Sister Johanna my teacher that year. I couldn't very well not go on the altar and miss out on being with the other nine guys in my class who also made it the first year.

The best part of being an altar boy was getting up there during a crowded Mass; it was like being on stage. If you got to serve the popular Masses, invariably some girl whose attention you were trying to attract would be there, and you had the perfect chance to show off. Maybe there was a method to Father Mick's madness. In third grade I wanted nothing to do with the Fears girls; in fourth grade I

122

## Down the Foggy Ruins of Time

was showing off for them on the altar. Another fun thing about serving Mass was the altar wine. If there wasn't a priest in the sacristy, my altar partner and I would sip from the quart bottle as we filled the cruets, and a couple of times I got a little goofy before the Mass started.

The worst part was when they had processions to honor the Virgin Mary during the month of May. It was usually just late enough in the spring that it was starting to get warm. For those events we had to spend an hour and a half in our cassocks and surplices walking a lap around the block in the hot afternoon sun. Luckily the cassocks were white linen and the surplices white muslin and lace (all gone slightly yellow with age), so it didn't get as hot as it could have if the cassocks had been black or red like some I'd seen in other parishes.

# Twelve

Then the worst thing that could happen did happen. One week after school got out, the United States got into a war over in Korea. Through the summer, all the news reports on the radio and in the papers were saying that American soldiers were dying over there. It was all a jumble of distant places and strange names brought terrifyingly close to home: the battle of Inchon, the thirty-eighth parallel, the Yalu River, General Douglas Mac Arthur and Singman Ree. It seemed like all of Sister Ruth's dark prophecies were being fulfilled. I'd just spent the school year hearing her tell of the horrors of Communism and how the Russians were going to attack us with atomic bombs. Now we were in an actual shooting war with the Communist North Koreans, and there was talk about the Chinese throwing in with them. It was pretty scary, and I was glad school was out and we didn't have to listen to Sister Ruth's ranting and raving about it.

To take my mind off of the bullshit that was happening all around me, I worked harder at and

## Down the Foggy Ruins of Time

concentrated more on baseball, and I was getting pretty good. Steven Gómez and I played a second season together on the sandlot at Yosemite. Come September, he was going into sixth grade, and he was thinking seriously about trying out for Saint Dominic's seventh and eighth grade softball team in the spring. He tried to talk me into trying out too, which really pissed Frank off, but I knew I didn't stand a chance so I didn't even consider it. In the end, Steven did try out, but they told him to come back next year.

At Saint Dominic's, Mass was celebrated every weekday morning and Saturday at 6:30 and 8:15. They didn't have sermons at weekday Masses, so the whole thing only lasted for half an hour. The only time I ever went to 6:30 weekday Mass was when I was scheduled to serve it, and I tried to get out of going at 8:15 whenever I could. The church was right across the street from the school, so if you got to school no later than 8:25, you were expected to go straight to Mass. Sister Adolf, the vice principal and seventh grade teacher, patrolled the schoolyard until then to make sure that those who got there early enough went into the church.

Ronald and I tried to leave my place by 8:15 or later. If it looked like we were going to get there in time to go to Mass, we'd skirt the school on Colorado and go down Caspar Avenue to Hobby Haven where we joined about a half dozen other kids who

125

were also dodging Sister Adolf's eagle eye. Hobby Haven was a small, neighborhood toy store at the corner of Merton and Caspar. The owner was a bald-headed old guy known only by the nickname Hobby. He toddled down Caspar every morning to open up shop at eight-thirty. He had every kind of model airplane you could imagine, from balsa wood gliders to pedestaled B-29s to different kinds of World War Two fighter planes and World War One biplanes with tiny one-lunger motors. He also had Duncan and Cherrio yo-yos, kites and toy cars and trucks. He had a rack of candy bars on the counter next to the cash register, and directly in front of the candy rack standing on the floor was a row of penny-candy globes on steel pedestals all in a straight line.

All we ever really did was hang out there and look at stuff. There was no way we could afford to buy something every time we went there, other than penny candy, like Double Bubble bubblegum or Tootsie Rolls or jawbreakers. The main reason we did it was to hide out from Sister Adolf until Mass let out at a quarter to nine. Then we'd wander over to the schoolyard to assemble for the morning's "Credo," "Our Father" and "Hail Mary's," "The Pledge.." and "The…Anthem."

Melo and I bought our B-29s from Hobby, and when we got them home and started assembling them, I found out in a hurry that he was much better at that sort of thing than I could ever hope to be. I

## Down the Foggy Ruins of Time

didn't have the patience for the detailed work it took to put one together, and I really wasn't all that interested in airplanes. Actually, I only bought it because he'd gotten one. After we assembled them, his looked like a good model of the real thing, and mine only looked like a bad imitation of his. The trailing edge of the wings on his came off the fuselage at the appropriate ninety-degree angle; the wings on mine were swept back more in the fashion of a modern jet airliner. His decals were all straight and smooth; mine came out crooked and wrinkled. I guess the real story there was that he was excited about the plane itself; I couldn't have cared less about it or any other airplane.

But that was okay because I started getting other ideas about what was important at that stage of my life. One Indian summer night shortly after I went into Sister Johanna's fourth grade class, Frank and I went over to Melo's house after dinner to watch television. Harriet had bought a fifteen-inch Muntz at the beginning of summer. That night I didn't get to watch too much though, because as soon as I walked in the front door, Phyllis put the arm on me and dragged me off to her room. When we got there, one of her girlfriends was already there and waiting for us. Phyllie locked the door, and the three of us spent the next half hour or so rolling around on her bed, kissing and hugging. Making out. Now, that just beat the hell out of messing around with some foolish model of a World War Two bomber.

When we came out, we joined Melo, Frank and Anita and watched the end of "Sandy's Dreams." After it ended, all of us went out to the backyard and smoked some cigarettes Melo had swiped from Harriet's purse. I only took a couple of puffs, which I didn't even inhale, and ten minutes later I was sick as a dog. I didn't throw up, but I felt like I was going to, and I ended up lying down and spinning around, at least that's how it felt to me, on the water-stained couch on the front porch, moaning and holding my guts. Nobody else got sick, so I just figured that they'd all done some smoking before. I was still sick as Frank and I crossed the Boulevard back to the trailer court at nine o'clock. He rode my ass all the way home.

"God! The girls didn't even get sick, and they inhaled," he said, using his most disparaging tone.

And so, his abuse and scorn continued, but I was getting used to it by then. He really got bummed anytime he thought I was upstaging him. Just two months after the smoking incident, Antoine and I did a musical gig together at the Christmas program in the parish hall. The act consisted of Dad playing "Silent Night" on his harmonica backstage as I stood at the footlights in my Cub uniform with a taped-over harmonica held to my mouth and mimed his playing

## Down the Foggy Ruins of Time

for the audience. It was my first time in the spot-
light, and I was digging on it, but Frank started ragging on me and putting my part of the performance
down just as soon as we got home that night.

That gig was about as musical as it ever got
for me. In fifth grade I took piano and violin lessons,
but I never followed through on either one of those
two instruments. The only thing I could ever play
was the radio and the record player. To my later dis-
appointment, I discovered that I just wasn't musical.
Frank, on the other hand, emerged as quite a musical
talent in his early twenties, learning the guitar and
the piano by ear, and doing saloon and coffee house
gigs with a folk trio in the early sixties. I never knew
why I was such a threat to him, or why he never
treated me like a brother when we were kids. Things
got a little better after we were adults, but by then I
regarded him with extreme suspicion. I'd learned
from the earlier years not to trust him.

# Thirteen

Sister Johanna was new to Saint Dominic's when my classmates and I went into her fourth-grade class. The complete opposite of old Ruthless, she was a first-year teacher, probably about twenty-three years old, by far the youngest, prettiest woman on the teaching staff. I was smitten instantly because, besides being young and beautiful, she was also an American-Mexican. I looked up "nun" in the dictionary Ramón had given me. I called her "Johanna la monja," using the correct Spanish pronunciation, and she was really impressed. Since my first conversations with Ramón five years ago, I tried to pronounce Spanish words the way he did, and the way I remembered George's mom saying them. I wanted my Spanish pronunciation to sound as authentic as theirs.

Her white habit and white smile highlighted her velvety brown cheeks and smooth-as-milk-chocolate hands. The nuns didn't wear makeup, not that Sister Johanna ever needed any. She was a natural beauty. Her dark, almond eyes and long lashes

## Down the Foggy Ruins of Time

needed no mascara, and the natural gloss and color of her cinnamon lips were flawless just as they were. She was gentle and soft spoken, another contrast to Sister Ruth. She just didn't use words like "Communist" and "iron curtain." The only way she'd even mention the war in Korea was to remind us that people were losing their lives over there and that we should say special prayers for them, all of them, both American and Korean soldiers, and innocent Korean civilians, too.

She was my favorite teacher in grade school. There was more than just a simple rapport between us. Indeed, she was the first girl I ever fell in love with (it was most certainly a one-sided affair; I'm sure she never entertained the same thoughts about me), but the judgment of society in general and the Church in particular rendered such thoughts and feelings taboo, since she was an adult woman more than twice my age, and a nun to boot. The taboo didn't stop me from having sweet dreams about her, though.

It was a clear case of unrequited love. I have no doubt Sister Johanna wasn't dreaming about me, or even thinking about me in any way other than as one of her pupils. The only real consolation I had was knowing I wasn't just any pupil, but a special one. This distinction manifested itself in the way she treated me and in the grades I was getting from her. I was such a punk, hanging around with the likes of

Melo Gervais, getting into trouble, generally not giving too much of a damn about school. Through my first three years in the classroom, I was a straight C student, but in Sister Johanna's fourth grade class I got an A in religion and a B in spelling. Her help with my Latin was probably the key to my passing Father Mick's test to be an altar boy. This time when he pulled quotes out of context, I was ready with the appropriate responses, even though I still didn't understand the language. He seemed duly impressed with my performance, and I owed it all to Sister Johanna.

One day when she was drilling me on my Latin, I started asking questions about her family. She said they still lived in the same house she grew up in down in Lincoln Heights.

"So, you have a lota' brothers and sisters like my mom?" I asked her.

"No. There are only three of us. All girls," she said.

"How old are your sisters, and are they go'n'a be nuns, too, or what?"

"Oh no," she said. "One in the family is enough for my papá. Josie's a sophomore at Los Angeles State College. She wants to be a high school Spanish teacher. My youngest sister, Lupe, is a senior at Sacred Heart High in the neighborhood, and she's preparing to follow Josie into State College. They're both good girls."

## Down the Foggy Ruins of Time

Besides getting a new teacher, we also got a couple of new kids in the class, the Schwarz twins, who were as obnoxious as Sister Johanna was nice. They were fraternal twins, so different that you wouldn't even think they were brothers much less twins. About the only physical characteristic they had in common was they both had freckles. The one personality trait they shared was that they were bullies, always harassing somebody into a fight. Lonny was a big, heavy-set, redheaded kid; Lanny was a skinny little kid about my size with sandy-brown hair. They were like a litter of kittens whose eggs had been fertilized by two different toms. Lanny, the smaller one of the two, got me into a fight with him within the first month of the new school year. I was no match for him because even though I was a little punk, I wasn't a rowdy little punk. I never was one much for fighting because of the pain factor. Also, I really wasn't mean or tough, which is what it takes to be a fighter. Lanny Schwarz was a mean, tough little son of a bitch.

I can't even remember what I did, if I did anything at all, to cause the guy to jump me the way he did. It happened one morning shortly before the nine o'clock bell. We'd just been over at Hobby's along with a bunch of other kids and were going through the alley that ran between the school and the Chevy dealer. It was the long way around and we were only trying to kill some more time before the

133

bell. I said something (I'll be damned if I can re-member what it was), and Lanny got really pissed off. He was a wiry, fast little son of a bitch and he made quick work of me. Sister Johanna came to my rescue when she heard me crying. My nose was bleeding from a right jab, and at the exact moment that she showed up on the scene, Lanny caught me with a left hook on the side of the head that sent me sprawling.

He took off up the alley the moment he saw her. She got me on my feet and took me to the nurse's room where she stanched my bloody nose and put an ice pack on the golf ball that was growing next to my right eye. No doubt about it, the guy had a good left hook. Sister made Lanny come to the nurse's room and apologize, and that was all well and good, but I learned to steer clear of the jerk after that. A couple years later, Lonny did the same thing to Jack Meador, a bigger kid who was never any-thing but a quiet, nice person. He damn sure never did anything to Lonny Schwarz.

I had to laugh the first time I heard Lanny explain how their last name was "German, not Jew-ish." He said that the same name with a T before the Z was Jewish—as if he had to explain anything. After all, he and his twin were going to Catholic school, attending Mass, receiving Holy Communion, serving on the altar. It should have been fairly obvious that they were Catholics, not Jews, but they were all the

## Down the Foggy Ruins of Time

time explaining that they weren't Jewish, and it
struck me that they must have been pretty insecure
about their own identity and heritage. Of course, I
had just the opposite idea in my mind. I wished my
name had the look and sound of something I wasn't.

Lanny was an excellent athlete, and he immediately began to dominate all of our games
−kickball, touch football, basketball and softball. He
was a southpaw who seemed to be trying, through
athletic prowess, to compensate for other shortcom-
ings, like his speech impediment. He had a funny
way of pronouncing words that began with ST, like
stucco, for example. The way Lanny pronounced it,
it came out "tsucco." Also, he didn't pronounce his
H's, which he pointed out was the way Englishmen
do (ha, cockney English, maybe, not the king's English), but he didn't sound anything like a Brit. He
sounded like an American who needed speech thera-
py. Lonny didn't have any of these problems, but he
also wasn't the athlete that Lanny was either. Now
that I recall all this stuff, I think I remember the reason Lanny jumped me was because maybe I mim-
icked his speech.

The twins's dad was an engineer on the
Southern Pacific railroad, and before they moved to
Los Angeles, they'd lived in Dunsmuir, a little railroad town in the mountains up in northern California. They bragged about it, talking like it was some
kind of mountain paradise, and putting down Los

135

Angeles the way people from northern California do, saying stuff like, "L.A. ain't nothin' but a desert that they brought water to." I never liked it when non-Angelenos, especially northern Californians, and more especially San Franciscans and Bay Areans slurred over the initials they used as an abbreviation for Los Angeles. Those same people would bring down the wrath of God on anybody who dared call San Francisco "Frisco."

      Robert Nez was the third new addition to the class. He'd come from Nogales, México. He was only in the fourth-grade classroom the first day. He didn't speak any English, so on the second day they took him away from the only teacher who could talk to him in his own language and moved him down to third grade supposedly only until he got a better grasp of English. For some reason he never achieved grade level. His English eventually got good, but they still kept him one year behind me and my classmates all the way through.

      He sure had a great arm; nobody could hit his fastball; and he was accurate too, able to throw strikes all day long, just as long as he didn't try to throw too hard. That was the only time he was wild, and then all he'd do was throw high. He told us he'd developed his arm by throwing rocks at jackrabbits back home. In October some of us got to see his accuracy when we went up into the hills above Hill Drive looking for pigeons, jack rabbits, squirrels,

136

## Down the Foggy Ruins of Time

whatever we could find, with bee bee guns and sling shots. Robert was the only one who didn't have a weapon, but he did better with rocks and his arm than anybody did with a Daisy or a slingshot. He got a jackrabbit, which made him the only one of us to hit anything. Besides having a great fastball, he had a big bat too, and that's probably why he ended up being a third baseman instead of a pitcher.

And what a cool guy! The complete opposite of the Schwarz twins. He was just as good an athlete as Lanny and could be just as bad-ass as both of them put together, but he never advanced either talent except in self-defense or in honest, fair competition. He became best friends with his next-door neighbor, a fifth grader named John Drew. They were inseparable in grade school and they stayed good buddies for a long time after. Once, when we were all in our early twenties, I saw them shooting pool in a bar near the Traffic Circle in Long Beach. I didn't talk to them, but I recognized them from across the room and could see that they were still tight partners after all those years.

The fourth weekend in January, my mom's youngest brother Casey, stopped in on us. He was fresh out of Air Force boot camp and heading for his duty station in Japan. He had orders to be on a plane on Monday afternoon at March Air Force Base out near Perris Lake. My parents took him to the horse races at Santa Anita on Saturday, where they got in

137

touch with one of his and Francesca's cousins from the farm in Waseca.

Billy Konig had recently gotten a job as a parking attendant on the racetrack circuit. He was at Santa Anita from Christmas to Easter, at Hollywood Park in the spring and then at Del Mar for half the summer. He also took a swing up north every year at the end of summer to Tanforan, Golden Gate Fields and Bay Meadows. He got Mom, Dad and Casey passes into the grandstand at Santa Anita. Frank and I got to go along, but it was pretty boring, and I wasn't there long before I started wishing I'd stayed home. We mostly just hung out in the infield looking for a winner among the discarded pari-mutuel tickets, but we never found one. The three adults were all losers. Not even the ones Billy touted them on ran in the money.

When we got home at about eight o'clock that night, Dad was pretty drunk, but Mom and Casey hadn't had any drinks and were sober. Billy was sober, too. We'd waited for him to get off work, and he followed us to our trailer. Antoine rode along with him, and Mom drove our car. He was staying in a hotel room in Hollywood, and our place was right on his way home from the track. He stuck around and had one drink with Antoine before driving to his hotel. Mom went to bed ahead of everybody, and Frank and I weren't far behind her, but there wasn't much sleeping until Billy finished his drink and left.

138

## Down the Foggy Ruins of Time

At that point Antoine and Casey turned in, and the trailer got dark and quiet.

Early Monday morning we all climbed into the Chrysler, drove downtown and dropped Antoine off at work. He shook hands with Casey and wished him luck. Then Francesca headed the car back out to Eagle Rock and dropped Frank and me off right in front of school at 8:15, so there was no getting out of going to Mass that day. Casey's flight out of March Air Force Base was supposed to be at one o'clock. Francesca was already back at the trailer when we got home from school.

As soon as Casey was gone, I began to worry about him. He was in Japan, not Korea, but they were only across the Sea of Japan from each other, about the same distance across the Gulf of México that New Orleans is from Cuba. And the war in Korea droned on. MacArthur wanted to march into China, and Harry Truman fired him.

The next day after the firing, a car hit me as I rode my bike down Colorado on my way to school. I was going the wrong way (clearly in the wrong), and a westbound car making a left turn onto Hermosa ran into me. I slammed my head on the curb and was unconscious for twenty minutes. I came to at Georgia Street Receiving with Mom and Dad at my side.

I went back to school the next day, Friday, and my classmates all gathered around and commiserated with me. The sympathy session lasted about five minutes, and then we got busy with the school-work at hand. Sister Johanna treated me so nice throughout the day that I just fell more deeply in love with her. I was hopeless.

# Fourteen

In mid-May, Mom and Dad sold the trailer and made a down payment on a little fixer-upper on La Roda Avenue a block over from the trailer court on the other side of the Pueblo Motel. To call it a fixer-upper was really to misrepresent the house. It was a half-finished, rundown little shanty built on a mudsill foundation. The lot was a good hundred and fifty feet deep, sloping from the street to the motel. The house was only set back about thirty-five feet from the rear property line, which resulted in the front yard being more than twice as big as the back-yard. The lot sloped to the degree that the front porch was only one low step up from the ground, and the landing at the back door was at the top of ten eight-inch wooden steps. Beneath the steps and a little to the right, there was a door that opened into a dirt half-basement. The front yard was a veritable jungle, but who was complaining? It was a house, our house, and my parents got it for only thirty-five hundred bucks.

*Jerome Arthur*

When school let out for summer vacation, we took our third trip to Minnesota. We only had ten days, so it was a quick one. We took off at five o'clock Friday morning and were going northeast out of Las Vegas by ten-thirty. We pulled in at Uncle Danny's place in Salt Lake at around seven that night. At three o'clock the next morning, we were up and out of there. From Salt Lake to Minneapolis it was a twenty-four hour, thirteen-hundred-mile push with my parents alternating driving and sleeping, keeping the car moving at all times, except to stop for gas and food. When we got to the end of that road, we were tried-and-true veterans of the broken white line.

We pulled up in front of Grandma's house at a little after three o'clock Sunday morning. The street was dark and deserted. It was a clear night, but the canopy of maples that lined both sidewalks only allowed us a faint glimpse of the moon and stars. Mom sent Frank and me to the door while she and Dad hung back in the car.

"Keep your heads down so they can't see your faces," she said. "Tell 'em you're lost and alone and you need a place to sleep."

The trees didn't extend over the front porch, so when we got up there, I looked up and saw an unobstructed view of the diamond-studded night sky. We knocked and I heard movement inside the dark house. Frank and I had our heads bowed as

142

## Down the Foggy Ruins of Time

Francesca'd told us to do when my grandparents, flanked by Edith and Jessie, opened the door. Mom and Dad were too anxious, and they rushed up behind us before we could even recite our lines. We were welcomed into the house, and everybody was so excited that we all stayed up talking for another forty-five minutes after we got there. Nobody had any reason to be up early the next day, except to go to church, and the adults all agreed that we could go to the last Mass of the day at twelve noon.

We only spent three and a half days in Minneapolis and didn't go up to the lake or the farm. Grandma put on another backyard fish fry that got going mid-afternoon Sunday and went on into the night. Monday was our day with the Bergmans and Tuesday we were back at Grandma's house.

We got back on the road on Wednesday morning. We made Casper, Wyoming eighteen hours later, and Dad pulled to the side of the road where he and Mom slept for three hours before sun-up the next morning. We got into Las Vegas Thursday night at around eight-thirty. After getting an early start Friday morning, we made Eagle Rock by lunchtime. It had been a hard trip, and we were all pretty exhausted at the end of it.

The next day after we got home, I went to Melo's house to see what'd been happening since we'd been gone. When we left eleven days ago, they'd just started grading the corner lot next door to his house, getting it ready for construction. A sign out front read, "Future Home of Bob's Big Boy." They were maybe half finished with setting the forms, rebar and plumbing when we got home. The ten-foot-high reinforced cinderblock retaining wall along Harriet's property line was near completion. It was Saturday and nobody was on the job, so Melo and I played King of the Royal Mountain on a huge sand pile at the job site. At one o'clock we went into his house and watched Bob Steele in *Ambush Trail* on television. After the movie I brought Melo home with me to show him our new pad. Dad tried to put him and me to work in the front yard, but Melo only stuck around for about five minutes.

Antoine got down to business and started fixing up our barely-habitable house as soon as we moved in. After working a full eight-hour shift at Dillon every day, he'd come home and put in a couple, three hours after dinner tearing out old walls and building new ones, reconfiguring the interior layout of the house. He did it all—framed the wall, hung the plasterboard and mitered the joints of the ceiling, door and baseboard molding. The living room and kitchen, on the left side of the house, were finished rooms by the end of summer. The two bedrooms, to the right of the living room as you entered the front door, and the bathroom, off the kitchen, never got completely finished for as long as we lived there. Bare studs were exposed in those rooms, and spiders

## Down the Foggy Ruins of Time

spun their webs and stored their eggs in the corners up by the ceiling. There were no more than eight hundred square feet of living space in the whole house (about the same size as my grandpa's house), but it was a big improvement over what we'd just moved from.

Antoine and Francesca enlisted Frank and me to help them on weekends defoliating the jungle in the front yard. Cactus, sage, rose bushes-gone-wild and other thorny berry vines crept along the ground and up on the fence that surrounded "the garden." When we were finished, the yard was cleared (only one rose bush remained out by the sidewalk), and the lawn was seeded. After the new lawn grew in, it looked pretty good compared to Mister Long's yard next door. His was still a jungle of foliage and junk, which made the contrast between ours and his all the more stark.

Dad was always doing something on the place, and most of what he did could truly be considered improvements on the property, but one of the jobs he did just didn't work out that way at all. He and his Canadian friend Gilbert poured a concrete driveway from the street to the house. They got drunk that day and wound up using too much sand in the mix, so within six months, after it got rained on the first time, the damned finish turned to sand. It wasn't a total loss, and Dad still parked the Airflow there, and later, his new Chevy, but it never looked like they did a good job on it.

Because of the trip, I'd missed the first day at Yosemite pool. Ronald and I went swimming on my first Monday back in town. On Tuesday I tried out for and got on the Eagles for the third summer. Steven and I had another good season of picking off runners on second. When we played the Comets, the team the Schwarz twins played for, we picked Lonny off twice. Robert Nez was our shortstop, and he and I became one of the best double-play combinations on the sandlot. Lanny hit into one when we played those guys.

One midsummer afternoon, Frank and I went over to Melo's house. We were fooling around out in the backyard when suddenly Phyllis scrambled up the bluff at the rear of the property, and, huffing and puffing, she told us to follow her. The four of us scurried back down the bluff to the rear of the apartment building that was located behind Harriet's property at street level. There was a concrete walkway enclosed on one side by the back of the building and on the other by a high, thick Eugenia hedge. About fifteen feet down the walkway, Anita was crouched down just outside the halo of a pool of light that glowed from a rear window. When she saw us, she turned and put her index finger to her lips, shushing us a little too loudly. We tiptoed down to where she was crouched, and I saw on the other side

146

## Down the Foggy Ruins of Time

of the open Venetian blinds, some guy, pacing around a brightly lighted room, bare-ass naked. The eyes in his big head were glazed over with lust, and his little head was all spit-shined and standing at attention. The girls were giggling, and Phyllie whispered in a voice I'm sure was loud enough for the guy to hear,

"Gawd, it's so big!"

Just as soon as she said it, the guy walked up to the window and started stroking his erection. It was pretty dim in the narrow little passageway, and the guy was inside the lighted room, so I don't think he could see us, but I was sure he heard us. He obviously knew we were there watching. He walked up to that window on purpose. We all five figured it out at the same time and took off running out of there.

When we came out onto the vacant lot between the apartment house and Melo's backyard, the girls started asking us all kinds of questions about erections. They wanted to see Frank's and mine (but not Melo's) just to see how big they'd get—with their help, of course. We all climbed back up the bluff and went into the darkened tunnel next to the abandoned barn. Once inside, Frank unzipped his trousers. All the dirty talk must've aroused him because his cock sprang out of his open fly, big and hard. Anita grabbed it and started massaging it just as she'd seen the guy do to himself a few minutes ago. Then, I'll be damned if she didn't get down on her knees, keeping a firm grip on Frank and leading him straight into her open mouth. A shaft of light, pregnant with dust motes, cut across her calves. Melo and I just watched, completely astonished. My heart was racing.

"Whew, that's hot!" Frank gasped.

"Let me have some, too!" Phyllie said, pulling off her panties.

She was massaging herself with her middle finger. When Frank pulled himself away from Anita and turned to Phyllie, he couldn't hold out any longer, and he squirted semen on her little eleven-year-old vulva, and it dripped off her finger and ran down her right thigh. Not ten seconds after Frank had his ejaculation, Melo's eighteen-year-old next-door neighbor Dorothy, whose backyard we were in, poked her head into the cave.

"What's going on in here?" she snapped.

But we three guys didn't stick around long enough to give her an answer. We ran out the other end of the tunnel and up Hermosa to Las Flores. I don't know how the girls explained themselves and us to Dorothy. She probably didn't put the finger on us because nothing ever came of her catching us. I was plenty scared that she would tell Harriet, who would in turn tell Mom and Dad, and then we'd all be in some deep shit. No such thing ever happened.

The next time I went to Confession, I told Father Segretti I'd had "impure thoughts," got five

## Down the Foggy Ruins of Time

"Our Fathers," ten "Hail Mary's," and an "Act of Contrition," and that was the end of it for me. Phyllie later told me that Dorothy lectured them on the evils of sex outside of marriage, especially for girls so young.

The summer ended as it began, with my family taking one more big step toward the middle class. One night about a week before school started, Frank and I went over to Melo's house after dinner to watch television. We got there at the beginning of "Time for Beany," and then we watched Buzz Cory, commander-in-chief of the Space Patrol, and his faithful sidekick, Cadet Happy save the galaxy one more time. When we got home at a little after nine o'clock, we found Mom and Dad sitting on the couch watching "You Asked For It" on a brand-new fifteen inch Philco console with a rabbit ears antenna sitting on top. They bought the house at the beginning of summer, the television at the end. Now all we needed was a new car, and then we'd really show 'em that we could keep up with the Joneses as well as any family around.

## Fifteen

Summer vacation had been a lot of fun; going back to school was a big letdown. My fifth-grade teacher, Sister Ingrid, suppressed any leftover enthusiasm I might have had with her strictly business teaching style. She wasn't mean and tough like Sister Ruth, but then neither was she sweet and gentle like Sister Johanna. She was a straightforward, no-nonsense teacher. I had her for both fifth and eighth grades, and I'd say she was the best teacher I had in elementary school. She had this strange little quirk where she opened her hanky and looked at its contents after she blew her nose.

Friday of the first week, she kept me after school because I made a wise-ass remark in religion class. As I was leaving the building after my detention, I looked across the hall and saw Sister Johanna sitting at her desk doing some paperwork. I stepped inside her door and said,

"How's it goin', Sister? You have a good summer?"

## Down the Foggy Ruins of Time

She was gathering some papers together and putting them into a manila folder. I couldn't get over how beautiful she was.

"Hello, Jerôme. How are you?"

"Pretty good."

"Yes, I had a wonderful summer. Bring that chair over here and I'll tell you what I did."

I pulled up the wooden chair that was in the corner by the window, and for the next half hour, she told me about the month she spent with her mother and father and sisters at her parents' house in Lincoln Heights and in El Paso, Texas visiting relatives. During the two weeks they were in El Paso, they crossed over into Ciudad Juárez to see her family who still lived on that side of the border.

"Wow!" I said. "How lucky! You got to go to México!"

"Oh, yes," she said. "My mother's sister lives there, but she crosses the border every day to get to her job as a domestic worker in El Paso. Juárez is actually quite nice for a border town. Very different from Tijuana y Mexicali. Our parents were so happy to have us all together with the family en Téxas y México. We had a wonderful time together."

It was very cool when she intermingled her Spanish and English like that, and like Ramón, she used the correct Spanish pronunciation. Hearing

151

about El Paso and her relatives who lived there only made me want to go.

"And what did you do for your summer vacation?" she asked.

I gave her the rundown, starting with our getting the house and taking the trip. She got a double-play-by-double-play account of my sandlot season. I skipped the part about the naked man masturbating in the apartment, and Frank and Anita in the cave. I wrapped it up with the new television set. When I finished, she picked up her manila folder with the papers in it, and we stood up together. I put the chair back in its place by the window, and we headed toward the door. We crossed the schoolyard, and I saw her to the front door of the convent. Then I went back to the schoolyard and got my bike.

Monday morning it was back to business for another week with Sister Ingrid. On Friday afternoon, I stepped across the hall again for another half-hour visit with Sister Johanna. From then on I tried to drop in on her after school every Friday that I didn't have something else going on. I'd erase her blackboards and clean her erasers. She taught me short sentences in Spanish and she'd drill me on the pronunciation. I was really dialed in to learning the language, so it came down to where I was getting more out of Sister Johanna's Friday after-school sessions than I was from Sister Ingrid's regular class-

## Down the Foggy Ruins of Time

room instruction. It just goes to show that if you're interested in the subject, you'll learn it.

All through fifth grade, Ronald and I rode our bikes to and from school daily. One of those days in early November, after he left me at my front door and headed home, the woman from across the street called out to me from the Longs's driveway. She said she needed some help with Mrs. Long who'd had a fall from her walker trying to negotiate the one step up to her front porch. When I got there, the old woman was lying on her back next to her upended walker. Her complexion was blue, and a fly was scurrying out of her slightly open mouth.

"I think she's dead," said the neighbor lady as she fanned her with a newspaper. "Do you have a telephone in your house?"

"Uh, huh," I said.

"Would you please go there and call for an ambulance. You just dial O and when the operator answers, tell her that we need an ambulance at this address. You think you can manage that?"

"I think so," I said and took off across the lawn to our front door.

We'd gotten a telephone since we'd moved into the house. We could afford it now since Mom had gotten a job after our return from Minnesota. Nobody else was at home, so I had to take care of it myself. I did as the lady had directed me, dialed the operator and told her to send an ambulance. She

*Jerome Arthur*

could tell by my voice that I was just a kid, so she asked me questions to make sure I was on the level, and not just pulling a prank. After I placed the receiver in the cradle, I went back over next door to wait with the neighbor lady.

It was hard to imagine that the old woman had died. I'd only known her for the five months that we'd been living there, and I'd had a conversation with her just two weeks ago on the sidewalk out front. She told me that they'd lived in their house for almost forty years, and it was only one of five on the whole block when they moved in. She sure did have some stories to tell about old times in the neighborhood. A couple times in the nineteen-twenties, when their two boys were old enough to do it, the whole family got up at three in the morning on New Year's Day and hiked over to Pasadena. Mister Long wanted to make sure they got there early enough to get a good spot on Colorado to watch the parade.

Now she was lying dead on her doorstep. It was the first time I'd ever seen a dead person and it spooked me. I only took the one look when I first got there and then I turned away. I never looked at a corpse ever again after that. In fact, from that time until now, I've never viewed a body in an open casket funeral. For my money it's just too morbid.

Mister Long came home from work just as they were putting his shroud-covered wife into the ambulance. The neighbor lady explained to him

154

## Down the Foggy Ruins of Time

what had happened. He was pretty broken up about it, and he went off in his pickup truck following the ambulance. Over the next week, his house was all-abuzz with his children and grandchildren, and when the funeral was over and they all went back to where they came from, he was left alone in his house surrounded by all his junk.

And that's where I got the idea of taking my Kodak Brownie to the Rose Parade that year and shooting some pictures. I set my alarm for three o'clock and started to hike over to Pasadena by three-fifteen. Eastbound traffic on Colorado was heavy. I got to the corner of Colorado and Orange Grove by four-ten. There was a big bash happening on Colorado Boulevard. It was well past the midnight hour, but a lot of people were still drinking and raising hell. One guy was weaving down the middle of the street swigging from a fifth of Wild Turkey that he had a one-handed chokehold on. When any car dared to drive through the melee (it was like running the gauntlet at two miles an hour), the guy with the fifth climbed up onto the hood from the front bumper, clambered over the roof and trunk, and stepped off at the rear bumper. He toasted everybody he passed and wished them a happy New Year, including the people in the car he'd just scrambled over.

Up and down the parade route, people were setting up chairs and bundling up in them, crawling

155

into sleeping bags spread out in the street, standing around huge flaming steel barrels, all trying to keep warm one way or the other. I walked to as far as Fair Oaks Avenue and back. At one point along the way, I found an open spot next to a fire drum, so I stopped to get warm. As the first light of day appeared right after the coldest, darkest hour, people were really starting to crowd in along the Boulevard, so I made my way back to Orange Grove where the floats were lining up.

I kept moving to stay warm. I really wasn't dressed for the cold morning. I had a good, warm winter jacket, but it just wasn't enough. A knit watch cap, a pair of long johns and some gloves would have been nice. As the dawn was breaking and the sun was lighting up the morning sky, I moved briskly along the lineup of floats, stopping only briefly at each one to take a picture. I headed back across the Suicide Bridge an hour after sunup, and shortly after that, the first floats in the lineup started rolling down Colorado. I was out of film, starved for sleep and beat to the bone. All I wanted to do at that point was to hit the sack. I was sound asleep in my bed when the parade really got going.

After the winter rains let up in March, Ronald and I got into horseback riding at the stable a quarter of a mile beyond the Eagle Rock where Figueroa came to a dead end. We'd go out every other Sunday and we usually rented the same two

## Down the Foggy Ruins of Time

horses. Kentucky was an ancient sorrel mare and Flame a docile five-year-old roan gelding with a patch of white right between his eyes. Kentucky was so old that she didn't always want to move once we got to the trailhead. One time when I couldn't get her going, I turned her around and went back to the stable. The people there gave me a switch and told me to give her a couple of strokes across her rump. Then one of them gave her a good whack sending her off at a canter, and when we got to the trail, she moved ahead and I didn't have to use the switch, which I was glad of because I really didn't want to be whipping the old girl. All she needed to know was that I had the switch, and that knowledge alone seemed to be enough to keep her moving.

The second Sunday that Ronald and I went up there, Bart, the guy with Down Syndrome Melo pushed me into at the movie theater that time, was there wearing cowboy boots and a too-large ten-gallon hat that was pulled down so low on his head that the tops of his ears bent under its wide brim. He was scolding one of the horses, shaking his finger at the poor, dumb animal as he rambled on making no sense at all. Even if he'd been making sense, the horse still wouldn't have understood him. It was funny and sad at the same time. The guy really couldn't articulate words, so his whole lecture came out in a wailing, garbled slur. I didn't see him out on the trail, but he was still hanging around the stable when we got back, so I guess the people there only humored him by letting him hang out but not letting him ride.

Up till then the only time I ever saw Ronald demonstrate any kind of athletic ability was summer afternoons in the pool at Yosemite. The Sundays that we went to the stable, Ronald proved that he was a good horseman as well. He handled Flame like he was born to it, and that was just the beginning. The next year we got into ice-skating at Pasadena Winter Garden, and he showed amazing skill wearing a pair of figure skates. By seventh grade, he got good enough on the gridiron that the seventh and eighth grade touch-football coach said he was a good candidate for All-CYO on that team. He later became a star football player at Eagle Rock High, and eventually he got a football scholarship to the University of California up in Berkeley. I saw him at a Saint Dominic's class reunion when we were twenty years old, and he was playing at Cal then and doing quite well.

# Sixteen

Now that Mom and Dad both had jobs, money was no longer the family's biggest worry; instead, Dad's drinking was becoming our number one problem. I know it can't be strictly true, but looking back on it now, I sometimes think he was drunk every night when he got home from work in those days. That's the way it was later on when I was in high school. He did like to put that booze away, and every once in a while Mom would try to keep up with him, but since she didn't have the stomach for it, she'd just wind up getting sick, while he got higher and higher.

When it came to drinking and partying, Antoine was on a mission. He had rheumatic fever when he was two years old, and the resulting damage to his heart hindered him throughout his life. He tried to enlist in the Army when he was eighteen, but he failed the physical. The Army doctor told him he'd be lucky if he made it to twenty-one, and so from then on he figured he might as well live it up for what little time he had left. He walked out of the infirmary at Fort Snelling, hitch-hiked into town, and got on a streetcar that took him straight over to Paul Konig's house. The two teenagers went out and scored a fifth of Jack Daniels. That was the beginning of Antoine's life as a career drinker, and, more often than not, Paul was his drinking buddy.

Paul was the guy through whom Antoine and Francesca had met. Their friendship began shortly after Antoine got home from his boxcar-hopping trip during the Depression. He was only fifteen when he ran away from home on Thanksgiving Day, and, anticipating the approach of another deep-freeze winter in Minneapolis, he headed for a warm climate. He and his pal Swede followed the sun, hopping freight trains south to New Orleans and west to Southern California, ending up in Seal Beach where he stayed for a year and a half. Four months before his seventeenth birthday, he returned to Minneapolis in the falling snow on a Greyhound bus, wearing only khaki trousers, a short sleeve shirt and the government-issue boondockers he got in the C.C.C. camp.

One day six months later, as he was out swimming in the river near the university, another kid got caught in the current and was being swept downstream. When the kid called out for help, Antoine, who wasn't much bigger than he was, but a lot better swimmer (he'd honed his skills skinny-dipping off the pier at Anaheim Landing in Seal

160

## Down the Foggy Ruins of Time

Beach), swam out and caught him and brought him in. That other kid was Paul, and from that day on they were best friends. Antoine met Mom one night two years later at Paul's house when she showed up to visit her Aunt Violet, Paul's mother. The way Antoine told it, he made his move early and before she knew what hit her, Francesca was conquered by his charm.

Paul and Antoine remained pals after Mom and Dad got married, and they hung around together a lot until we moved to California. They'd been notorious rounders in north Minneapolis in the parks and on the streets when they were still in their teens, and in the bars and three-two joints after they reached the legal age. Their scene was to hustle pool games and then end up in a brawl, which, nine times out of ten, they'd win, leaving their opponents bruised and bloodied, and sometimes unconscious. They were little shits both of them, but wiry, mean, and tough as nails. As they moved into adulthood and took on their adult features, they bore uncanny resemblances to two famous contemporary movie actors, both in looks and size, and they were not averse to impersonating them when they were out drinking. Paul was a dead ringer for Alan Ladd, and Antoine could've been a stunt double for James Cagney, but when someone called them on it, they'd end up getting into a fight.

*Jerome Arthur*

In mid-January, the dead of winter, when it was freezing-ass cold in Minneapolis, Paul and his family showed up on our doorstep in Eagle Rock. At first we were all glad to see him with his second wife, Estelle, and her son from a previous marriage and their own little baby girl, but it didn't take him long to wear out his welcome. Three weeks after their arrival, Casey came stateside on leave. He didn't go home to visit Grandma and Grandpa during his two weeks leave because he didn't want to go to Minneapolis in February. In fact, he specifically took the leave when he did because he wanted to check out Southern California in the winter. He stayed at our house the whole time. It had been a little over a year since we'd seen him last, and he'd changed a lot. He was no longer the callow kid he'd been the year before, overly sensitive to the slightest discouraging word. Now he was a little more self-assured, a world traveler of sorts; however, he never lost his sensitivity and shyness; he was a complete contrast to his brother Luke.

Since Paul had been Dad's main drinking partner in the past, when he came to town, they picked up where they'd left off. On each of our three trips to Minneapolis, Antoine had managed to spend a little time with Paul, and they'd carried on as if they'd never been separated. When Paul arrived in Eagle Rock, it was just like old times. They'd go out barhopping, taking Casey with them, leaving the

## Down the Foggy Ruins of Time

women and kids at the house. One time I was awakened by their arrival back home after a night out on the town. I cracked the bedroom door and peaked out at them sitting at the table having a nightcap. They were both all pumped up, their fists bruised black and blue, not a scratch on their faces, and they were talking about how they'd kicked some guys's asses and how much fun it was. Casey was with them, but he wasn't drinking (he was just barely twenty years old), and it didn't look like he'd been fighting. He only seemed to be going along with them. He wasn't a fighter—too shy and reserved to be brawling.

Another time after they'd been out on a binge, Casey got caught in the middle of an argument between Paul and Estelle. Paul had got drunk every day since they'd arrived in Eagle Rock. This one Saturday afternoon when the three guys got back to our house, Dad and Paul drunk as hell, Estelle started ragging on Paul as soon as he got out of the car. He put up with it for about five minutes, and then he turned on her and cussed her out, calling her a bitch and every other name he could dredge up from his drunkard's vocabulary. Then he got into his car and took off with her groping for the passenger-side door handle and almost getting dragged down the street in the process. As the door handle slipped out of her grasp, she was left standing on the curb screaming after him with tears rolling down her cheeks. She became hysterical, falling at first to her knees, arms raised, as though she were praying, and then to her back, shrieking on the grass strip between the sidewalk and street.

Casey, who was sober, went out to try to calm her down and get her to go back into the house, but he wound up getting kicked in the groin for his trouble. As he doubled over in pain, Antoine and Francesca hurried out to the sidewalk together. They picked Estelle up bodily and brought her back to the house, kicking and screaming all the way. Frank and I stared in astonishment, mouths open; Estelle's kids were crying hysterically. I couldn't believe what I was seeing. The whole scene was like a bad dream.

I got roped into one of Paul's alcohol trips shortly after my eleventh birthday. One day after school not five minutes after Ronald had pedaled off home leaving me alone in the house, an urgent knock came at the front door. When I answered it, Paul pushed past me into the living room demanding to know where Antoine was. He moved around the room in a miasma of whisky reek, and I could tell right away that he was, as my grandpa would've put it, "three sheets to the wind." He wasn't falling-down drunk; his high was an angst-buzz, not a happy glow. This incident happened after Casey's leave was over and he'd gone back to Japan. Paul had settled his family in a one-bedroom cabin in the trailer

## Down the Foggy Ruins of Time

court, and he got a job selling used cars over in Glendale.

"God, I guess he's still at work, Paul," I said, watching him pace around the living room hitting his left palm with his right fist. His anxiety was making me nervous and scared, but I was trying to be cool. "He usually don't get home till around six, another two and a half hours away. What happened, man?"

"Ah, I just decked some son of a bitch over in the Can Can," he said. The Can Can Club was a bar around the corner on Colorado. It was part of the Pueblo Motel complex. "Fucker didn't move after he went down. I think I might've killed him." No sooner did he utter those words than the high whine of a siren split the afternoon lull. He paid no attention to it. "You know, I didn't mind the asshole sayin' I was obnoxious. What pissed me off was when he started jabbin' me in the chest with his goddamn finger. That's when I cold-cocked the son of a bitch."

He kept pacing and slugging his right fist into his left palm. I never quite understood why he was telling me all this. If he was trying to scare the shit out of me, he was doing a good job of it. He probably wasn't trying to do anything. He was just drunk and didn't really know what he was saying or doing.

"I'm goin' home," he said suddenly. "I hate to do it. Old Lady's just go'n'a ride my ass. 'Least I got a jug there. Take a couple slugs, calm my nerves down."

He went out the back door, down the steps to the yard, over the fence, and through the Pueblo Motel, thus avoiding the front door of the Can Can Club. While he was pacing around in our living room, you could cut the tension with a knife. I was glad that it went out the door with him. It was quiet once again as I poured myself a glass of milk and dug some peanut butter cookies out of the cookie jar. I was relaxing, trying to calm down, when Frank got home. We'd both gotten Daily News routes in March, so, after he had some milk and cookies too, we went across the street to Benny Hartack's house to fold our papers and do our routes.

I finished my route that day about the same time Mom got home from work, and when I saw her, I told her about the episode with Paul. He had been around long enough that she was getting used to his shenanigans. She shook her head and rolled her eyes and went about the business of fixing dinner. She told Dad about it at the supper table, which prompted him to leave right after he finished eating. He said he was going out looking for Paul. About ten o'clock they came in drunk and laughing their asses off. I couldn't believe the change in Paul's demeanor. He was carrying on as though he hadn't even had the fight earlier or been so upset about it in our living room.

166

## Down the Foggy Ruins of Time

I never found out positively, as I'm sure Paul and Antoine hadn't either, whether or not he'd killed the guy in the Can Can Club that afternoon. I read the comics and parts of the sports section every day before I did my route. For five days after the episode, I also skimmed the front section of the paper, looking for the story, and when it didn't show, I figured Paul hadn't killed anybody.

Paul was one of those guys who lived his life on the edge. Every time he entered a room, tension, fear and angst followed him. And it was always a double dose. He also threw racism and prejudice into the mix. These latter two emotions only heightened the intensity of the former three and made them immediate and real.

He came by the house one evening as we were finishing dinner. He and Antoine were going up to Topper's to have some highballs and to shoot pool. The national news was on television as he came into our living room, and they were doing a story about that day's hearings of the McCarthy committee in the U.S. Senate. The reporter was saying how Roy Cohn and David Schine seemed to be playing fast and loose with the law.

"Who's the shine?" Paul asked when he heard the name. "I don't see no shines in that crowd."

"What're you talkin' about?" Antoine replied. "Ain't no colored guy there. That's the guy's name. David Schine. 'Sides, they don't call 'em shines on national television. Call 'em Negroes."

"Oh," said Paul with a sinister giggle. His laughter was as sharp-edged as the siren sound the day of the Can Can incident.

Two weeks later, old man Forcette accused me of stealing his newspaper money while he was right there behind the butcher counter. His wife ran the groceries and checkout stand of their little family grocery store; he ran the butcher shop. She usually showed up for work a few minutes before nine o'clock to open the store for business. The old man was in the butcher shop by a quarter to eight six days a week.

I was passing in front of the store at about eight o'clock on that Saturday morning, and my eye caught the cover of a magazine I'd never seen before on the rack inside the locked front door. It was called *Mad* magazine, and the grinning kid on the cover grabbed my attention. I stopped and stood next to the empty newspaper rack and looked at it through the window in the door. The price in the upper right-hand corner said, "10¢ Cheap!"

I wasn't looking down as I backed away from the door, and I almost tripped over a bundle of that morning's *Examiner*. The Times bundle, right next to it, had four nickels on top of it, and the string had been cut and some papers were missing from the stack, but I didn't go anywhere near that bundle. As

## Down the Foggy Ruins of Time

I walked away from the store, I looked over my shoulder and saw the old butcher moving around behind his counter.

I went around the corner to the house where the rest of the family was getting ready to face the weekend. Mom was in the kitchen frying up some bacon; Dad and Frank were just rolling out of the sack. I wasn't in the house more than five minutes when there was a heavy knock at the front door. When I opened it, Mister Forcette stood before me on the porch, and with a cold stare, asked to speak to my mother. I stood next to her as he accused me of stealing a nickel from his stack of newspapers. He told her there were only four nickels, but five papers were missing. I didn't take any of his money, certainly not one nickel where there were five, and I just kept denying it. I was persistent and Francesca believed me. The old butcher finally left when Antoine, hung-over and on a short fuse, told him to beat it. Dad believed me too, but I don't think Frank did.

No way was I going to steal the guy's newspaper money. I'd just gotten my own paper route a couple of months ago, and I knew how hard it was to collect from my customers. Somebody must've taken one of his papers without paying for it. Besides, I just wasn't into stealing. That was more Melo's style than mine. Maybe the old butcher thought I'd done it because Melo and I were such good buddies–guilt by association. The real irony in all this was that Billy Forcette, old man Forcette's youngest son, was the worst thief of anybody I knew.

About a year after his father accused me, Billy went with Melo and me to a stamp store in Pasadena. Stamp collecting was probably the last hobby Melo and I got into together. When we went to Pasadena, I stood over Billy's shoulder and watched him stuff maybe fifty stamps into his shirt pockets. In fact, he even bragged afterwards that it was his special shirt, and he only used it for stealing stamps. It was a large, baggy shirt with big pockets and button-down flaps that he left loose until he stood up to leave, and then he'd secure the flaps, safely concealing his take of the loot. To tell the truth, I always thought Billy was stealing from his dad's till.

# Seventeen

By the time Robert Nez arrived at Saint Dominic's, the only kids at the school, or in Eagle Rock for that matter, of any color or ethnicity were the Gómez brothers, Steven in Frank's class and Seth one year behind me. There were a couple of American-Chinese brothers going to Rockdale School at Yosemite and Wiota. I think they and their family were the only American-Asians in all of Eagle Rock. There were no black people in Eagle Rock or Glendale—indeed, those were the days when Glendale cops ushered black people out of town if they showed their faces after dark. Pasadena, on the other hand, was about the most integrated place around, with an enclave of upper income American-Europeans and a mix of middle-class whites, American-Africans, American-Mexicans and American-Filipinos, but the place wasn't truly integrated because those ethnic groups didn't mix with one another, and they most certainly didn't mix with the American-Europeans.

Eagle Rock was as homogeneous as the milk Mom brought home from the grocery store (same color, too), the result of which was that I rarely came in contact with any black or brown people, and that left me feeling culturally deprived because I thought I was a Mexicano. Even on the rare occasion when I laid eyes on black people, it was from the isolation of the backseat of the car when we went to Pasadena and cruised down Green Street to stay out of the traffic on Colorado Boulevard. The closest I ever actually got to any black guys, was in the bleachers at Wrigley Field. There must have been some Jewish people around Eagle Rock, but the only one I ever knew about was Mister Pillar, who owned a discount clothing outlet originally located on Colorado a couple of blocks from the Glendale line. He later moved his operation into the Safeway store at Colorado and Argus after Safeway left for bigger digs down near the Center. I don't even think he lived in Eagle Rock. If there was a synagogue anywhere in town, I never knew where it was. The Italians were the only large group of people in Eagle Rock who could be called an ethnic minority, but they hardly seemed any different than the other mongrel European nationalities that made up the majority population of the town.

Many of the people I knew and talked to and listened to (other than my parents, who were much cooler than a lot of folks in Eagle Rock) only rein-

## Down the Foggy Ruins of Time

forced my ignorance with their Jim Crow attitudes and comments. The kids who went to Saint Dominic's didn't always display a lot of tolerance themselves. They weren't all that unbiased and filled with brotherly love. There was a certain amount of anti-Semitism in the Schwarzes' protestations against being Jewish, and even though I can't remember ever hearing any blatantly racist language on the schoolyard, it was pretty obvious the Saint Dominic's kids didn't have much use for black or brown people. And Melo and his buddies from Eagle Rock Elementary were worse. Whenever we were in front of the television watching "Our Gang" comedies, they'd call Stymie and Buckwheat "niggers" at the bat of an eye.

So, until I was a fourteen-year-old freshman at a Catholic boy's high school, whose enrollment was eighty percent American-Mexican and the other twenty percent a mix of white, black, Asian, and other brown nationalities hailing from Central and South America, my experience with other cultures was painfully limited. Most of whatever I knew about people of African, Hispanic and Asian ancestry was learned secondhand and was, for the most part, erroneous and misinformed.

Eagle Rock was a Henry Aldridge kind of neighborhood all right, not merely indifferent, but hostile to any kind of cultural diversity. I remember seeing that hostility early on when I used to hear

Greg Forest, back in the days when we were living in the lower court and the Forests were in the upper court, carrying on in his superior way about how the lower court was nothing but "a slum, only one step up from nigger town." After he finally got his family out of there, his criticism took in the whole trailer court. Talk about forgetting where you came from! If Greg Forest was saying such things about poor white people, you can just imagine how he felt about black and brown people. The general sentiment around town was pretty much a mirror reflection of his feelings, and the citizens made sure for many years that the place stayed as white as Weber's bread.

It was a mystery to me why the Forests even stayed so friendly with us. Greg was anti-everything, including Catholic, and I never understood why Antoine didn't take offense to that, and also to Greg's trash talk about where we lived. Because of the way Greg talked in that regard, you'd think he believed us to be nothing but low-class peasants, beneath his elevated station in life. Not so. For some reason Greg and Louise really liked Antoine and Francesca, and Frank and Bobby were as tight buddies as Ronald and I were. It was just hard to listen to Greg spew his racial and religious bigotry.

There was probably no neighborhood in Eagle Rock that epitomized Greg's arrogance more than the one he moved his family into. It was cer-

174

tainly the most elitist neighborhood in town. Most of the houses on the tree-lined streets that ran between Colorado and Hill Drive were spacious one-story California bungalows, stucco-and-red-tile haciendas and two-story Craftsmans. Interspersed among these were custom miniature mansions whose architecture ran from ante-bellum southern plantation (Robert Munson's house on Hermosa, for example) to New England colonial. Most of the houses on Hill Drive were big rambling estates with circular driveways. The Forests moved into a good size Mexican hacienda on Mount Royal between Las Flores and Hill Drive. They were in their own element in that neighborhood, but they still stayed friends with my parents.

The worst racist incident that I ever heard about in Eagle Rock happened not long after Robert Nez arrived at Saint Dominic's. Someone threw a rock with a note tied to it through the front window of his house. The note was a threat and it demanded that Robert and his mother "go back where you came from." His mom, a maid at the Pueblo Motel, sought solace and comfort from her pastor. Father Mick went on a rampage from up in the pulpit, roundly denouncing the incident and its perpetrators in his Sunday sermon, finally calming down with a special request for prayers from the congregation. That's how the rest of us found out that it happened. After he railed against it in such a heavy-handed way, the Gómezes got scared too, even though they hadn't been threatened.

It was really sad to see those three guys during that time. They were really intimidated by the harassment, put in their places as it were. Then it all died down. Nothing else happened, and the one isolated incident came to be thought of as a trick of petty pranksters, and who knows, maybe Father Mick's sermon had an effect. However, the terror was real; at least for me it was real. Because I thought I was a Mexicano, I started thinking I was next, but when I saw that Ronald (who really was a Mexicano) wasn't even next, I realized how foolish I was acting. I'll always remember how cool Sister Johanna was through the crisis. She was especially nice to Robert Nez and Seth Gómez, who welcomed her kindness; they damn sure weren't going to get any from their own teacher, Sister Ruth.

Once when Ronald and I were at the pool, I overheard a conversation between Lynn, the sorority girl lifeguard who looked good enough to be a contestant in the Miss Eagle Rock beauty pageant, and Steve "Stunning," one of the guy lifeguards, a real Charles Atlas-type. She was telling him she'd gone to a movie in Pasadena the night before, and there were a few "colored people" in the audience.

"I'm not prejudice or anything like that," I heard her say to Steve. "It's just that you can smell them."

## Down the Foggy Ruins of Time

"Yeah, I know what you mean," he replied.

Of course, he was just trying to pull her pants down, so he would have agreed with anything she said to achieve that objective.

Lynn's comment puzzled me because I kept thinking how I never smelled anything out of the ordinary when we sat next to black men in the bleachers at Wrigley Field. All you could smell out there were hot dogs, beer and burning cigars. But even though I knew this to be true, I was still taken in by her inadvertent racist logic, thinking she might have a point, rather than trusting my olfactory sense and my own better judgment. And I couldn't rationalize my gullibility by claiming to be seduced by her beauty. That certainly didn't excuse her racism, nor did it excuse my part in it. I was racially and culturally ignorant, and most of the people around me were only pushing me deeper into the hole I was already in. It wasn't until I got to high school and got a job downtown and spent some time there that I recognized the ignorance of her statement and my own complicity in it.

And ultimately Lynn got hers. Not only was racism rampant in Eagle Rock, but sexism was also pervasive. Hardly a night went by during the summer without someone climbing over the eight-foot chain link fence that enclosed the pool and going for a late-night swim. One night a couple weeks after Lynn's comment, vandals, not swimmers climbed the fence. Using thick black crayons, they tagged the lifeguard tower that she usually sat in with remarks that suggested different kinds of sex acts they'd like to perform on her, and on the side of the lifeguard's shack that faced the pool and her tower, in letters a foot high, they scrawled something about her abilities with oral sex.

It looked to me like something Melo might do, and it wouldn't surprise me a bit if he were involved in it with two of his buddies from school, Beau Winwood and Chester Newman. You could always count on something turning up missing when Melo and Beau got together. Melo blackmailed Beau into stealing things for him by threatening to expose Beau's past transgressions to his mother. Melo told me all of this with a big show of pride, as if he had Beau under his control, but after watching Beau in action, I decided that he really wasn't afraid of Melo's threats. He actually got off on stealing. He probably stole the black crayons to do the job on Lynn. The other guy, Chester Newman, was probably the one who wrote the nasty obscenities on the lifeguard tower and shack. He was a weird, racist jerk who told really ugly ethnic jokes. He wore long-sleeve shirts, "to keep the dirt covered up," as he said his mother put it. I could see those three guys being the ones who'd vandalized the pool.

Since there were no black people living in Eagle Rock, whoever did it had to be white, but I

## Down the Foggy Ruins of Time

think the irony in that was lost on Lynn. She wasn't clever enough to see that one. I didn't particularly care for her racist attitude and her sweetheart-of-Sigma-Chi personality, but there was no way she deserved such brutal abuse, and since she was the one who opened the pool the next day, she was the first one to see the graffiti.

Nor was Eagle Rock the only place in Los Angeles where such incidents occurred. Some racist punks burned a cross into Nat King Cole's front lawn shortly after he moved into Hancock Park, the gated community on the west side. I heard about that one at the breakfast table as Antoine, sipping from his first cup of coffee of the day and smoking a Camel, read a story from that morning's Mirror about it aloud to Francesca, who was hovering over the stove cooking bacon and eggs. For as young as I was, I was smart enough to know injustice when I saw it, and I found it hard to believe that such things could happen in Southern California, as though it were Mississippi or Alabama. And why pick on Nat King Cole and his family? He made some of the sweetest music of the time. He was cool!

Racism among the white citizenry of Los Angeles was only half of what black people had to worry about at that time. They got as raw a deal from the cops as Ramón had told me the Mexicanos got. Resentment of police brutality against black people built up over the years, and it finally erupted

179

when the Watts riots broke out and swept through south central Los Angeles in the summer of sixty-five. The Mexicanos followed suit a year later when county sheriff's deputies started a police riot by shooting Los Angeles Times reporter Rubén Sálazar with a tear gas rifle at very close range during an equal rights rally at Laguna Park in East Los Angeles.

# Eighteen

I quit my paper route at the end of fifth grade. I wanted to spend my summer afternoons (the same time I was supposed to deliver papers) playing baseball or swimming at the pool or body surfing at Playa del Rey. Also, delivering newspapers was boring work, and collecting was always a big pain, not to mention Frank's ragging on me the whole twenty minutes it took to fold our papers.

Frank got pissed off every time any of his friends, whom he was always trying to convince that I was a jerk, started taking to me and liking me more than him. It first happened when Steven Gómez and I got to be buddies and stayed tight through three summers on the sandlot. Of course, Frank was at a definite disadvantage in that one. Steven was a Mexican and so, I thought, was I, or at the very least, I had aspirations to mexicanismo, and that's the last thing Frank would ever aspire to or consider himself to be. I'm sure Steven recognized that, and that's why he was my friend and not Frank's.

*Jerome Arthur*

And it happened again with Benny Hartack and Marv Wiggins, the two Eagle Rock gavachos Frank and I folded our papers with. Like Steven, they were Frank's age and really his friends when we started folding our papers together, but as time passed and they got to know us better, they gradually became better friends with me than Frank. This only made him more hostile toward me, and he'd probe my vulnerable, sensitive spots until I'd get so pissed off that I'd fly into a blind rage and do something really stupid, like the time I went after him with a butcher knife or the other time when I threw an ax at him from across the backyard, missing him by inches, only because he ducked just in time.

About a month before I quit the route, Antoine bought a new car, a fifty-two Chevrolet Deluxe Styleline four-door sedan. He got a hundred dollars for the Airflow on a trade-in at Wynn Chevrolet, the dealer across the alley from school. He'd bargained the salesman down from the $1492 sticker price to $1350, so after he threw in three hundred that he'd saved, he got financing for the remaining $950. He made the car a present to himself and picked it up on May fifth, his thirty-sixth birthday.

That was my first experience with a new car, and I was amazed at how luxurious it was on the inside for just a Chevy. New cars have always been plush, and in the fifties even the bottom of the line models, like Chevies, Fords, and Plymouths, were

## Down the Foggy Ruins of Time

very luxurious cars. They had fabric seat covers and door panels, and the headliners were of the softest, finest brushed cotton. They were plush, and they had a certain distinctive smell that was no longer typical by the mid-seventies when the Japanese and Europeans started to have such an impact on the American car market. During those years new car interiors started to smell like plastic and vinyl, a trend that has continued on into the present. Somehow it just isn't the same.

Dad was like a kid in a candy store with his new car. He carried on like Frank and I did when we'd gotten our Columbias four years ago. His birthday was on Monday that year, and he took the afternoon off to go pick the car up. On his way home, he stopped by Topper's for a couple of birthday shots and to show it off to his drinking buddies. He was buzzing when he got home, and he got us all together and took us on a cruise along Hill Drive. We passed a big rambling estate with a Cadillac and a Lincoln parked in the driveway.

"They ain't got nothin' on us, 'cause we got us a new Chevy Deluxe," Antoine said to no one in particular, and he sat tall and proud behind the wheel just like when we crossed the Minnesota line.

I got to ride shotgun that first night; Mom and Frank rode in the back seat. For the first month that he had the car, Dad took us out cruising at least two nights a week when he got home from work.

Frank and I took turns riding shotgun, and a few times Mom took the wheel and Dad rode shotgun. By mid-June, the newness had worn off, and the evening cruises ended. Instead, Antoine had a few more "tasties" after dinner, watched "Dragnet," "The Honeymooners," and/or "Your Show of Shows." and then wobbled off to bed.

In late June, the Bergmans—Uncle Luke, Aunt Megan, and Kenny—came to town on their vacation. Frank and Kenny hooked right up as they'd done in Minneapolis, and once again I was just the jerky little kid-brother neither of them wanted anything to do with, and that was okay, but what really pissed me off and hurt my feelings was when Frank started disparaging me to Uncle Luke.

"My route's real level," Frank said. "My little brother's is all hills, and he's so dumb he actually pedals up and down 'em."

Hell, by that time, I'd already quit the damn route. I was making double plays with Robert and pick-offs with Steven at Yosemite, but Frank was still using the route to put me down. In the end, it really didn't matter much because Uncle Luke was such a cool guy that Frank's put-downs didn't affect his attitude toward me, and he actually told Frank that he shouldn't be so mean.

They were driving a new car too, a fifty-two DeSoto, when they arrived on a Wednesday afternoon. Antoine had taken a week's vacation to spend

## Down the Foggy Ruins of Time

time with them, so on Friday morning we all took off for Tijuana in two cars. I was finally taking my first trip into México, and I didn't care one bit that Frank and Kenny tried to keep their distance from me. Uncle Luke and Antoine told them to quit being jerks, so they lightened up a little bit, but it didn't matter to me what they did, because once we crossed the border, I'd be "home" and I wasn't going to let them spoil the experience for me.

The drive down the coast was really cool. Huntington Beach, Newport Beach, Laguna Beach and Oceanside, now all good-size cities, were only little coastal villages back then. We stopped in San Juan Capistrano for lunch and to check out the mission. We had to drive around for a while to find three vacancies in a motel on the northern outskirts of San Ysidro. After we got settled, we crossed the border into Tijuana.

I could see that this was going to be an experience I'd have to share with Sister Johanna. The main drag in town was like a carnival midway. The sidewalks were jammed with gavacho tourists. Shop keepers were out in front of their stores working the crowd, hawking their wares: silver bracelets and necklaces, leather belts and billfolds, guaraches with tire tread soles, wool zerapes and straw sombreros. The sidewalk barkers in front of the strip-joints tried to hustle Antoine and Luke inside by offering them a peek. We three kids got pictures taken sitting on a donkey, painted with black and white stripes so that it looked like a zebra, and all of the adults got charcoal sketches drawn of themselves. You could really see the resemblance between Antoine and James Cagney, and Francesca and Judy Garland in those pictures.

As we strolled down Calle Benito Juárez before sundown, I looked longingly down the side streets into the neighborhoods (I wanted to find some Mexicano kids to play with, but the only ones I saw were selling chicles on the street). The adults weren't showing any interest in going that way, so we were stuck on the neon midway of the main street where it was all honky-tonks and shops selling junk to turistas Americanas. Late in the evening, after Antoine had been doing some pretty hard drinking and was feeling no pain, we all went back to our motel and collapsed from exhaustion. After breakfast the next morning, we went back across the border and played around until about two in the afternoon. Then we headed on home.

The Bergmans stayed with us for a week, and I was sad to see them leave. Two days before the Fourth of July, they packed up and headed out of town. It had been a fun week. True, Frank and Kenny had given me a pretty rough time, but all the fun things we'd done had offset it. We'd gone to México! One of the days, all the guys went to an Angels/Stars game at Wrigley, and one night the whole

## Down the Foggy Ruins of Time

gang went over to Hollywood and saw Hannah Lee, a 3-D western.

In August Paul packed up his family and headed back to Minneapolis. They'd only been in Eagle Rock for eight months, but it seemed like a much longer time. A week after they left, Antoine dropped the big bombshell. He came home one night, drunk as usual, and told us he'd quit his job and had spent the afternoon in the Brass Rail down on Hill Street across from Pershing Square.

"Sons a'bitches tried to fire me, but I quit before they could. Showed 'em they can't fuck with ol' Antoni Faroni."

Old feelings of insecurity surfaced right away. I remembered how it had been the last time he was out of work, and I was afraid of going back to that. How was he going to make the house and car payments? I think he bought the television set on time, too. I was having visions of losing all of those things, and worse, the possibility of having to move back to the Minneapolis deep-freeze. But soon I found I had nothing to worry about, not then anyway, later maybe, but not then. The next day he got a job running a thirty-six-inch Harris offset press at a place called Impressions Incorporated in Hollywood. The owner of the shop was an ice cream eating diabetic named Garthwaite. Antoine didn't miss a paycheck.

187

# Nineteen

One day about three weeks before I went into Sister Nimrod's sixth grade class, Melo and I hiked up La Loma Road to go crawdad fishing at Johnson Lake near the Pasadena line. It was hardly a lake (I've never been able to find it on any map), more accurately a wetlands. It was nothing more than a group of small, crystal-clear pools, a larger version of the spring at the trailer court. There were plenty of crawdads creeping around the rocks in those pools, but we didn't catch anything on that hot August afternoon. We found a really huge one, as big as a Maine lobster, or so it appeared to my eleven-year-old eyes. We baited our hooks with raw bacon and dropped our strings in the water, but the crawdad had good instincts and wouldn't take the bait. After we spent almost an hour trying to catch him, Melo lost his patience and got up to his old tricks again. He pushed me into the water, and my left leg got wet up to my knee. The damn crawdad started snapping at my blue jeans. I was wearing the U.S. Keds high-tops I'd gotten at the beginning of

## Down the Foggy Ruins of Time

summer vacation, and the insole and black canvas upper soaked up the water like a sponge.

I wasn't going to take that from him, so I grabbed him from behind, got him in a bear hug with his arms pinned down at his sides, pulled him over to the crawdad hole, kicking and yelling, and dumped him in feet first, making sure that both of his feet got wet. I didn't get much satisfaction from doing it though, because I still had to walk all the way home with water squishing in my right shoe. It was a pretty warm day so my trouser cuff was dry by the time I got back to the house, but my insole and sock were still pretty damp.

In the waning days of summer, Melo and I had one more little incident. We were hanging around my house on the Saturday following our hike up to Johnson Lake. It was really a hot day and we were thirsty, so we headed over to Forcette's to get a couple Grapettes. On our way out the driveway, we saw a piece of garden hose lying in the gutter in front of the house next door. As soon as he laid eyes on it, Melo got another one of his bright ideas—siphoning gas out of a nearby forty-eight Chevy convertible just to see if he could do it. He took the gas cap off and stuck the hose down into the tank as I stood by and watched. Just as he started to suck on it, a guy and his girlfriend stepped out onto the sidewalk from the entry door that led to the apartments up the stairs from the laundromat on the corner. As soon as he saw us, he started yelling and came running after us, leaving his girlfriend standing by the door through which they'd just emerged.

Melo escaped up the alley next to Benny Hartack's house, and I ran back home, but the guy caught me by my left arm as I was running down our driveway. Mom and Dad both came out of the house to see what was going on. The guy let go of my arm as they approached. He continued on down the driveway and met them half way. I went and stood next to Dad.

"That your kid?" the guy asked.

"Yeah," Antoine said. "What's the problem, and why in hell are you layin' hands on 'im?"

"Him and another kid were puttin' somethin' in my gas tank," he said gesturing in the direction of his car. He was pretty pissed off, but he had the good sense to hold it in check because he could see Antoine was pissed off too, and pity the poor bastard if he thought he could take him just because he was bigger.

"We didn't put nothin' in your tank," I piped in. "Just the hose. We were tryin' to siphon the gas, and we only did it to see if we could."

"You didn't put any sugar or sand in it, did you?"

"Nah, just the hose. And I'm sorry we done it, man." I was holding my hands up in surrender.

## Down the Foggy Ruins of Time

He cooled down a little bit when he heard that. After Mom and Dad apologized for my bad behavior, he started back up the driveway to the street where his lady friend was waiting. He'd mentioned to my parents that I wasn't alone, but it didn't do any good, because they knew Melo was the other kid, and there was nothing they could do about it, so once again he didn't get any punishment for his part in the incident. When the guy turned and walked away from us, Francesca gave me the dirtiest look and said something like, "I ought'a brain you." She made me stay in my room for the rest of the day. Antoine called me a "knucklehead" and that was just about the worst punishment he could have meted out.

The Thursday before school started, a semi-truck, hauling a shipment of wine grapes down Colorado on a staked flatbed trailer, jack-knifed and the flatbed twisted and flipped right in front of Bob's Big Boy restaurant. No other cars were involved, and the trailer was the only part of the rig that flipped over. Nobody was hurt.

I was going home from Nally's near the Center when the accident happened. I'd just picked up a new school uniform for Monday and was walking past Chic's Liquors when I actually heard the racket from the wreck. I stepped out into the street and could see the semi three blocks off sprawled across the Boulevard. Instead of going home when I

191

got to the scene, I crossed the street and went up to Melo's house. Boxes of grapes, some broken and some intact, had spilled off the flatbed and literally filled the intersection where Argus met the north side of Colorado. The driver had gotten out of his truck and started directing traffic through a narrow space between his front bumper and the center divider of the Boulevard. Stepping gingerly around the mess, I made my way up to Melo's.

"Come on in," he said, leaving me to close the front door.

"Did you see this wreck out here," I called after him as he walked through the dining room toward the kitchen. He was flipping through the pages of a booklet.

"Heck yeah. Even swiped me a box. I's right here in the house when it happened, and it made one hell of a bang," he said. "Heard it and went down to see what was goin' on. Was the first one to get there after it happened."

I followed him to the pantry, which was on the left just inside the kitchen door. He'd dug up a three-gallon vat from among Harriet's pots and pans and had set it on the floor in front of the pantry door. A big colander was a perfect fit on the vat's rim. He tossed the booklet into the colander, picked up the vat by its handles, took it into the service porch and set it in the laundry tray. The booklet he'd been flipping through was titled "Fermenting Wine Grapes,"

192

## Down the Foggy Ruins of Time

and he opened it to the first page and read. Then he went out to the back porch, got the box of grapes, and filled the colander. Using his hands, he pressed the grapes through the holes in the sieve. He talked the whole time, telling me about how he'd heard the crash and gone down to the corner to check it out, and how he'd swiped the unbroken box of grapes when the guy was directing traffic and wasn't looking.

After he pressed all the grapes, he rinsed the sieve and his purple hands in the kitchen sink. He then put the lid on the vat and took it into his room. There was plenty of space for it in his huge walk-in closet. Over the next month and a half, we did a few tastings. After the first week it didn't taste much different than grape flavored Kool-Aid or Grapette, but by the second week, we could actually get a little buzz from the stuff. It was only six weeks along the last time I had a sip, and it still didn't really taste much like the altar wine I'd sampled in the sacristy, but it had a good kick.

Some big changes had taken place at school since I got out in June. In midsummer they'd begun construction on the new school building. The work was in full swing when school started. What had been the sand box with rings, trapeze and parallel bars for the big kids, and jungle gym, merry-go-round, teeter-totters and swings for the little kids when we'd left fifth grade was now a maze of concrete footings, foundation and sub-floor for the building we'd be spending seventh and eighth grade in.

You could see the shape of the building by Christmas, and by Easter it was up and enclosed against the weather. The workers were doing the interior finish by May. The parish owned the vacant lot next to the nun's convent across Merton Street from the schoolyard, so before they started construction on the new building, they paved the lot with macadam and painted a softball diamond and basketball court on it. The diamond had a backstop made of chain link behind home plate, and the basketball court had hoops and backboards at each end. It became the yard where fifth, sixth, seventh and eighth grades spent recess and the lunch hour. The primary grades still had recess and lunch hour on the old schoolyard, which was reduced in area during the construction, but would return to close to its original size after the old building had its date with the wrecking ball.

When the construction project was completed, we had a modern reinforced brick structure with a slightly canted roof, sloping toward the alley with a row of windows high up close to the ceiling on that side. All you could see out of those windows was a little bit of sky and the flat roofline of the Chevy dealership. There were also windows on the other side of the building that faced the schoolyard. This

## Down the Foggy Ruins of Time

new building would replace an old seismic catastrophe-waiting-to-happen—a wood frame structure with beige stucco siding and a gabled red tile roof on top of skip sheeting instead of plywood and no shear strength in the cripple wall. It would be torn down when they finished the new building.

The footprint of the old building was a rectangle consisting of eight rooms, four on each side of a central hall. A basement with a low ceiling held the girl's and boy's restrooms, a room where the nuns could administer first aid and a good-size broom closet for the janitor. Grades one through four were on the playground side of the building, and five through eight were on the Maywood Avenue side. The new building was a rectangle too, a long rectangle, stretching almost two-thirds the length of the ally-side of the property, all of the rooms in a straight line with the doors opening directly onto the schoolyard.

# Twenty

I went into Sister Nimrod's sixth grade class the Monday following the grape truck wreck. Obviously, she'd taken a name other than her given Christian name. She said she took it for two reasons. The first was that it was her brother's name; he'd been a sailor aboard the Arizona at Pearl Harbor. She also liked the name because the Old Testament character was a hunter, which, she said, symbolized her personal search for her Savior. We all thought it was a very appropriate sounding name for her. Behind her back a lot of the kids called her Sister Dimwit, or when we really wanted to get mean, Sister Numbnuts.

She was the first teacher I'd had up till then who absolutely could not control her class. She tried to be strict like Sister Ruth and Sister Adolf, but she just didn't have the toughness that those two had, and the class knew it. A few of the kids would band together—Ronald, the Schwarzes, the rich kid Sterling Holden and his pal Gene Glad—and literally take over the class, and she was powerless to do anything about it.

She was absent-minded and never learned anybody's name, so she'd just refer to a kid as "boy" or "girl," like, "You, boy, stop disturbing the class; it's rude!" or "Girl! Girl! Gum chewing is vulgar and not permitted in this classroom. How bold!" And, of course, Ronald got the most mileage out of this odd way she had of addressing her pupils and her regular use of the words "vulgar," "rude" and "bold," mimicking her behind her back. He was still doing a good Sister Nimrod imitation nine years later at the class reunion we had when we were twenty.

She was a chubby little moon-face (she looked like she'd taken too much cortisone for too many years) with a malicious look in her eye, but that was the only place she revealed any meanness. She certainly didn't have any in her personality. You couldn't really describe her as a nice little old lady (she was probably only about thirty-five years old), but when it came to keeping order in the class, that's exactly how she came across. She meant to be a harsh taskmaster, but she simply didn't have the temperament for it, only the looks. When she'd be challenged by Ronald, or anyone else who felt like usurping her class, she'd simply stare out over the heads of her pupils at the rear wall of the classroom, bewildered and confused, and then move on in dismay to another subject.

197

It was the second year for us to be on the street side of the building, and for the second year in a row, we got to see the arrival in late September of the new cars at the Chevy showroom next door. They got unloaded from the truck right outside our window. At the time it seemed so important to see them as they rolled down off the truck, to get the very first look at the brand-new Bel Air, Deluxe and Special models. One time when a guy was delivering a shipment, Sister Nimrod remarked on how he wasn't wearing gloves as he was moving and adjusting the ramps that he used to drive the cars off the trailer. She deliberately interrupted her sentence-diagramming lecture on the blackboard to take note of it.

"Anytime a person does heavy labor like that, he should wear work gloves to protect his hands," she'd said. She was no one's fool, no doubt about it, even though the class treated her like a buffoon and made fun of her.

I went back into the newspaper business a week after school started. I got the corner in front of Bob's selling the afternoon edition of the *Harold Express*. A corner was a much worse deal than a route, and I knew after the first day that I wouldn't last long doing it. The hours were terrible, three to six five afternoons a week. The job involved standing out on the curb on Colorado Boulevard for those three hours hawking papers to the passing motorists

## Down the Foggy Ruins of Time

and the early dinner crowd at the restaurant. The highlight of every day was when the Eight Star edition showed up at three-thirty. There was always a good run of customers when it got there, and I even had a regular Eight Star customer. Mister Richards always had a smile and an anecdote when he picked up his paper. One day he got there right when my boss was getting ready to pull away from the curb after he'd delivered my papers.

"See you tomorrow, Mister Goodall," I said, leaning down to his passenger-side window just before he pulled out.

When I turned around to sell Mister Richards his paper, he said to me,

"I once knew a fellow name of Goodall. Rufus Goodall. Negro chap. First time I shook his hand, he said, 'Name's Rufus Goodall, that's all.' Get it?" Then he turned and headed up Argus back home.

There weren't too many good reasons for working the corner, but Mister Richards and the Eight Star edition were definitely two of them. Another one was that Bob's, still not even a year old yet, had become an after-school hangout for the Eagle Rock High crowd, and it was fun to watch them all converge on the place in their souped-up Deuce Coupes and thirty-eight Fords and forty-one Chevies. The restaurant also had the best cherry Cokes and cinnamon doughnuts in town, but the bad thing

199

about that was I'd end up blowing all my daily prof-
its on them. Ultimately, there were more liabilities
than assets to working a corner newspaper stand, so I
quit, and on November first I got my old paper route
back.

One afternoon less than three weeks after I
started doing the route again, one of my customers
stopped me and asked if I wanted a dog. She lived in
a flat-roof stucco house on Linda Rosa Avenue right
where Argus ended. I got off my bike and followed
her into her backyard to take a look. What I saw was
Penny, a fluffy little gray dog with a square beard
and a fringe of bangs that hung in her eyes, almost
completely concealing them. The lady said she was
five years old. I thought she was cute and wanted to
take her home right then and there, but I couldn't do
that without first asking Francesca if it would be
okay. I told the lady I'd try to come back later with
my mom. I finished the route and got back to the
house about the same time she got home from work.

"Sounds like a cute dog," she said, after I
described Penny to her. "Let's go take a look."

We walked back down the hill to the lady's
house, and it was love at first sight for Mom too, so
we took Penny home.

We didn't have her two weeks before Mom
cut the fringe of hair that covered her eyes. She said
it impaired the dog's vision, so, with the best of intentions, she cut it, and in less than six months, Pen-

## Down the Foggy Ruins of Time

ny lost most of her eyesight. The hair never grew back, and Penny's vision got progressively worse until she was almost blind by the time she died three years later. She started to shy away from the light the very next day after the hair was cut. She shook her head and snorted when I let her out the front door in the bright morning sun. Up till then, she'd been doing her business out front, but this time she slinked around to the backyard where it was shady and did it there. When she finished, she took refuge in the shade behind the back wall under the steps.

At the beginning of December, Burden informed us that our routes were going to mornings after the first of the year. The *Daily News* became the *Mirror News* when it was bought by the Times Mirror Company and merged with the *Mirror*. There was no way Frank was going to get up at four o'clock every day, and Benny and Marv weren't fond of the idea either, so they all quit after the switch, and that left me folding my papers alone, which was fine because Frank was nothing but a pain in the ass anyway. I did kind of miss hanging with Benny and Marv, though. We'd gotten to be pretty good friends.

I liked working alone and I liked the early morning hours. It was great to see the sunrise on the clear days. I watched so many of them from the top of the hill on Wildwood Drive where my last delivery was that I became a connoisseur of the dawn.

*Jerome Arthur*

I developed my own routine. After I folded all of my papers but one, I'd skim the sports section and read the comics. I didn't read all of the strips, only the ones I liked: Gordo, Peanuts, Beetle Bailey, Blondie, and Mutt and Jeff. The only two serials I'd read were Alley Oop and Mandrake the Magician. I just couldn't get into stuff like Dick Tracy, Rex Morgan, M.D. and Mary Worth. After I finished the comics, I'd put that last paper on the table for Antoine and Francesca when they woke up. Then I'd take off to do my route on the new Defiance three-speed English racer I got for Christmas the year before. My last delivery was on the hillside of the street, so after I threw that paper I crossed to the other side and watched the sun come up over the hills of Pasadena.

# Twenty-one

After the holidays, Frank and I sold our Columbias, which were still good, serviceable bikes, for ten bucks apiece. They were pretty stripped down by then. Fenders and chain guards had long since disappeared; the paint jobs had worn and chipped away; rust was setting in. The new bikes were a welcome upgrade. Having three speeds, a lighter weight frame and narrower, lightweight tires made my route a lot easier. Now I could climb all the hills, whereas with the Columbia I had to get off and walk it up most of them.

Frank was careless with his. He'd leave it lying out overnight on its side on the front lawn near the sidewalk. One November night less than a year after he got it, a thief came along and stole it. It was hard for me to muster much sympathy for him or his misfortune. It's a big drag to get your bike stolen, and it really wasn't nice of me to be unsympathetic, but he was being such a jerk to me that I couldn't help secretly laughing at his bad luck. I shouldn't have, though, because all it did was come back around on me. Now that he didn't have a bike, he'd try to sneak off with mine.

Nor were any of my other possessions secure from his grasp. He wore my clothes without so much as asking me, and I couldn't lock that stuff up and keep it away from him like I did the bike. We lived in the same room together and shared the same closet, and he'd just help himself to one of my shirts if he saw one he liked. He thought he was squaring it with me by telling me to go ahead and wear anything of his, but I didn't want to wear his stuff. I wanted to wear my own clothes, because they were mine, and besides, his were too big for me. Why weren't mine too small for him? His use of my clothes against my wishes was an ongoing problem for the next five years. That was when he finally moved out on us and into his junior college fraternity house over in Glendale.

When a holy day of obligation was on the same day as a national holiday and it wasn't Sunday, they had a ten o'clock Mass on that day. That year New Year's Day was on Thursday, and I served the ten o'clock, and Mom and Dad went to it. Frank had gone to the 8:15 with one of his friends. I rode home with my parents after I got out of my cassock and surplice. The first thing Dad did after we walked in the front door was turn on the radio, and at that very moment the deejay was announcing that Hank Williams had died in the middle of the night. The guy

## Down the Foggy Ruins of Time

on the radio said he was on the road with his manager heading for another joint when it happened. I was saddened by the news. I'd heard Hank's music many times on Dick Haynes's radio program, and I'd always liked it—"Your Cheatin' Heart," "Kaw-Liga," "Jambalaya." After the commercial break, the deejay played a couple of Hank Williams songs in a row. Then when he broke in with another commercial, he announced Hank's passing once again, and said he was playing his songs all through the show as a tribute. Then Antoine had to go and scare me.

"Goddamn, I think Hank was younger'n me. Quite a bit younger, matter of fact," he said, as we sat down to the pancake breakfast Mom had put together. "He was a heavy boozer and I'd bet that's what croaked 'im."

At around noon, after the breakfast dishes had been put away, Antoine fixed himself his first drink of the day. I sat with him and we listened to Hank sing "Ramblin' Man." As he sipped from his drink and listened to the music, Dad dissolved into the melancholy world of his youth. He picked up his harmonica, which he usually kept on the end table next to his chair and started playing along with the record. When Hank sang, "...till I hear an old freight rollin' down the line," Antoine made his harmonica sound like a train whistle, and then he picked up the melody on the next line.

"Song like that one takes me back to my freight hoppin' days," he said when it ended. Then he fixed himself another drink, turned the radio off and tuned in to the Rose Bowl game on television.

Three weeks later Dwight Eisenhower took over as president of the country, and a month after that, the Russian dictator, Josef Stalin, died. His death caused a lot of commotion on the television and in the newspapers. What would Russia do next? Who would take Stalin's place? Americans were so afraid of a nuclear attack from Russia that they were building bomb shelters in their backyards. In the face of all the hysteria, I was actually feeling less anxious and uptight than I'd felt before when Sister Ruth used to rail against "the red horde behind the iron curtain," and she had us diving under our desks during air raid drills. What could be better than Stalin's demise? I'd been hearing all along that he wasn't much different than Hitler, and that seemed to me reason enough to want him gone. It looked to me like America's politicians and newspapers were all in it together, actually convincing the public that they had something to fear from a backward country like Russia. It's hard to believe that the people fell for it, but they did.

The paranoia reached its peak at the beginning of summer that year when the U.S. Government executed Julius and Ethel Rosenberg for allegedly being Russian spies. That was weird and I didn't understand it at all. It actually scared me to think that two average Americans not unlike Antoine and Francesca could be executed in the electric chair. They were a married couple, and I kept wondering if they had kids and what happened to them after their parents were killed. Antoine didn't minimize my fears when he suggested that the way to get them to confess was to put her in the chair and give her "a couple a' jolts" with him watching.

"That'd get 'im to talk," he said.

The shooting stopped in Korea a month after the Rosenbergs were executed.

Sixth grade really marked the time when Melo and I started seriously going our separate ways. After our trip to Johnson Lake, I only saw him once before school started, the day he swiped the box of grapes and got the wine going, and then I checked him out just a few times after that to see how it was doing. Shortly after Halloween, I quit going around to his house altogether. I was now hanging around almost exclusively with Ronald Day.

A couple weeks before we went into sixth grade, Ronald and I started going ice-skating at Pasadena Winter Garden on Friday nights. At first I was using the hockey skates that Jessie and I had found in Grandpa's basement three years ago. Last year when we were back there, she dug them out and gave them to me. I only tried them out a couple

207

times, and they were really hard to use, so the third time we went to the rink, I left them home and rented a pair of speed skates. Ronald rented figure skates from the beginning. I wanted to go as fast as I could, and he'd fool around doing pirouettes and stuff like that.

I had to admit, he was good at it. He was a natural, and that athletic ability along with his Latin lover's good looks (even though he was still only a kid) really attracted the girls. At the ice rink they were falling all over themselves trying to get close to him. They followed him around like dogs in heat, and they oohed and aahed when he'd glide through a figure eight or leap into the air, turn and land gracefully on one skate going backwards.

None of Ronald's coolness at the rink rubbed off on me; I was the consummate punk on speed skates. I only came close to his kind of cool once, and that's all I did was come close. One Friday night a couple girls were following me all over the rink, laughing and giggling, pointing at me, talking about me in hushed voices. I finally went up to them and asked what the hell was going on.

"Gina says you're Ricky Nelson," the cutest one responded. "Are you him?"

The attention and flattery had me pumped up there for a couple minutes. I'd been told before that I bore a slight resemblance to Ricky (Ronald's mom Rita had said it a couple of times), so the mis-

## Down the Foggy Ruins of Time

taken identity didn't come as that much of a surprise to me, but rather than just going along with it, I had to blow the whole deal by reminding them of what night of the week it was.

"I can't be Ricky Nelson," I said. "It's Friday night. He's on television right now."

As the organist played "Lady of Spain," they skated off and joined the other mooners vying for Ronald's attentions. The first time I was pursued by a girl since Phyllie and her girlfriend dragged me off to her room back in fourth grade, and I end up scaring her off with some bullshit story about not being the guy she thought I was.

There was one girl whom Ronald paid more attention to than the others. Her name was Charlene Thompson, and by about the third time we went to the rink, they were doing some pretty fancy pairs skating. They were usually the two best skaters on the ice. They got to be such good friends that her parents started picking us up at Ronald's house on their way to the rink. That was a good deal for Rita and Francesca because it saved them from having to take turns chauffeuring us back and forth. It was a good deal for us, too, because we got to ride in Mister Thompson's cool fifty-two Ford woody. As we skated, he and his wife sat contentedly by the fire drinking hot chocolate, watching with pride as Ronald and Charlene did their routines. At the end of

*Jerome Arthur*

the evening, they dropped us off at Ronald's house on their way back to Glendale.

As time passed Ronald and Charlene got to be such good buddies that they were doing a lot of stuff together outside the ice rink, and sometimes he'd ask me to go along. One Saturday in late April, he and I took a bike ride over to her house. We crossed the railroad tracks on Colorado and took San Fernando Road West up through West Glendale. The hills of Griffith Park rose up on our left. I'd wanted to get a closer look at this little town ever since that day we drove by it on our way out to visit Uncle Luke's friend in Van Nuys. We got back onto San Fernando Road at the north end of town and took it up one block past the Verdugo Wash to Charlene's house.

Her house and her dad's upholstery shop (Dallas Upholstery; his name was Dallas) were in one building. It was a big, old one-story commercial structure (it looked like it might have housed a grocery store in another lifetime) with the shop in front and the house behind it. Theirs was a family business and Charlene's mother, Margaret, worked on a heavy-duty sewing machine behind a three-foot-high counter in the front part of the shop. Dallas' work area was in a fluorescent-lit back room that was directly behind the storefront. The back door of the shop led straight into the living room of the house, but the front door and entry to the house were on the

210

## Down the Foggy Ruins of Time

side of the building, and you got to it by a three-foot-wide walkway from the front sidewalk. The whole back part of the building had been remodeled and was set up as a two-bedroom, two bath house. There was a small, fenced patio and lawn behind the building, accessed by French doors from the dining room.

Margaret and Dallas closed the shop at one o'clock on Saturdays, so shortly after we got there, she made some sandwiches and we all had lunch. When we finished eating, Charlene got her bike out, and the three of us rode over to where the wash bordered on the Roger Jessup Dairy. We left our bikes up on the levee and hiked down the rocky slope to the muddy riverbed where there were murky pools with catfish swimming around and rushes and reeds poking through the cloudy surface. There was also some debris: a tire, a gallon jug with the neck broken off and a Ralph's shopping cart half submerged on its side. After we fooled around down there for a little while, we went back up to the levee and walked our bikes over to the dairy where there must have been a hundred cows lined up at the feeding troughs. When we got back to Charlene's house, Margaret served us some milk and chocolate chip cookies. Ronald and I headed back to Eagle Rock at about five o'clock, and we got home by a little after six.

Just when I thought I was never going to see him again, Melo called me on the phone on Saturday morning, the day before Palm Sunday, to see if I wanted to go with him and Billy Forcette to a stamp store in Pasadena. Billy knew a lot about collecting stamps, like which ones were the most valuable and which ones we didn't need to bother with (the Gadsden Purchase, for example, was worthless), and of course, he probably stole most of the stamps in his own collection.

Watching those two in action that day convinced me that they were not cool guys. Forcette was just another example of what kind of person Melo was, and it was becoming increasingly clear to me that I didn't want to be hanging around with the likes of them. Besides, I'd dealt with Melo's bullshit long enough and I could see the toll it was taking. So, after that little excursion to Pasadena, I quit hanging around with him altogether.

All through sixth grade, I kept up the tradition I'd started in fifth grade and went to visit Sister Johanna's room after school from time to time. One Friday in April, I went to see her, and she told me that she'd be leaving the school in June. They were transferring her to Sacred Heart in Lincoln Heights, where she herself had gone to school. I made sure I got over to see her at least twice a week from that day until the end of the semester. On the last day of school, I went to say one last goodbye. It was all I could do to keep myself from telling her how I really felt about her, and as I was saying goodbye, I got the

## Down the Foggy Ruins of Time

feeling that I didn't need to tell her. Her smile was so warm, her gaze so sincere and knowing, that I think she understood my feelings completely.

# Twenty-two

I met Carol Tremaine on the first day of summer vacation while I was collecting for my paper route. I had just turned twelve and she was fifteen. I was in the process of quitting the route. Friday was going to be my last delivery day, and I was planning on sleeping in on Saturday morning for the first time in six months. There were only three houses that I still needed to collect from, and Carol's was the first one on the list. As I mounted the steps to her porch, the front door swung open and she came out. She had a towel rolled up under her left arm and she wore sandals, shorts and an unbuttoned Hawaiian print blouse over an azure one-piece Catalina swimsuit. We said hi to each other, and after I told her why I was there, she said her parents weren't home, and I'd have to come back later. She was very friendly, and I could've sworn she was making eyes (about the same color as her bathing suit) at me.

I didn't even try to collect from the other two houses that day. Instead, I pedaled home as fast as I could, got my trunks and a towel, and headed over to the pool. I'd guessed right; she had been making a play for me earlier. She walked right up to me when I came out onto the pool deck from the shower in the men's locker room, and we spent the rest of the afternoon swimming and hanging around together.

We wound up spending a good part of the summer with each other—at the Yosemite pool, and at her house. She was an only child, and her parents both worked, so there were a lot of times when she had the house to herself. The first time we spent an afternoon together in her room was Friday, five days after we met. I sat on the edge of her bed and watched as she used rubber bands and bobby pins to put curls in her dark brown hair. We were all alone in the house. I got off my perch, walked up behind her and cupped my hands over her breasts. She looked up at me with a dreamy-eyed smile, pulled me closer to her and kissed me. I was absolutely amazed at how soft her breasts were and the reciprocal pleasure we felt when I touched them. They were so soft that it sent a warm feeling into my heart. She said she experienced the same sensation from my touch. At that moment with the whole summer still ahead of us, I thought we might go all the way, but we never did. What we did on that first Friday afternoon was about as much as we did all summer long. We never did "do it," never even got past the foreplay.

*Jerome Arthur*

No sooner had I met Carol than we were off on another trip to Minnesota. The Monday following our little tryst in her room, Antoine and Francesca packed us up and took us on our biennial pilgrimage "back home." We left at seven o'clock in the evening because Antoine wanted to make sure we hit the desert after sundown. It didn't make much difference; it was still ninety degrees by the light of the crescent moon. This trip, I really noticed how much Los Angeles-to-Las Vegas traffic had increased. The car lights ahead of us were continuous for as far as the eye could see, a string of pearls on the left and a strand of rubies on the right. We saw them lined up across the desert, climbing and descending the Halloran summit grade, as we dropped down off the mountain from Barstow heading toward Baker.

The whole trip back to Minnesota, all I could think about was Carol. I didn't want to go half way across the country; I wanted to stay right there in Eagle Rock and hang around with her. It wasn't until our second full day in Minnesota, when a group of us went up to Lake Osakis for three days that I finally got her out of my mind. We had two carloads of people. Antoine, Grandpa, Luke Konig and I went in Dad's Chevy. Casey, who was home on leave, went along with Kenny and Frank in Luke Bergman's DeSoto. Paul Konig was already at the lake when we got there. That was the first time we'd seen him since he'd left Los Angeles. His Mercury out-

216

## Down the Foggy Ruins of Time

board was mounted on the stern of a boat pulled up on the beach next to the dock. Uncle Luke Bergman had brought along his Evanrude, and the first thing he did after he got out of the car was mount it on the stern of the other boat.

What a great fishing trip! Paul really knew Lake Osakis ("drunk or sober," Antoine said), and where the best spots were. We trolled with lazy ikes and caught our limit of northern pike on two of the three days we were there. We didn't have that kind of luck with walleyed pike; in the whole three days, Paul was the only guy in our two boats to catch one.

On the last day, while the other guys went off to troll for more northern and walleye, Luke Bergman took Kenny, Frank and me across to the opposite shore, and we found a spot among the reeds and rushes in an isolated cove where we fished for bass, but we didn't have much luck. Kenny caught a fair size sunfish, but it was too small to keep, so he tossed it back. When we got back to the cabin, we pulled the boat up on the small beach and parked it between Paul's Merc. and the dock. Inside the cabin Antoine and Luke Konig were cleaning the walleye that Paul had caught that day. Frank asked Paul if he could use the Merc. Paul had already had a couple of stiff shots and was feeling pretty loose. For all he cared, Frank could have taken the Mercury outboard to the moon.

When we got back out on the water, we cruised the two boats around off the end of the dock, putting them through their paces. Paul's Mercury had a lot more get-up-and-go than Luke's Evanrude, but that didn't stop Kenny from making a bet with Frank.

"I bet my dad's Evanrude could beat that Merc.," he said.

"I got a quarter says it can't," Frank said. "Let's race 'em and find out."

"Let's go," Kenny said, "and I'll even take Jerôme with me."

They started at our dock. The next dock down the shoreline a quarter of a mile was the finish line. Kenny knew what he was doing. I headed straight for the rower's bench amidships, but before I could sit down, he told me to grab the tackle box and to put it under the bench in the bow and then to sit on that bench.

After we got lined up, we stepped off. It looked like Frank had the Merc. opened up to full throttle, and because he didn't have any weight in his bow, his hull just shot up to about a thirty-five-degree angle. He left a wide wake as the centerline of his hull merely slapped at the water it was supposed to be cutting through. In the meantime, Kenny opened his throttle to about two-thirds, and with me and the tackle box in the bow, his prow cut through the water, leaving a smaller wake, and by the time

## Down the Foggy Ruins of Time

we crossed the finish line, we were one full boat-length ahead of Frank.

While we were having our little race, Paul had put away a few more highballs. Antoine and Luke Konig had joined him after they finished cleaning the walleye. When we got back in, they were all partying heartily, and Grandpa let it be known to Luke and Paul, but not Antoine, that he didn't approve. That was our last night at the lake, and I was glad it was coming to an end. I was missing the city, and I'd grown weary of Antoine's and Paul's daily and nightly drunken antics.

Antoine and Luke Konig kept it up on the ride back to Minneapolis. When we were twenty minutes down the road from the lake, Grandpa finally made a meek complaint to Antoine about it. Casey had switched over to our car to do the driving. Luke Bergman was driving his own car, and he still had Kenny and Frank with him. I was in the back seat of our Chevy behind Casey; Grandpa was riding shotgun; Antoine was sitting behind him. Luke sat bolt upright between Antoine and me, his straight back about six inches from the back of the seat, his feet planted firmly on either side of the hump in the floorboard where the drive shaft ran, his hands holding onto his knee caps. They tried to be discreet, attempting half-heartedly to sneak drinks, but Grandpa wasn't fooled, and he kept complaining. The two guys finally did quit before they'd killed off the pint they'd been passing back and forth in a brown paper sack. Nevertheless, they were fairly hammered by the time we got back to town.

Saturday morning, July Fourth, the day after we'd returned from the lake, I was eating a bowl of Cherrios in Grandma's kitchen, when suddenly a lightning bolt of pain shot through a decayed upper molar and up into my left temple. The doctor's office that Mom had gone to the day I was born had since become a dental office, and she was able to get me an emergency appointment on the Saturday holiday. Once again she and I took a walk across the schoolyard to see a doctor. I was putting up such a fuss that she had to go in with me, stand next to the dentist's chair and hold my hand. He put me under with ether, but his supply was low, and right when he was in the middle of pulling the tooth, I started to regain consciousness. I jumped at the first inkling of pain, and the dentist broke the decayed crown off of the tooth, leaving three roots exposed in my upper jaw. Since it was Saturday, and a holiday to boot, he couldn't replenish his supply of ether, so he was unable to finish the job.

We got back on the road for Los Angeles on Monday morning. Grandpa had taken two weeks vacation so he, Grandma and Jessie came with us to California. The plan was to meet Danny in Salt Lake City, and he'd drive them the rest of the way to our place where they'd all spend a few days. Then

## Down the Foggy Ruins of Time

they'd return to Salt Lake City, and my grandparents would catch a train from there back to Minneapolis. Edith was going to stenographer's school so she wouldn't be making the trip.

I was suffering the whole trip west, and Grandma was doing anything and everything to take my pain away, but I was such a thoughtless and inconsiderate pre-adolescent boy that I was being a real jerk to her. When we got to Las Vegas, we went for a late night walk up Fremont Street shortly after our arrival. As the others walked on ahead, Grandma pulled me off to the side, and we ducked into a cafe on one of the cross streets. We sat down at the counter and she ordered each of us a piece of apple pie alamode. I flared up at her when she suggested that I use a spoon instead of a fork so I wouldn't hurt my bad tooth. If I'd been smart and showed a little kindness and consideration for her feelings, I would've listened to her and taken her advice. But instead of doing the smart thing or the kind thing, I went ahead and used the fork and promptly, though accidentally, jabbed my bad tooth with it and went shrieking out of the restaurant.

From time to time, Antoine gave me a little sip of whatever he was drinking, encouraging me to swish it around the tooth, and then spit it out. That did kill the pain, but not for long. He himself had had all of his molars pulled before he reached twenty-five years of age, so he was telling me all of his gruesome tooth stories the whole way home. How he came to lose all of his molars, according to him, was that his teeth were so hard that dentists' drills would break off when they tried to fill the cavities.

"Hard sons a'bitches," he said. "Couldn't stop 'em from achin', and couldn't drill 'em, so I just told the tooth sawbones to pull 'em."

The next day after we got home from the trip, Mom rushed me to an oral surgeon in Glendale, and he put me under with sodium pentothal and surgically removed the three roots. I was only out of commission on the day I had the surgery, and within three days, I was as good as new.

That trip was the first time ever that Grandma had been out of Minnesota. The only other time Grandpa had been out of the state was when he went off to Germany during the First World War. They were both born and raised on the farm, Grandpa outside Waseca and Grandma midway between Bird Island and Cosmos.

Grandpa was the youngest of nine boys, and his mother, an American-Irish woman whose maiden name was Casey, died when he was only two years old. My great-grandpa, a strict Catholic of German heritage, raised the five younger boys, including my Grandpa, by himself. The four older brothers were already helping out on the farm, and after their mother died, they pitched in and helped my great-grandpa raise their younger brothers. All of them,

## Down the Foggy Ruins of Time

except Grandpa and Tom, his closest brother in age, stayed on the farm or in the vicinity of Waseca when they grew to adulthood. Conrad moved to Minneapolis when he was nineteen years old, and at the same time Tom, twenty-one, went to Sioux City, Iowa. They both got jobs with the local streetcar companies.

Grandma's parents were Lutherans who'd emigrated from Germany before she was born. Her name before she married Grandpa was Gretchen Haas and she had two brothers who stayed on the farm. One eventually got his own farm near Cosmos while the other ran the family farm. That was Uncle Elmer's farm where we'd gone on our first trip back to Minnesota in forty-seven. When she met Grandpa at an ice cream social in Mankato, she was nineteen years old and he was twenty-one. They got married a year later. Grandpa joined the Army and was sent to Germany. Francesca was born five months before the armistice was signed. Grandpa once told me the story of how when he got home after the war, he found his seven-month-old daughter learning German as her first language and worshipping with her mother at the Lutheran church.

"I be jiggered if I didn't put my foot down," he'd said. "I told your grandma that I just spent a year and a half at war with Germans, and I didn't want my daughter speakin' their language. This is America and we speak English. When I finished layin' the law down about the language we was go'n'a use in my house, I told her we was Catholics and 'by God, we'll be goin' to Saint Anne's from now on.'" From that point on Grandma, like Antoine and most other converts to Catholicism, became more devout than those born to the faith.

Mom and all of her siblings called their parents Pa and Ma. Sometimes Antoine and Uncle Luke would call Grandpa "Stub" because he was about five feet six inches tall, bald as a cue ball, and he had the trademark Konig potbelly. Every once in a while, Luke would call him "Dutch" or "Connie," but only on rare occasions, and those names were always uttered with the greatest of respect and affection.

Grandpa and Grandma were great in California. The first time we took Grandma to the beach at Santa Monica, she pulled her skirts up to her knees, waded out into the surf and started to sing,

"From the mountains/to the prairie/to the ocean white with foam/God bless America...."

Grandpa took the Five streetcar to the end of the line in Hawthorne and back to Eagle Rock a couple times while he was in town. He sat in the seat across from the driver next to the front door and chatted with the guy the whole trip.

From the day he arrived, he kept saying he wanted to go out to Orange County to visit a buddy, a fellow streetcar conductor who'd retired in Anaheim.

## Down the Foggy Ruins of Time

"So, where is Alaham?" he kept asking, no matter how many times we pronounced it correctly for him.

"It's Anaheim," Mom said, rolling her eyes, "and it's in Orange County, about an hour and a half drive from here."

On Sunday after Mass, we all piled into the two cars and drove out to Anaheim. As soon as we passed through Whittier, all we saw on both sides of the road were orange groves, except when we came to the occasional small town, like Fullerton. There were a couple of new housing developments in Anaheim, and Grandpa's pal lived in one of them. His house backed up to an orange grove.

During the time my grandparents, Danny and Jessie stayed with us, we really did a lot of different stuff. On Saturday all the men and boys went to a game at Wrigley Field. Another night all eight of us saw Shane at the Pantages in Hollywood. Earlier that same day we took them all over to Farmers Market.

# Twenty-three

For a solid month after Grandpa and Grandma left, I spent most of my waking hours with Carol. Then the last week in August, Antoine and Francesca got together with Greg and Louise Forest and rented a house down on the Newport peninsula. Gregy, who was seventeen years old by then and no longer using the diminutive nickname, had gone up to Lake Arrowhead with one of his buddies, so he didn't make it to the beach with the rest of us. A few days before we left, Antoine and Greg took us kids to Palley's war surplus store out on San Fernando Road in Burbank where they picked up some fishing gear, and we three guys got green three-tined spearheads. On the way we passed Dallas Upholstery. I glanced in the front window and saw Dallas talking to a customer at the counter. Margaret was working at her sewing machine.

On the way home, we stopped at a lumberyard in Glendale and got doweling to attach the spearheads to. Our idea was to do some spear fishing in the surf. What the hell did we know about it? I

## Down the Foggy Ruins of Time

still don't know what was going on in my head when I thought about hanging out with Frank and Bobby when they were both armed with spears. Their idea of a good time would've been to tie me up to one of the pilings of Balboa Pier and use me for target practice.

In those days the trip from Eagle Rock to Newport was a real ride in the country. Southgate and Lynwood were just beginning to be developed, so there was still a pretty good stretch of open country in that area between Los Angeles and Long Beach. Pacific Coast Highway south out of Long Beach was wide open all the way to San Diego. No housing and condominium developments littered the virgin hills and lowlands east of the highway. You didn't see any oil drilling platforms on the western horizon in Seal Beach and Huntington Beach. It wasn't all pristine coastline, however. Even though they weren't out on the water, some wells were pumping on the bluff in Huntington. Tin Can Beach, across the highway from the unsullied wetlands of Bolsa Chica lagoon, was a wasteland of discarded bottles and cans.

We stayed in a three-bedroom, one bath California bungalow with an outdoor shower in an enclosed patio. The two couples each had a bedroom and we three boys shared the third. As soon as we got our stuff unpacked, we took our spears down to the beach (we were such flatlanders, such valleys),

227

and I left mine leaning up against the wall outside the public rest room while I went inside to take a leak. When I came out, the damn thing was gone; I never even got a chance to try it out. Rip-offs are always a big drag and it pissed me off to get it stolen, but it wound up not being any loss, and in the end I was glad to be rid of it. What the hell was I going to do with it anyway?

As I dove into the surf, Frank and Bobby, looking like a couple of valley geeks, paced back and forth in the sand, not knowing what to do with their spears. After a minute or two of that, they took them back to the cottage and returned to the beach. By the time they got in the water, I'd already caught three nice waves and was working on the fourth.

That week at Newport gave me a good taste of the beach-bum life I'd live later on when I was in my twenties. I was on the beach and in the surf every day we were there. I had no desire to hang out with Frank and Bobby; let them try to hang out with me. I had the beach and the surf, and nothing but time to think about Carol and wish she was there. The only time I spent with them was at night when we went down to the little amusement park next to where the Balboa Island ferry landed. One night we went to the movie theater in the little village of Balboa and saw Jimmy Stewart and June Allison in *The Stratton Story*.

## Down the Foggy Ruins of Time

I lost track of the adults through most of the week. Greg and Antoine took a charter out of the bay one afternoon and made use of the gear they'd gotten at Palley's. Dad got pretty drunk that day, but he caught a seven-pound lingcod and Greg caught an eight-pound rock cod which were enough to feed us all for dinner that night. Our last night in the beach house, the adults stayed up late playing poker in a fog of Camels and Seagram's. All in all, it was a great five days, and a very cool end to a really righteous summer.

On our last morning there, I got into trouble with Francesca because I got wet when she told me to stay out of the water. I woke up at a little before daybreak because I wanted to go down to the beach and watch the sunrise. Mom and Louise were already awake and bustling around the kitchen. They had the Wheaties and Cherrios out on the table along with a half-loaf of Weber's bread and what was left of the butter and peanut butter. They were just setting the bowls, plates and silverware out as I was heading toward the door.

"Don't go in the water," Mom said. "We're tryin' to get on the road as soon as we clean up after breakfast, and I want you back at a decent time so you can get packed and be ready to leave when the rest of us are ready."

"Aw, Mom..." I started to say, but she cut me off.

"I mean it. We will leave before nine o'clock, and you'll be here no later than eight or there'll be hell to pay. You hear me?"

"Yeah, I'll be here," I said over my shoulder as I closed the door and headed out into the gray dawn. I really wasn't worried too much, though, because everybody else was still in bed.

The sunrise from the Balboa Pier was beautiful! A lot prettier than any I'd ever seen in Eagle Rock. I got out there just seconds before it broke over the horizon. It was a crystal-clear morning, not a cloud in the sky. The purple arc on the eastern edge of the planet was right above where water meets land on the south coast. The wet sand below the high tide mark and the burnished-copper surface of the water reflected the magenta sky. The air smelled of the briny ocean. A flock of tiny shorebirds scampered just ahead of the ebb and flow of the tide. As the sun made its way over the Santa Ana Mountains down close to the shoreline, it cast a shimmering gold column across the water's crinkly surface, forming an inverted exclamation point. The shaft broke up just below me and scattered sparkling stardust across the backside of the breaking surf. I only stayed on the pier until the flaming ball was fully above the horizon. The silent energy of the sun rising above the powerful roar of the surf struck me as paradoxical.

## Down the Foggy Ruins of Time

About ten feet from where I was standing, a Latino couple, with lines in the water, carried on in Spanish as the sun burst over the horizon. I caught bits and pieces of their conversation.

"¡Qué amanecida bonita! ¿Verdad, amante?"

"Sí, es muy bonita."

Of all the people out there, they were definitely the most animated and appreciative of the beautiful sunrise. The others (mostly gavachos, except for one black guy and a couple of Filipinos) didn't seem too impressed. If they were, they weren't showing it. They stared at their lines, smoked tobacco, and talked in small groups, not really paying a lot of attention to either the breaking dawn or the breaking surf.

The shore break was perfect, and I just wanted to go dive in and get a few rides before I went home, but I was a good boy—at first anyway. I walked up the beach until I was right in front of where our cottage was located. The foamy whitewater was creaming the sand, leaving sand-crab air holes as it ebbed. At first I only got my feet wet as I waded into ankle-deep water. Then I moved in a little deeper where the surf was breaking around my shins. Suddenly a pretty good size wave broke at my knees and splashed up and got my trunks wet. At that point I thought, *Oh, what the hell?* and dove into the next wave.

*Jerome Arthur*

I don't know how long I'd been in the water when I saw Mom, all dressed and ready for the trip home, walk barefoot across the beach toward the surf. She stood at water's edge, elbows akimbo, an angry look on her face, so I rode the next wave in, and for the next couple of hours, suffered through her wrath. I found out what she meant when she said there'd be hell to pay. I paid. When she and I got back to the cottage, the Forests were pulling out. Antoine and Frank were putting the last of our stuff into the Chevy. I took off my wet trunks and got dressed, and then we were on our way, too.

Because I'd been in the water and didn't get back to the beach house when I was supposed to, I didn't get any breakfast, so before we even got to Huntington Beach, I was grouchy with hunger pangs, but Francesca said I'd just have to put up with it and it served me right for disobeying her. She was not in a good mood.

I felt like I was in heaven the last two weeks of summer vacation. I spent almost every day hanging around with Carol, either in her room or at the pool. On the last day, I made a final trek over to her house. I'd been doling out my leftover paper-route rubber bands to her ever since we started hanging around together. She was using them and bobby pins to put curls in her hair. Now I wanted to give her all of what I had left, so I took them over to her place on Sunday afternoon, the day before school started,

## Down the Foggy Ruins of Time

and, while her parents were at a matinee at the Eagle theater, we fooled around one last time, feeling and touching each other as we were making out. When we finished, I pedaled over to the pool, which had been drained the day before and was deserted. I stood next to the chain link fence and thought about her and reminisced our time together. That was the last time I saw her.

# Twenty-four

Mom and Dad started looking at real estate at the beginning of the new school year. Francesca said we'd lived in the unfinished house long enough, and she wanted a real home with a nice kitchen and interior walls in the bedrooms instead of open studs. The lady who owned the house where we got Penny had hers on the market, and Antoine and Francesca were interested. They put our house up for sale after the first time they looked at the Linda Rosa house.

They'd hooked up with a real estate broker named Nate Santor and he was showing them property all over Eagle Rock, but they kept coming back to the house on Linda Rosa. Frank and I got to meet Nate one night when he brought over a counteroffer. The three of them sat down at the table with drinks and went over the agreed-upon terms. After he'd had a couple of stiff shots, Antoine said,

"You know, Nate, you're a real swell fellow. You know how to cut a deal. Name like Santor, you a Jew boy or what?"

## Down the Foggy Ruins of Time

I know it sounds like a weird comment to make, but Antoine had a way of making that kind of a question seem completely innocuous. Maybe that was because it was so patently obvious that he wasn't, by any stretch of the imagination, a racist or anti-Semitic. Nate must've recognized that fact because he didn't seem to be offended at all.

"No," he said. "Santor is an Italian name. There used to be an i at the end, but my father dropped it. Or maybe I should say the fella's at Ellis Island dropped it for him when he got off the boat."

The counter-offer was accepted and the deal went through. We sailed right through a thirty-day escrow and by Halloween we'd sold the old unfinished fixer-upper on La Roda and moved down to Linda Rosa. Penny got to go back to where she lived when she was a puppy. And for the first time, we were living in a finished and complete house. All the interior walls were lath and plaster, no more open studs strung with spider webs. The front door opened directly into the living room. The dining room (it was the first house we lived in that actually had a dining room) was to the left as you entered. The kitchen was behind the dining room along the wall that bordered the driveway. A door opposite the front door led to a central hall with doors to the bedrooms and bathroom. The house had a twenty-foot setback in front, almost exactly the opposite of the house on La Roda. Hence, the backyard on Linda

Rosa was about the same size as the front yard on La Roda.

It was only a two-bedroom house, so Frank and I still had to share a room, but that didn't take any of the luster off the fact that it was a regular house like all the other kids lived in, and not a trailer or a hovel, which is what the house on La Roda felt like. I think it was at this point in time that the Farot family changed social classes. We moved, unnoticed, from the lower class right into the middle class (albeit lower-middle), and for the first time ever, I was feeling equal in social status to my peers.

One of the good features of the Linda Rosa house was its proximity to Yosemite playground, and its location on the main walking route to Bob's Big Boy from the playground and Eagle Rock High. I'd see a lot of kids I knew passing by all the time. Because the park was only two blocks away from the house, it was easy to go there after school. And now that I was in "junior high school," even though it was still only Saint Dominic's and Sister Adolf, the playground became more of a hangout place than the schoolyard because there was more to do there.

The new school building was up and running when I went into seventh grade. They had finished construction toward the end of summer vacation and completed the demolition on the old building one-week before the start of the fall semester. The crew and all of the equipment were out of there

## Down the Foggy Ruins of Time

by October first, after they'd finished the work on the new sand box.

The individual rooms were spacious, airy and new smelling, and they all had new, free-standing metal desks with laminated wood writing tables minus inkwell holes. In fact, it had been a couple years since we'd used inkwells in the old desks because by that time we'd quit using fountain pens in favor of Scripto ballpoints. The restrooms were all modern and sanitary. I actually looked forward to going to school every day because everything was so clean and comfortable and unused.

From the beginning of the semester until we moved, Ronald and I did our morning bike ride down Chickasaw. Every time we got to school during the first couple months, I was struck by Sister Johanna's absence. I missed going to her room on Friday afternoons.

On Wednesday of the first week of the new school year, Ronald and I were coming out of Bob's with cinnamon doughnuts and cherry Cokes, and Mister Goodall, my old boss, was dealing with the kid who was working my old corner. When he saw me, he called me over and offered me a job. This one was in Glendale at the intersection of Verdugo Road and Colorado Boulevard in front of a Van De Kamp's bakery that sat on the corner of the parking lot of a Ralph's supermarket. He offered me a good guarantee, so I took the job.

*Jerome Arthur*

I went to work the next day, and once again I was hustling the two o'clock and Eight Star editions of the *Herald Express*. The clientele were the afternoon commuters going north on Verdugo heading home from their jobs in Los Angeles. It was actually a pretty busy corner. A guy named Frank took care of all the newspaper racks at the entrance to Ralph's, and he was a lot busier than I was. He had maybe six different newspapers to sell. We'd get together a couple of times during our shift and compare notes on how we were doing with the *Herald*. He was a freshman at Glendale High School, the same age as my big brother, and as soon as we started working together, he began treating me like my big brother never treated me, like my brother should have been treating me. This Frank was nice to me, took care of me, watched over me, protected me.

During the first week of school, the Glendale Junior High boys had a screwball rite where the eighth graders called the seventh graders "scrubs," and then they'd pick a few seventh-grade boys at random and smear (scrub) lipstick all over their faces. Marauding groups of eighth graders would roam the streets after school looking for seventh graders to scrub. When a group of them tried to grab me on my first Friday on the corner (my second day on the job), Frank pulled them off of me, telling them that I was a freshman at Glendale High just like he was. He was a cool guy, and I really liked working with

## Down the Foggy Ruins of Time

him, but selling papers on a corner just wasn't my thing, so I quit after only a month and a half on the job.

While I was doing the corner, Ronald was practicing with the seventh and eighth grade touch football team so we didn't ride home together. Later on, after we moved, he came down the steeper backside of La Roda in the morning, and we'd go down Yosemite to Maywood where we'd pick up Ralph Meister who lived in a house on that corner. From his place it was only two flat blocks past Eagle Rock Elementary to Saint Dominic's.

After I quit the corner, I'd ride straight home, dump my books, and go hang out at the rec. room at Yosemite. A kid named Quade and I got into playing chess a few days a week (every day when it was raining) through the fall and winter. When we started out, we only read the first part of the instruction booklet that Mister Cimarelli had in the office, the part about what kind of moves the various pieces could make. For Quade and me the rest of it was the learn-as-you-go method. We played for a couple of weeks before we found out about check and checkmate. One day when Quade was "taking" my king, another kid who was watching the match said,

"That ain't the way you do it in chess. It ain't at all like checkers where you can jump everything on the board. You don't take the king. You put it in check, and then you try to get checkmate. That's where your king can't make no more moves."

At that point Quade got out the instructions and we read the rules about those two moves. From then on we did it right.

Since Frank had graduated from Saint Dominic's and was now going to Cathedral High School down near Chinatown, this was the first year since I was in first grade that I didn't have my big brother putting me down when our paths crossed during recess and lunch hour. Since we never got along all that well in most other situations, I found myself trying to avoid him whenever I'd see him on the schoolyard. He hung out with his friends, and I hung out with mine. Nevertheless, we weren't always able to avoid contact, and when we had it, it usually worked to my disadvantage, so the less I saw of him, the better. When he went to Cathedral, I at least got him off my back for the few hours every day that we were in school, and I must admit, my life was improved greatly. In two years I'd be at Cathedral too, and, soon enough, I'd again be seeing more than my share of him at school.

Sister Adolf proved to be the toughest teacher I had at Saint Dominic's. She was a very nice lady, but she was just as firm as the name she chose to serve her Savior. As the seventh-grade teacher, she was also the vice-principal, and hence the main disciplinarian for the whole school. In all

## Down the Foggy Ruins of Time

the time I was there, I couldn't remember ever seeing her smile. What a difference going from Sister
Nimrod to Sister Adolf. Nobody got out of line in
Sister Adolf's class because she had a lesson plan,
and she stuck to it. She was strictly business-like
Sister Ingrid, but a lot tougher, and completely fair,
unlike Sister Ruth who was just plain mean and nasty. I worked my butt off in Sister Adolf's class and
felt good about getting C's. She came down on me
one time, and she made the discipline feel like a
learning experience.

During the lunch hour on the schoolyard, we
sat on some benches lined up along a chain link
fence on the back property line. With our backs
against the fence, we ate and watched the day-to-day
disappearance of the foothills behind a curtain of
smog, and anything we said about it could be easily
overheard by the neighbors in the houses on the other side of the fence. On more than one occasion, I
might have said something like,

"Where the fuck're the mountains disap-
pearin' to? Goes to show, fuckin' smog's takin'
over."

The houses weren't even fifteen feet from
the fence, and the people in them could hear stuff
like that loud and clear. One day a couple weeks before Halloween, as we were heading back to class
after lunch, Sister Adolf came out of the convent and
intercepted me.

*Jerome Arthur*

"Jerôme, I would like a word with you before we return to class," she said, separating me from the three or four guys I was walking with. She took me aside to a small patch of lawn that was situated between the church and the convent, bordered by some sweet-smelling roses of all colors. "Someone in one of the houses behind the schoolyard has complained about the language out there."

I could feel the blood rising in my cheeks. This was embarrassing.

"She's pointed you out as the leading culprit. What do you have to say?"

"Nothin', Sister. I don't know what to say, 'cept I'm sorry." I was shuffling around, feeling all-hangdog.

"You're too smart to be using such language. That kind of talk only makes you look and sound foolish. It's a sign of ignorance, even illiteracy. You should try to overcome the impulse to use it." She paused in her lecture, I guess, to give me a chance to say something.

"I'll try to do better. I'm sorry, Sister," I repeated with my head down.

I couldn't look her in the eye. And I truly was sorry. I certainly appreciated it that she didn't lay a religious trip on me, didn't even try to tell me cussing was a sin.

"Now, let's get back to class."

## Down the Foggy Ruins of Time

She went into the convent, and I went ahead and ran across the street. I got to my seat just as the last person to enter the room before me sat down. Sister Adolf followed a minute later. She walked right past me without a word or even a sidelong glance. That was Sister Adolf, no nonsense, nothing more said about it. For my part, I tried to cuss less, and I had all good intentions of doing so, but I'm afraid my attempts weren't very successful. I still cussed a lot, but I always tried to make sure that when I did, I wasn't over near that fence.

That little episode happened on a Wednesday in mid-October, and two days later I had my first run-in with the cops. It marked the beginning of my lifelong fear and dislike of the police. I'd heard plenty of cop-hating talk from Melo over the years, but I never gave it much thought until they came down on me that night.

Norm Cline, an Eagle Rock Junior High kid from down the street asked me to go with him to the Eagle Rock/Franklin game at Occidental College. We left the game about halfway through the fourth quarter, and as we headed up Campus Road toward the back gate of Yosemite playground, we saw a customized forty-nine Merc. parked at the curb. It was a real beauty: nosed and decked, channeled, full moons, and dual chrome tailpipes. We got down on our hands and knees and looked underneath. The guy's mufflers were glass-packs, and his tires had four-inch-wide white sidewalls. The candy-apple-red paint job had the deep shine of multiple coats of lacquer. The car was so beautiful that we just stood there and stared at it, walked all around it, admired it.

A car pulled up beside us and two plainclothes cops got out, patted us down and hustled us into the back seat of their car. They asked us what we thought we were doing, and they accused us of trying to steal something–they didn't know what –off the car. Bottom line, they were rousting us, and I got scared, so suddenly I broke down and started crying, which prompted them to ease up, and let us go on our way, telling us to go straight home.

Now that I was in seventh grade, I was eligible to go out for the seventh and eighth grade sports teams. I didn't try out for the touch football team because I didn't like how rough the sport was. I didn't like getting knocked around, and besides, I was doing the corner during the season. Ronald, Ralph Meister, Jack Meador and the Schwarz twins made the starting lineup. Lanny made first string quarterback. I wasn't any good at basketball, so I didn't try out for that team either, opting instead to spend my afternoons playing chess with Quade.

Spring training for fast-pitch-softball began in early February. I made the team and early in the season had the starting position at second base, but I got benched when an eighth grader came out late,

## Down the Foggy Ruins of Time

after he'd recovered from a sprained ankle he'd gotten in the last basketball game of the season. Just as he'd done on the football and basketball teams, Lanny made first string on the softball team, the only seventh grader to do so. He was such a good baseball player that Coach Flanagan made him the starting shortstop even though he was a southpaw. Coach was pretty cool, though, and he let everybody play a little bit in each game. So, I did get some playing time in at second, but not enough to earn the little flannel oblong they called a letter. I wouldn't shine on that team until I got into eighth grade, and that's when I got my letter.

We played our home games on the blacktop schoolyard next to the nuns's convent. All of our opponents also played on blacktop except Saint Bernard's down in Glassell Park. Their schoolyard wasn't big enough to have a diamond, plus it wasn't level, so they played their home games at Glassell Recreation Center near the corner of Verdugo Road and Eagle Rock Boulevard. Glassell Rec. Center was a regular City Parks and Recreation Department playground like Yosemite, and its diamond had a dirt infield and a grass outfield.

Shortly after the start of the baseball season, Sister Adolf began preparing us for our next sacrament, Confirmation. They only did them every other year, so they always involved the seventh and eighth grade classes together. Confirmation marked the time when I started seriously going my own way with my religious beliefs. Doubts had started to crop up the previous year when we read a couple of stories from the Old Testament—"Abraham and Isaac," and "The Book of Job." No matter how hard Sister Nimrod tried to put a kind and merciful face on God in those stories, I was turned off completely by Him, because He seemed so vengeful and cruel, and ultimately, I decided for myself that He wasn't my god.

Sister Nimrod was always telling us to "pray for the poor "pagan" babies in China." Applying such an epithet to those poor Chinese kids seemed cruel and un-Christian to me. And then the clincher was when she told us that animals didn't have souls and therefore didn't get to go to heaven. That was the one that made my mind up once and for all; I didn't want to go to heaven if Penny wasn't going to be there, too.

So, by the time I got confirmed, I was only doing whatever was necessary to keep Francesca and the nuns off my case. I found I was begging off more and more on serving on the altar. I just couldn't get into Confirmation the same way I got into First Communion, even though I knew they were both of equal importance, but by then I was turned off by Confession and Communion, too. So, I went to all the instruction sessions and just kind of nodded my head and went along with the program and got confirmed. About the only thing I really dug about it

## Down the Foggy Ruins of Time

was that you got to choose a Confirmation name, and I took Ramón, in memory of my friend from kindergarten, but after I got confirmed, I never used the name again.

# Twenty-five

Casey got discharged from the Air Force in April, and he showed up at our place again around the same time the McCarthy hearings in the U.S. Senate started to unravel. The first night he was with us, we all sat around the television and watched the "C.B.S. Evening News" with Douglas Edwards. He showed a news clip of the senator accusing everybody and his brother of being a Communist. I was beginning to reach a certain level of maturity in my adolescence, because I could plainly see McCarthy was not cool. How scared I used to be when Sister Ruth ranted and raved about the Communists. Now, I just laughed as McCarthy, with his boy wonders Cohn and Schine at his side, railed against the international Communist conspiracy from the bully pulpit of his committee. At this stage of the game, I thought the guy was nuts, and if I could figure it out, I thought everybody else must see it, too. Antoine and Francesca both agreed that he was crazy. Dad said that anybody who'd accuse the Army brass of being Communists had to be off his rocker, and that was enough for me. I lost all fear of McCarthy and

## Down the Foggy Ruins of Time

his phantom Communists. It's really too bad that his depravity wasn't recognized for what it was and exposed earlier. So many innocent people's lives were ruined as he trampled all over their First Amendment rights.

At the dinner table, Casey had told us he was only going to Minneapolis to straighten up his affairs, and then he'd come back to Los Angeles to settle down and try to get a job in the printing business like Antoine. He stayed with us for a couple weeks, and one of the first things he did was buy a car. He'd arrived on Thursday, and on Saturday Frank and I went with him and Antoine to Glendale to look at used cars. As he was looking over Johnny Lail's selection, Frank and I went over to the showroom and looked at the new Chevy sports car, the Corvette. It stood white as a bride on the showroom floor, and Frank and I thought it was a really cool car. When we got back to the used cars, Antoine and Casey were getting ready to take a forty-six Chevy two-door sedan for a test drive. We got into the back seat with dad. Casey was driving; the salesman was riding shotgun. As we passed by the showroom window of the dealership, Frank said,

"Hey, Casey. Take a look at that Corvette."

"Yeah, sure," he said without turning his head. "And how much they want for it? Three thousand, thirty-five hundred?"

"Closer to thirty-five," the salesman said.

"Too rich for my blood. 'Sides there ain't no room for the stuff I wan'a bring back out here with me from Minneapolis."

We took Brand Boulevard out of Glendale to Atwater and crossed the Hyperion Bridge to Riverside Drive. Casey stepped on it, getting it up to fifty-five going down Riverside. We took a left on Fletcher Drive back across the river and cruised up San Fernando Road back to Johnny Lail's. The Chevy was clean and it was a good running little car. Casey bargained the salesman down from two hundred and fifty dollars to two hundred and drove it off the lot. Frank and I rode home with him, and Antoine drove on ahead of us. Frank tuned the radio in the dashboard to a station that was playing a really cool up-tempo rhythm and blues version of "Marie, the Dawn is Breaking." Casey snapped out of his new-car-daydream long enough to say,

"These guys sure fucked up a good song."

Then he went back to enjoying the drive. I disagreed with him, but I didn't say anything. As far as I was concerned, those guys were just doing another, better version of the song.

Casey had two weeks of fun in the sun; it looked like he was grooming himself for his return and a long stay. He went to the beach a few times, and he spent a couple days with Antoine at Impressions Incorporated. I think he even got himself lined up with a job for when he came back out. His last

## Down the Foggy Ruins of Time

Saturday in town, he took Frank and me up to Mount Waterman and tried to show us how to ski, but that turned out to be a cold and miserable experience, a real disaster. At the end of the two weeks, Casey went home, and just as his brother Luke had done before him, he got a job in Minneapolis (as a feeder at Brown and Bigelow, the same printing company Antoine worked for when I was born), met a Mexicana (one of the very few in Minnesota) named Josie, got married, started a family, and he never came back to California again.

On the Saturday after Casey pulled out, I called Ronald on the phone to see if he wanted to go down to Yosemite and hang out in the rec. room, play some caroms or ping pong, but he said he had a matinee date with Charlene at the Alex theater. He was on his way out to catch the Asbury bus that went to Glendale, so I went to Yosemite by myself. I was hoping to play some chess with Quade, but he wasn't around, so I went up to the ping-pong table that Nick Sunseri and Rod McFadden were playing on.

I said, "Hey, can I play the winner?"

"Sure. We're at ten-seven right now, my favor," Nick said.

I took a seat on a bench at the side of the table and watched Rod beat Nick twenty-one to eighteen. I beat both of them the next two games, and then all three of us went over to Larsen's market across Yosemite from the park and got some Grapettes. I hung out with them for the rest of the afternoon, and that led to a friendship that saw me spending quite a bit of time with them through the spring and summer and on into fall. They were both cool cats.

I had met Rod a couple years ago through Melo. They'd been classmates at Eagle Rock Elementary, and they were still classmates at Eagle Rock Junior High, but their friendship had gone the same way that mine and Melo's had gone. Not only were they no longer friends, they were, in fact, enemies. Rod didn't like Melo mostly because of the crowd he was running with, a club whose members were wan'a be hoods, but they weren't bad enough to be truly called a gang. The Knights had club jackets with the symbol of the chess piece as their logo. Frank was a member. When he'd gone to high school downtown, he didn't leave the neighborhood the way I would two years later. He was still hanging around with the Knights who were all Eagle Rock High guys. He was the only member of the club who didn't go to school there. Bobby Forest and Ronald's older brother Richie were also members. Ronald joined in the fall of that year when he went into eighth grade at Eagle Rock Junior High.

Rod truly hated the Knights; he despised what he perceived as their phoniness. He was constantly bad-mouthing them, and he was pretty open

## Down the Foggy Ruins of Time

and loud about it, so they knew exactly what kind of trash he was talking about them, and he did it all with impunity because he was a big thirteen-year-old, and a bad-ass to boot. Plus, his seventeen-year-old brother, Roger, was also big and bad and highly respected among his own peers, so only a very few of the Knights individually would think of choosing Rod off, and most certainly no group of them would ever jump him because then they'd have to deal with Roger and his friends. I always felt safe and secure when I was hanging around with Rod. I was glad I had him for a friend at that stage of my life.

Nick was Rod's best friend. I had played against him three summers in a row on the sandlot. He'd been on the Comets' roster. Now he belonged to a club called the Gauchos. They had club jackets too, but their members didn't have any gang aspirations at all. They weren't tough guys like the Knights considered themselves to be. The Gauchos was a social club. They had meetings at a different member's house each time with refreshments like the way we used to do it in Cubs. One really cool thing about Nick was that he, like Ronald, had dark-hair and an olive-complexion. His heritage was Italian, so as far as I was concerned, he was just another Latino like Ronald with his Mexican heritage and me with my French heritage.

Some of my perplexity on that subject cleared up when Frank brought home his freshman yearbook at the end of May. I saw my destiny in its pages, and things were looking pretty good. I spent long stretches of time looking at the pictures of the different classes and was blown away by the names I read under them: Nieto, like George; Sandoval, like Ramón; Cota, like the name of the street we lived on in Long Beach. I suddenly felt a rush of excitement. All I had to do was complete another month of seventh grade and then the nine months of eighth grade and I'd be outa' there at Saint Dominic's, and off to Cathedral, where I'd be home at last and hanging around with a bunch of guys whom I would develop a much closer kinship with than I ever would with my own brother. I could hardly wait.

My friendship with Ronald ended fairly abruptly. I was still doing a lot of stuff with him all through the spring after I'd started hanging around with Rod and Nick. And then in June when school got out, he said he was going to Eagle Rock Junior High in the fall. I saw him at Yosemite only two or three times during summer vacation, and each time he was with his newfound pals from the Knights, smoking Chesterfields out in left field near the pool. I was usually with Nick and Rod on those occasions, but we were in the opposite field, and we'd be making jokes about them and putting them down, but we were far enough away from them that they couldn't hear us doing it.

## Down the Foggy Ruins of Time

The last week in June, Uncle Danny came into town from Salt Lake City. His friend Bob, who was going into the seminary in the fall, came along with him. They'd stopped in Las Vegas to pay their dues on the way down Highway Ninety-one, and when they arrived at our house, Uncle Dan was full of stories about his adventures in the casinos. He'd hit a hundred-dollar jackpot on one of the dollar slot machines at the Mint. He said he'd only been that lucky once before when he'd hopped over to Wendover and won fifty silver dollars holding a handle in his hand.

"I won't be able to go to Wendover anymore, though," he said. "When I get home from this trip, I'm being transferred to the parish in Monticello, near the Navajo Reservation a couple hundred miles southeast of Salt Lake."

They were with us a full four days, and, just as we'd done in the past when we had out-of-town guests, we did something with them every day. One day Dan and Bob took Frank and me to the beach at Santa Monica; another day Mom and Dad took off from work and the four of them got on the train at Union Station and went to the horse races down at Del Mar.

On their last night in town, all six of us went in two cars to Hollywood to see a Cinerama movie. After four days Frank and I were pretty wound up and we were acting like jerks. The movie was *The*

*Seven Wonders of the World,* and it was over our heads. The adults really liked it because it was an interesting documentary, but Frank and I were bored. The other Cinerama movie we'd seen was all about thrill rides like roller coasters and guys jumping out of airplanes with parachutes and other guys taking you for a ride in a Navy jet. Now, that was the ticket for Frank and me; the Wonders of the World were boring. When we came out of the theater, we were scoffing at how dumb we thought the movie was, and how the other one we'd seen was so much better.

Uncle Danny had taken Frank and me in his car, and Bob had gone with Antoine and Francesca in the Chevy. On the way home I was riding shotgun and Frank was in between Uncle Danny and me in the front seat. We two boys just kept going on about how boring the movie had been. When we got to Rosemary Drive on Yosemite, Danny missed the turn and started to pass by the playground. I was very hyper at that point and really being a jerk, and I blurted out,

"Hey, wise guy...."

I was cut off when Father Dan's backhand snapped across the seat in front of Frank and caught me flush on the nose. Tears sprang to my eyes and the blood flowed, covering my upper lip. I pinched my nose to stop the bleeding, but I didn't act fast

## Down the Foggy Ruins of Time

enough to keep it from dripping on my new beige peggers.

"I am not a wise guy," he said. "I am a Catholic priest, and I deserve more respect than that, so stop your whining and complaining."

Pinching my bleeding nose between my thumb and forefinger and tilting my head back, I blinked back my tears and glanced out of the corner of my eye at Uncle Danny. His lower lip was quivering. He was pissed! And I don't blame him! He made his left turn at La Roda and doubled back to our house. Behind us, Dad didn't miss the turn at Rosemary, so they were already in the driveway getting out of the car as we pulled in behind them. I made a dash to the bathroom to clean up.

When I came out, I went straight to my room to think about what had just happened. I was in a daze. My own father, Antoine, had never hit me before. As a matter of fact, no adult had ever laid a hand on me when I was a kid, except Bart, the mongoloid, but that didn't really count. Frank and I were both being jerks and I knew it, but I thought Uncle Danny overreacted to our rudeness and stepped over the line. Just another reason for me to re-evaluate my feelings about the Church and its ministers. Four years ago, when Father Mick snookered me out of going on the altar a couple of months early, I saw it as the church rejecting me. I saw Danny's backhand as the church assaulting me. I was afraid of the church, now more than ever. Those Old Testament and Inquisition stories were just classroom lectures; my own experience with my uncle and my parish priest were hands-on seminars (literally, in the case of my uncle).

It was late when we'd gotten home, so I just went ahead and hit the sack. The next morning I was up before everybody else and out the door to Yosemite playground. I stayed there by myself doing nothing until I was sure that Father Dan and Bob had gone back to Salt Lake City. I walked home and didn't say a word about it to either Antoine or Francesca. I don't know if Uncle Danny said anything to them or not.

# Twenty-six

About a week after Danny and Bob went back to Salt Lake, we found out about Casey's marriage and decision to stay in Minneapolis in a letter from my aunt Edith. She wrote to tell Mom and Dad that she and a friend she'd attended stenographer's school with would be moving to Los Angeles around the end of August, and would it be okay to stay with us until they found their own place. They arrived at our house the Thursday before Labor Day, and by the weekend, they'd found a furnished bungalow in the court next door to Carmine's liquor store on Colorado at Mount Royal. They started work at Occidental Insurance Company in downtown on Tuesday after the holiday.

Finally, after we'd been disappointed when Luke and Casey didn't come back as they'd said they were going to, a relative from Minneapolis, their little sister Edith moved to Los Angeles. It was my first experience having extended family living close by. It's true we had Paul and his family for a while, but they were really a burden with his drunken antics, and hardly qualified as any kind of family. Edith was a good-hearted, stable person who was lots of fun to have around. Good people. Family.

Two weeks after we received her letter, Antoine took Frank and me over to Milne Brothers Motorcycles in Pasadena and bought us a couple of motor scooters. Frank got a Cushman that was in pretty good condition; I got a Mustang Colt that barely ran. The Colt was a small version of the Mustang motorcycle—smaller frame and engine, and eight-inch wheels versus twelve-inch. The Mustang was a Harley Davidson look-alike in miniature with a teardrop gas tank, wide saddle with big springs, and Harley-style handlebars. About the only thing missing was the V-twin engine; Mustangs and Mustang Colts had powerful little one lungers. My Colt's engine was just barely bigger than a Briggs and Stratton Doodlebug engine, but a lot more powerful.

Frank's Cushman was bigger and had more power than my Colt, but the Colt looked like a motorcycle, whereas the Cushman was truly a motor scooter with a floorboard where the kick-starter rested, and a big, rounded, sheet metal skirt with a cushion to sit on. The engine and gas tank were inside the skirt underneath the seat cushion. The rigid sheet metal lid that covered the storage box served as a very hard buddy seat.

My Colt had foot pegs with a shift lever on the left, a brake pedal and kick-starter on the right.

## Down the Foggy Ruins of Time

The Cushman didn't have gears; power was engaged to the wheels by means of a centrifugal clutch. Both scooters were fire engine red: Frank's all red with white handlebars, mine white on top of the gas tank with chrome handlebars and a chrome rear fender which I used for a buddy seat. Since there were no buddy pegs on either scooter and the sheet metal surfaces were hard, it wasn't a very comfortable ride.

And so, I was thirteen years old and poised to go into eighth grade, and I had a miniature motorcycle that I wasn't even old enough to ride legally. I was still two years away from getting my learner's permit which would've made me street legal, but I rode it anyway, rode it, that is, when it was running, and mostly limited to the four-block area of my neighborhood. Antoine did allow me to go over the hill on Argus and cruise down Chickasaw to as far as school, and I could also go over La Roda to Tenshaw and Mount Royal, but I had to stay off Colorado Boulevard, Eagle Rock Boulevard and Yosemite Drive, and I wasn't allowed to cross any of those three streets. I did the La Roda-Tenshaw-Mount Royal ride a few times in the fall to go visit Edith and Agnes in their bungalow. Frank had gotten his learner's permit that year, so he could ride his anywhere he wanted. He'd also grown to his full adult height of five-ten, a good three inches taller than Antoine and almost a foot taller than I. I was just

*Jerome Arthur*

barely over five feet tall when I entered eighth grade, a good size for my little motorcycle, which, it seemed, I was working on more than I was riding.

Antoine was a good mechanic and he was always willing to help me out whenever I had to do any work on the Colt, and from those sessions, I learned some valuable mechanical skills. He'd always been at the ready to fix a flat tire on our Columbias or replace a broken indicator chain and rod on our Defiances. Over the years I'd watched him do oil changes and tune-ups on the Packard, the Airflow and the Chevy. His left index finger had been amputated at the knuckle, the result of a Chevy six he was working on accidentally cutting loose from a hoist and landing smack on that one finger. He also did his own maintenance and repairs on his press.

Antoine was a good mechanic all right, but there wasn't much he could do to help me fix the carburetor on the Colt. There wasn't much anybody could have done on that one, and I never did get it right. It was a funky needle valve setup that someone who'd owned the scooter before me had taken a file to. Lacking a brand new un-mutilated needle valve, it never would be right. One cold, crisp autumn night we worked on the damn thing until ten o'clock. It was so cold that two sweatshirts weren't enough to keep me warm. All they did was accumulate a heavy smell of gasoline and so did I. And there was no im-

## Down the Foggy Ruins of Time

provement with the needle valve when we finished
the job.

Shortly after we got our scooters, a couple
of Frank's buddies from the Knights, Lee Proctor
and Alan Andrade, started hanging around our
house. Lee had a standard-size Mustang, and he and
Frank were the only two guys in the Knights who
had scooters. Alan was Lee's best friend and also in
the club, so he was like a permanent fixture on Lee's
buddy seat. Lee was also going out with Al's little
sister, Frances.

A couple days before school started, they
showed up at our house to see if Frank wanted to go
with them over to the Los Angeles River near Atwater to cruise their scooters down on the concrete riverbed. Since Frank wasn't riding anybody on the
back of his Cushman, Lee suggested that he take me,
and when Alan told him it would be more fun if
there were four of us, Frank grudgingly agreed to
take me along.

We took off down Yosemite Drive to Eagle
Rock Boulevard, went down to Verdugo Road and
picked up Fletcher Drive, which we took straight out
past San Fernando Road till we hit the river. Just
past Gladding Mc Bean, the terra-cotta tile company,
we got onto a service-vehicle ramp that took us
down to the riverbed. We rode the scooters down to
where the Arroyo Seco flows into the river. There
were four Mexicanos, my kind of guys, hanging

around under the Arroyo Seco Parkway overpass. They wore sharply pressed khaki trousers that were just slightly too long at the cuffs, black, spit-shined French-toe shoes, and over white T-shirts, baggy Pendletons, also slightly too big, buttoned at the collar and cuffs. One of them had a spray can, and he was tagging the overpass with the word "Bullet." Directly under it he sprayed C/S in neatly formed letters and R under that.

"What's that stand for?" Lee asked him.

"It's like this, ese," the guy doing the tagging replied with a heavy accent. "Boollet's my nickname, eh, and C/S stands for con safos, and that means ain't nobody can put notheen bad down on my name, 'cause whatever they say goes back to them, and the R stands for rifa controla, and that means that whatever they put down goes back to their mother, eh."

We hung out with them for a while, and Lee and Frank took turns giving them rides on their scooters. I didn't particularly like them spraying their graffiti around on the overpasses and bridges down on the riverbed, but when all was said and done, they were cool cats. We spent a good hour with them, and then we took the riverbed back up to Fletcher Drive and headed home.

# Twenty-seven

For the first time in six years, except the year we lived on Wiota, I rode to school alone on the first day of the new term. Ronald had transferred to Eagle Rock Junior High, which was no surprise to anybody; he'd told us all in June that he wouldn't be coming back to Saint Dominic's for eighth grade. Another kid came in and took his place, the first new addition to the class since fourth grade and the Schwarz twins.

At 8:45, I rounded the corner of Maywood and Merton and saw the new kid leaning up against the fence near the front gate. Five other guys, the Schwarz twins, Seth Gómez, Jack Meador, and Ralph Meister surrounded him. Ralph and Jack were the only two guys who were anywhere near as tall as the new kid. He and Ralph were about five-ten, Jack was five-nine and Lonny Schwarz was five-seven. Seth and Lanny were the littlest ones in the group, my size, about five feet tall.

## Down the Foggy Ruins of Time

I locked my bike up and joined them. Seth, who already seemed to be acquainted with the new kid, introduced us. His name was Tommy Riley, and he was a good-looking guy with wavy auburn hair, blue eyes and a Paul Newman smile. Despite his appearance and the last name, his heritage wasn't all Irish. His mother, Gabriela, came from Italian stock. But neither of those two bloodlines applied to Tommy in the world we lived in. Just like me, he'd spent his entire childhood believing in his own mind that he was a Mexicano, but he went me one better. He actually had a name for what I always believed myself to be—Chicano.

He'd moved to Eagle Rock from San Francisco, but before that he'd lived in Lincoln Heights. He'd done his first four years at Sacred Heart. He was a full year older than the rest of us, suggesting that somewhere along the line he'd been held back in school. That explained his size; he was already close to his full adult height.

Tommy's arrival at Saint Dominic's marked a new chapter in my life. He was the first gavacho I ever met who tried to show Mexicanos and other people with dark skin in a positive light. It was a far cry from Lynn's negative stereotypes of black people. Tommy thought he was a Mexicano, a Chicano, so if he ever heard anybody bad-mouth them, he took it personally.

"I got a friend goes to Queen of Angels down Chinatown. Vato's puro Chicano but he's as light as you and me," Tommy said. "A real güero."

He did a decent job with the pronunciation, and it sure was nice to hear the language again, no matter that two of the words he'd used were colloquialisms. It had been over a year since I'd seen Sister Johanna, and that was the last time I'd heard any version of Spanish spoken. It was pretty cool, but it got spoiled a little bit when Lanny Schwarz latched onto "vato" and went around spouting "vato" this and "vato" that, not even knowing what the hell he was saying, using the labial-dental instead of the bilabial pronunciation of the "v." Of course, Tommy pronounced it that way too, and so did I and all the others at the time, but when I got into Brother Samuel's Spanish class at Cathedral, I learned that, for at least the last four hundred years or so, the F is the only labial-dental sound in the Spanish language. The correct pronunciation for the "v" is the same as for the "b." "¿B de burro o V de vaca?" Brother Samuel would prompt, when he drilled us on spelling and pronunciation.

Right before the bell rang Tommy made some disparaging remark about my riding a bike. He said only little kids rode bikes. Well, so be it. I guess I'll always be a kid then, because I'll never be too old to ride a bike. If it ever comes to the point that I'm physically unable because of old age to stay up

## Down the Foggy Ruins of Time

on two wheels, I'll ride an adult tricycle, and, if necessary, get a battery for it. His scorn certainly didn't dissuade me from riding during the time we were friends. Too bad I wasn't allowed to ride the Colt to school; if I'd showed up on it, maybe that would've shut him up. His superior attitude certainly didn't make for a good first meeting, but we did become friends, and he eventually took Ronald's place as my best friend in eighth grade.

The friendship really began when he invited me over to his house on Wednesday night, two days after we met. He lived in a second story apartment on Eagle Rock Boulevard near Avenue Forty-five. I cut through Yosemite and Oxy to get there. It was a three-bedroom apartment and Tommy lived there with his mom and dad and his older brother Robert who was a senior at Franklin High. He'd tried to get into Cathedral but he didn't get accepted. The apartment was only a temporary place for them. They would move into a three-bedroom house on Campus Road directly across the street from Oxy before Thanksgiving.

The first thing Tommy did that Wednesday night, after he closed us in his room, was put a Dave Brubeck Quartet album on the turntable. Then he opened a window and lit up a Lucky, and as he smoked and listened to the music, he told me that he first started listening to jazz in San Francisco on KJAZ, a station that broadcasted out of Berkeley.

*Jerome Arthur*

One of the coolest things about Tommy was that he really dug the music. All kinds of music, including rhythm and blues, and rock 'n' roll, which were my favorites. I told him about H.H., Hunter Hancock, the deejay with a late-night radio gig down in South Central Los Angeles, and Tommy said he already checked him out. He was a white guy in his thirties, and he played black musicians exclusively. His sexy-sounding sidekick, Margie, was a beautiful young black woman in her early twenties. They were a married couple. At the time I didn't know any of this about them because until then I'd only heard their late-night voices coming through the speaker of the radio I kept on a nightstand next to my bed. The first time I actually saw them and guessed their ages and ethnic backgrounds was two years later when they emceed a Sunday afternoon rock 'n' roll show that I went to at the downtown Paramount theater.

I was supposed to be home by nine o'clock that night, but I wanted to stick around at Tommy's a little while longer so we could listen together to a little bit of H.H.'s show. I phoned Mom to see if she'd let me stay for another half hour. She told me to be home no later than ten o'clock. We tuned Tommy's radio to H.H., and, during the half hour I stayed, we got to hear the Chords's original version of "Sh-Boom," "Cherry Pie," by Marvin and Johnny, "All Night Long," Joe Houston, "Saint James

## Down the Foggy Ruins of Time

Infirmary," Bobby Blue Bland and "Drinkin' Wine Spo-Dee-O-Dee," Stick McGhee.

"Here, check this out," Tommy said, when the last one before I left came on. It was Big Joe Turner doing "Sweet Sixteen." "There, yuh hear those drums? Check out that cool snare. That's Connie Kay, man. This was when he was a session drummer in the house band at Atlantic Records. Now he's Lester Young's drummer, and he's jammin' with a new group that only has a couple records out—the Modern Jazz Quartet, M.J.Q. He's great, ese."

And that was just the start. From then on it was so cool listening to H.H. at night and then talking about the songs with Tommy the next morning at school. Most of the other kids in the class didn't know what the hell we were talking about. It was especially fun to see the Schwarz twins in a quandary and clueless. They were listening to Dick Hugg, "Huggie Boy," who played stuff like the Crew-cuts' cover of "Sh-Boom," and Georgia Gibbs's cover of "Tweedlee Dee," instead of the original and much better version by La Vern Baker.

I really had this sense that something special was happening with that music at that time. Rhythm and blues and rock 'n' roll were so completely different from anything that had gone before them in popular music. The two genres were in the vanguard of a musical revolution, and I felt like I was right

271

there with them. I was only audience, but what the
hell, the audience is a pretty big part of it. It was
about then that I began to regret not being able to
sing or play an instrument, because it really
would've been cool to be in a band like the guys I
idolized, Chuck Berry and Bo Diddley, and my all-
time favorite, Fats Domino. I had a bunch of his forty-fives. Rock 'n' roll music. My favorite kind. At
my twentieth high school reunion in 1979, after we
had watched rock 'n' roll bud in the fifties and blos-
som through the next two decades, my sophomore-
year English teacher, Brother Declan, quoted me as
saying, back then in fifty-seven, "rock 'n' roll is here
to stay."

 Earlier in the evening when we were listening to Brubeck, Tommy showed me his tattoo,
which was a cross with three "god signs" shooting
off the top, located on the outside of his right calf.

 "My carnal, Efren, did that for me right after
I got back in town, and I did one for him," he said.
"Phoned him my first day back, eh. I been hangeen
aroun' with him and Loro all summer down Lincoln
Heights Rec. Center, and Louise, a malt shop down
North Broadway in the Heights. We started a club,
Los Deuces. We get our jackets, we're go'n'a have
the four deuces fanned out with a top hat on one side
and a cane on the other. Go down with me this Sat-
urday, ese. Meet Efren and the other vatos."

 "Really?" I said.

## Down the Foggy Ruins of Time

"Simón, ese."

"How'll we get there?"

"Five car, same way I got down there all summer."

That next Saturday we took the Five car down to North Broadway. Loro got on at the corner of Cypress Avenue and Maceo. We got off at the north end of the North Broadway Bridge, and Efren was waiting for us across the street. As we walked down the hill on North Broadway, we passed a sign that said, "Lincoln Heights District." It dawned on me as soon as I saw the sign that this was the neighborhood Sister Johanna grew up in.

"The vatos that live down here call this neighborhood 'The Avenues,' ese," Tommy said to me when we got to Avenue Twenty-one. "I used to live down this street right here."

When we got to Daly Street, we went right and walked one block to the playground on Manitou. It was a smaller version of Yosemite, more like an inner-city playground. Most of the kids here were Chicanos. There were a few American-Italians hanging around, but they blended right in. Tommy and I, and maybe about two other gavachos from that neighborhood, had the lightest complexions of anybody, and he was right about Efren being light, but he had dark hair and he looked like a Mexicano. Before we got on the streetcar to go home, we went over to Louise's and got malts.

273

I went to see Tommy in the house on Campus Road right after he moved in. Again, the first thing he did was put another Brubeck record on, and again he opened the window, but this time, after he lit up his Lucky, he took a little pinner joint out of a Bayer aspirin tin (he said a tin of three cost him fifty cents) and fired it up. I didn't actively smoke the leño with him, but I definitely got my first contact high that night.

"You know, man," he said. "If I could take a couple tokes a' yesca and have Brubeck playeen over a loudspeaker when I'm runneen, nobody'd beat me in the hunnert yard dash, eh."

I knew he was fast on his feet because by then I'd seen his lightning speed at a couple of the seventh and eighth grade touch football games.

Tommy was anxious to get the year at Saint Dominic's over with so he could move on to Cathedral High School. I, too, had been anxious to get there ever since last spring when I spent so much time looking through Frank's annual, the Cathedral *Chimes*. But I wasn't nearly as enthusiastic as Tommy. All through that eighth-grade school year, he was pumped up with school spirit for Cathedral, and unlike his brother before him, he got accepted, so he did end up going there, but ironically he didn't graduate with our class. He dropped out toward the end of junior year to marry a girl he'd knocked up in early spring. He eventually did get his Cathedral diplo-

## Down the Foggy Ruins of Time

ma a few years later by persuading the school to accept the courses he'd passed in adult education at Eagle Rock High.

I think the main reason he befriended me and not some of the other guys was because I was the only other boy in our class who was going to Cathedral, and I think he thought he was acting as my guide into the Chicano life I was just then entering. The Schwarz twins and most of the other guys wound up joining Ronald and Melo and Nick and Rod at Eagle Rock High. A few guys went to Saint Francis over in Pasadena, and a couple went to Loyola down on Venice Boulevard. Tommy was also impressed with the fact that Frank was already going to Cathedral, but that attitude would change later.

Tommy's friend, Loro, was in his first year at Cathedral. He was an American-Italian kid, born Nelson Lira, and he pronounced it the way you would if you were speaking Spanish rather than Italian. The name itself could go either way. In sophomore year I knew two girls in the same class at Sacred Heart, the girls's Catholic high school and co-ed. grammar school in Lincoln Heights, and they both had the last name Lira. One of the girls was an American-Mexican and the other an American-Italian.

Nelson, like Tommy, considered himself to be a Chicano. His nickname, Loro, was Spanish for parrot, but also a variation on the pronunciation of his last name. By sophomore year he would drop the nickname, preferring to be called Nelson while at the same time trying to maintain his own chicanismo. He was a chubby guy with dark hair and blue eyes against an olive complexion. He had a classic Roman nose, which was where he got his nickname. He was a hell of a good tenor saxophone player, and I envied him his skill with his instrument.

The Saturday after we went to Lincoln Heights, Tommy and I took the Five car down to Loro's house in Cypress Park. He lived with his mother in a small bungalow on Thorpe Avenue one block off Cypress. They called each other by their first names, and they laughed and cussed together and carried on like they were brother and sister rather than mother and son. His mom was cool and his neighborhood was really cool. There were a lot of Chicanos all over the place, like Lincoln Heights. It was neat! Compared to Cypress Park and Lincoln Heights, Eagle Rock was uptight and bland.

It didn't take long after I met Tommy to start dressing like him and his buddies. I started to wear khakis instead of peggers when I got out of my uniform after school and on weekends. I wore them exclusively when I went to Cathedral. Uniforms were not required there, but they did have a dress code. You could pretty much wear anything except blue denim, T-shirts and black peggers.

## Down the Foggy Ruins of Time

One Friday night in mid-October, Tommy brought Loro, and a couple of other guys from Cathedral to the Eagle Theater when East of Eden was playing. I was in the theater that night, but I got there by myself, not with Tommy and his boys. That movie was James Dean's screen debut and it had made him into the brightest new star in the Hollywood galaxy. He'd only been in the one picture, but his performance was so strong that the writers and critics were calling him the icon of his generation. His persona was just beginning to be infused into teenagers' collective consciousness. He was a cult figure on the verge of super stardom. His presence on the screen towered above me as I sat in an aisle seat a good ten rows behind Tommy and his pals. Paulino Luca, an Eagle Rock High badass who knew me and knew I knew Tommy, came up to my seat and told me to go with him out to the lobby.

"I been hearin' a lot about your buddy, Tommy Riley," Lino said. He didn't look like he was pissed off, but with Lino, you never knew. "I wan'a meet him, so go back in the movie, bring him out, introduce me."

"Okay," I said, as my heart started beating faster.

I walked back down the aisle to where Tommy was sitting and passed Lino's message on to him.

"Oh, shit," he said, getting out of his seat and walking with me back out to the lobby. I introduced the two guys and went back to my seat. Not five minutes went by before Tommy re-entered and took his seat. When the movie was over, I joined him and his friends.

"So, what'd Lino want, man?" I was curious to know.

"Not much," he replied. "Just wanted to meet me, eh, and then he wanted to know if I brought these vatos up here to start trouble, and I tol' 'im no, so that was it. I went back in and watched the rest of the show."

We went up to Bob's where there was a whole crowd of people who'd been at the movie and at the Eagle Rock High football game. Lino was there so Tommy went up to him, and they hung out together, observing the action and, without gesture or nuance, quietly commenting on it.

"It's cool," Tommy said when he came back to where we were standing. "I tol' Lino my mom was Italian and that makes us paisanos, so now he thinks we should be blood brothers, man."

During this whole time when Tommy and I were getting to be friends, I was still running with Rod and Nick. The next Friday night after the movie, I got together with them for an Eagle Rock High/Canoga Park High football game at Oxy. After the game a couple guys got into a fight. One of the

## Down the Foggy Ruins of Time

guys was in the Knights and a bunch of them, including Ronald and Melo, were rooting for their guy. Rod then, of course, became the rooting section for the other guy, and by the time that fight ended, he and Ronald were duking it out.

Rod, Nick and I headed back over the hill and split up at the entrance to Yosemite playground. When I got to my front door, I stood in the shadows of the overhang and watched Melo and Ronald, with about five other Knights, round the corner and head up the hill on Argus in the direction of Bob's. Just as they started up the hill, one of the group, a kid named Roger, who lived down the street from Ronald at the corner of Mount Royal and Tenshaw, shouted out to me,

"Hey, Little Farot, Melo wants to kick your ass."

"Really?" I replied. "Well, just send him right on over, and we'll see who'll kick whose ass."

Like I said before, I never was a fighter, but I knew damn well I could kick Melo's ass, no sweat.

"Knock it off, Roger," I heard Melo hiss in a loud whisper that drifted over the still night air. As I stood there, I listened to their voices withdraw as they made their way up and over the hill.

# Twenty-eight

One Thursday afternoon in late October as Tommy, Jack and I were hanging around the schoolyard by the front gate getting ready to walk over to Jack's place, Karen Snyder came up to us and asked if we wanted to come by her house for Cokes and to listen to some of her records. It was on our way, so we walked along with her and hung around at her place for a while. She was probably the most sophisticated and one of the prettiest girls in the class. She was most definitely the best developed physically at the beginning of the school year, and for as young as she was, she really knew how to carry her hourglass figure with poise and composure.

I snuck sidelong glances at her the whole fifteen minutes it took us to walk to her house. She took four Cokes from a six-pack in the refrigerator, and we all sat in the living room and talked. Her parents were at work, so it was just us four kids in the house alone. We started out with small talk, and then she got to the point, saying how she was a good wrestler and she wanted to wrestle with Tommy. He

## Down the Foggy Ruins of Time

took up the gauntlet, and they both stood up, clinched like a couple of wrestlers, and, very gently, he took her down and rolled around on the floor with her. He played it straight, just wrestling, not grabbing. At one point, when both of them were on their knees and he had her in a headlock, I couldn't resist the fun of just once reaching down and tweaking her boob, which Jack thought was pretty brash, and I guess it was. Tommy didn't see me do it, so he didn't think anything of it. Karen didn't see me do it either, but she sure as hell felt it, and liked it, I think, because she came out of the headlock leering at me with lust in her dark-blue eyes, and then she acted disappointed that Tommy hadn't tried to do something similar when she was in his clutches. That soft touch took me back two summers to memories of Carol.

When they quit wrestling, Tommy showed her what he called a "Mexican inhale." It was pretty ridiculous, but she went along with him, and she seemed to be enjoying the experience. He took a big drag from his Lucky, grabbed Karen, pulled her to him, and gave her a long kiss during which he blew the smoke into her mouth. It had to be one of the most ludicrous things I ever saw. After that we went to her room and hung around for another twenty minutes killing off our Cokes and listening to some of her records. She had a collection of forty-fives by pop singers like Teresa Brewer, Kay Starr and Georgia Gibbs.

At about ten after four, we three guys walked the three blocks over to Jack's house. The underground fort he'd had when Ronald and I were there at the end of second grade had been filled in. From Jack's backyard you could see Glendale High's G limed on the side of the hill overlooking their football field. As we looked at it, Tommy said,

"Hey, let's take some shovels up there tomorrow night and change that G to a C, for Cathedral."

Shades of Melo all over again. I could see us going up there and I'd be the one who'd get caught. There was no way they'd catch Tommy because, like Melo, he knew how to get away. He'd already shown how adept he was at getting over an eight-foot high chain link fence using only two moves. And he was fast, too. I was worried that he might be too much like Melo and only into saving his own skin, but I liked the idea of taking the chance, so I went ahead and met them on Friday night at Jack's house. His dad had a couple shovels, a rake and a hoe in a shed in the backyard. Jack and Tommy took the shovels and I took the hoe.

We set out right after dinner. Since we were back to standard time, the night sky was already full dark at that early hour. We crossed Colorado and

## Down the Foggy Ruins of Time

climbed the hill up Lincoln Avenue and got on the street directly above the G.

As we moved down the hill toward the letter, about ten guys came in from another direction with shovels and hoes, and two of them were carrying a fifty-pound sack of lime. We all converged on the G together. Besides outnumbering us, these guys were also older than we were. They went to work on the letter right away, leaving us three standing on the sidelines. The lights were on down on the football field, and some players were doing pre-game warmups. A few people were taking their seats in the bleachers. The letter and the surrounding area were lighted by two big spotlights, so as soon as the people down below looked up and saw what was going on, some of them started off the field and were coming our way.

"So, what're you changeen it to?" Tommy asked the one who seemed to be in charge of the operation.

"An O, for Occidental. We're fraternity brothers in the Teke house at Oxy. What were you guys go'n'a change it to?"

"Ah, we were just go'n'a mess it up," Tommy replied with a shrug.

About then we could see that some of the people from the bleachers were crossing Colorado, so we decided to split before they got there. They were heading toward Langley, the street on the opposite side of the hill from Lincoln, so, moving away from the crowd, we went back down the same way we came up.

"Let's get these shovels back to your chante," Tommy said to Jack, "before somebody catches us with 'em. See how I threw 'em off when I tol' 'em we's just go'n'a mess it up? If I tol' 'em what we was really planneen on doeen, they probably would've jumped us, ese."

We made it back across Colorado to the safety of Jack's backyard without mishap. We put the tools in the shed, went to the middle of the yard and looked up at the crowd gathered around the lighted letter O on the side of the hill. The Oxy guys got the job done, and I was feeling pretty good. Only a month and a half into the new school year, and there I was taking a little risk and going along with someone I barely knew and not getting caught. What a change that was for me! Completely different than if I'd been with Melo.

The following Monday morning, one of the girls in the class, Louise Zentner, told me she wanted to be my steady girl. The only problem with her suggestion was that she was already someone else's steady girl. He was a kid from Eagle Rock Junior High named Russell Knopik. My reticence to take her up on her proposal only made her pump me up the more with encouragement.

## Down the Foggy Ruins of Time

"Sure, I'm going steady, but I'm breaking up with him tonight. We're in this ballroom dance class together up at the Women's Club, and I'm go'n'a break the news to 'im before the class starts. Come by at nine o'clock and meet me when the class gets out. Let's go steady."

It was such a flaky proposition that I still hesitated, but she was so pretty, and she kept coming after me, and I didn't want to blow it again like I did that night a couple years ago at the ice rink, so I went for it and met her that night, and after that she was my steady girl. It only lasted a month, though, and ended one night at a party at Karen Snyder's house when Tommy brought a couple more of his buddies up from Lincoln Heights, Alfredo Rheinhardt and Carlos Contreras. They weren't Cathedral guys; they were Lincoln High freshmen. Alfredo made a run on Louise as soon as he laid eyes on her, and she fell for his jive. That whole scene was only so much bullshit.

Not only was my girl making out with the pendejo right in front of me, which I guess I should have expected after the way she'd done Russell, but when Nick Sunseri, who lived next door to Karen, came to the party wearing his Gauchos jacket, Alfredo told him that he'd better go back home and take it off or "we're go'n'a jump your paddy ass." That was a weird thing to say to Nick because his complexion was darker and his hair was blacker than

285

both of those two pendejos. Since Tommy didn't know Nick, he couldn't intervene and tell the two punks that Nick was a cool cat and to leave him alone. I don't think he would've intervened in any case because he was scared of his own camaradas. I still get a laugh out of how we were all so intimidated by them, and I do mean all of us, including Tommy. The simple truth was that he brought a couple of jerks to the party and he couldn't control them.

That little incident happened right after Thanksgiving. There was another one at the end of the school year at Louise's birthday party. It was a swim party at her cousin's house in Pasadena, and she invited a bunch of us from school. By that time Loro had come along with Tommy to plenty of our social functions, so it was only natural for Louise to tell Tommy to invite him to her party. Louise's mother, her aunt and another woman friend loaded their three station wagons with fourteen-year olds and ferried us all over to Pasadena. It was a great swim party, but it ended on a sour note when Loro, who got a stupid thrill out of punching hard surfaces just to show how tough he was, started punching holes in the plaster board of the pool house. Needless to say, Louise's aunt was thoroughly pissed off, and she refused to give Loro a ride back to Eagle Rock, leaving him to walk the four miles back to Tommy's house.

## Down the Foggy Ruins of Time

Tommy walked with him, but there's no way I'd join them. I had no sympathy for Loro, and by that time I was no longer on friendly terms with either one of them. I was glad that he got some punishment for the vandalism. It certainly was reassuring to know that the punk paid for his bad behavior, but the time before, those other two jerks got away with it.

By Christmas time, Tommy and I were tight partners. I was just as tight with him throughout most of the eighth-grade school year as I'd been with Melo from kindergarten to sixth grade, and with Ronald from first to seventh grades. Ronald was the only one of the three who ever really gave me my due. Sometimes Tommy would pull some of the same kind of bullshit that Melo used to pull. Where-as Melo's harassment had been physical, like when he pushed me into Bart at the movie theater, Tommy's was psychological, like when he told me I was a pendejo because I still rode a bike. Sometimes he treated me not unlike the way Frank treated me, acting like a big brother, putting me down in front of Loro and his other carnales chicanos. But I still hung around with him because he hung out with me, and he was my current connection to my adopted heritage. It took me a long time to realize that one of the reasons he befriended me was so that he could use me as a whipping boy for his mind games.

*Jerome Arthur*

By the time school got back in session after Christmas vacation, Tommy was spending a lot of time with Margot Major. He was hanging around at her house after school at least three days a week, and I'd hang with them. One spring day he invited Loro up, and the three of us went over there and hung out for the afternoon. Margot's friend Priscilla Natwick was there that day, too, and at one point she and I were sitting side by side on the stoop. Loro came up to us, and with his palms pressed together, he pointed his fingers between us as though he wanted to separate us and sit down next to her.

"Scooto, Fart-over," he said and laughed like hell. Tommy laughed along with him, but I wasn't laughing and neither were the girls. Making fun of my last name was another one of the things Melo had done when we were hanging around together, but Ronald had never done it.

# Twenty-nine

We had a good softball team that spring. I was the starter at shortstop, and at the last practice of spring training, our coach, Mister Flanagan, told the whole team that Lanny Schwarz, our catcher, and I, both had a good chance of making all-C.Y.O. if the team had a good season. That goes to show how good a ball player Lanny was. He was a southpaw and both years on that team, he started at the two most important right-handed positions on any baseball team. They don't even make a left-handed catcher's mitt, so Lanny had to use a first baseman's trapper when he was behind the plate.

I don't know why Mister Flanagan didn't mention Tommy's name, too, because he was our best player, the star of the team at first base. He was perfect for that position—a southpaw, now over six feet tall, and he could jump. He was fast on the base paths, too; he ran a ten-five hundred yard dash. With his strong throwing-arm at third base, Robert Nez more than once threw the ball high over Tommy's head, but Tommy was such a good jumper that none of those throws ever got past him. If there was a runner on second who thought it was going to be a passed ball, nine times out of ten, Tommy'd throw him out trying to take third base. He made those amazing catches all through the season, but the team didn't go anywhere that year, and none of us made all-C.Y.O.

Our last game of the season was against Saint Bernard's at Glassell Rec. Center, the only one we didn't play on blacktop. I think I got more intense in a game when I played it on dirt and grass versus asphalt. I was a chatterbox on the field and in the dugout. For me, talking it up was part of the strategy of the game, and I just seemed to do more of it on a dirt infield. I thought it made the opposing batters and pitchers nervous, forcing them to make mistakes.

There was only one problem on that day— my chattering got on some people's nerves. There were these three Chicanos from Irving Junior High, two my size and a big, skinny one about as tall as Tommy, hanging around in the bleachers. Dan Bariteau, a buddy of mine from sandlot ball at Yosemite, was sitting near them. Around the fifth inning, Dan came over to our bench and told me he overheard one of the little punks telling the other two that he was going to kick my ass because I talked too much. We won that day, and as I walked with Lanny and

## Down the Foggy Ruins of Time

Tommy across left field in the direction of the cars we'd come to the game in, the punk came up to me.

"Hey, pendejo," he said, as he approached. "You got a big mouth, ese."

His two buddies hung right behind him. He was one of the little ones, my height but heavier. The other little one was giving Lanny some dirty looks, and the tall, skinny guy was looking pretty hard at Tommy. As we faced each other, and before anybody could say anything more or throw any punches, Coach Flanagan and the coach from Saint Bernard's came over and sent the three punks on their way.

As I got ready to sit down to dinner that night, Tommy called on the phone.

"Hey, Jerôme, I just got revenge for us, eh!" He sounded all pumped and excited.

"What's happenin', man?" I asked.

"When I got back to my chante after the game, Robert was here with his carnal Sidney Owens. I tol' 'em what happened, and both those vatos tol' me let's go down and kick some ass. So, we went down, eh, and Walter, the big skinny vato, was still hangeen aroun' in the park by himself. His two camaradas'd just split. They were walkeen down Verdugo when we pulled up. They saw us three guys get out of the car and they took off runneen. I tol' Walter to step outa' the park. He really didn't wan'a fight, eh, but he came out when I tol' 'im. I punched his ass out, ese. He's such a punk. I only hit 'im

291

three times before he had enough. Didn't even touch me. He looked pathetic walkeen home all by himself, bloody around his nose and mouth. I felt sorry for 'im, man. So right there's our revenge, eh."

"Cool," I said, glad that he hadn't come to pick me up on his way over there, because then I might've had to fight the punk who chose me off.

Saturday, a week later, was the day of the entrance exam for the fall semester at Cathedral. I went over to Tommy's on the Thursday night before to talk to him about going together on the streetcar down to the school. After he shut us in his room, he put on a Shorty Rogers record and lit a Lucky.

"I ain't goeen down with you, eh," he said, to my astonishment. "I got a problem with your brother, man. Frank don't got such a good reputation at that school. I figure if I show up with you, it's go'n'a rub off, ese."

That was one of those times when I was absolutely speechless; I had no idea how I was supposed to respond to what he'd said. Such a different attitude since just a week ago when he duked it out with Walter and got "our revenge, eh." But that was cool, because in the end, my scholastic aptitude did the talking for me. I got a higher test score than Tommy, and I ended up in one of the three college prep. homerooms. There were five homerooms altogether, three for college prep. and two for vocational ed. In the top college prep. class, they had Latin and

## Down the Foggy Ruins of Time

algebra, and most of those students did indeed go on to college. In the other two prep. homerooms, they took Spanish and algebra, and I ended up in one of those classes. Tommy was in one of the vocational ed. homerooms, and that actually turned out to be a good deal for him, because he eventually went to Frank Wiggins and learned the printing business.

But Cathedral was a college prep. high school, and its primary goal was to send as many as possible of its graduates off to college, so I guess you could say I was a better prospect than Tommy because of the higher test score. So much for anything rubbing off. That little episode marked the beginning of the end of our friendship. We only stayed on cordial terms after that. We didn't socialize much out of school for the rest of that term, and I never even saw him throughout the summer vacation. When school started in the fall, he became a star on the J.V. football team, and then he really didn't want to have anything to do with me.

On the day of the test, I got on the Five car and when it got to Avenue Forty-five, Tommy didn't get on, but two gavachos got on at Avenue Thirty-three in Glassell Park, and four Chicanos came aboard at Maceo in Cypress Park. It looked like they were going where I was going, and sure enough, when the streetcar pulled up at the corner of Broadway and Bishops Road, we all got off together. When we were crossing the North Broadway bridge,

I saw some guys fooling around down in the riverbed and wondered if it was Bullet and his buddies. Tommy's friend, Efren Pacheco, was walking on the sidewalk in front of the car dealer's showroom as the streetcar was pulling up to the safety zone.

Dominic Bosso Chrysler/Plymouth occupied the two corners of the T-intersection at North Broadway and Bishops Road. A train yard was located on the river bench lands at the bottom of a bluff on the east side of the street. Bosso's new car showroom and service department were on the northwest corner. The used car lot was on the southwest corner. The Annex, the brick building that housed Cathedral's shop classes, backed up to Broadway next door to the used cars. The rest of the campus sprawled to the west up a gentle slope above the used car lot and Annex to the frontage road next to the Arroyo Seco Parkway, and south to a row of bungalows on Cottage Home Street. The closest neighborhoods to the school were Chinatown and Bunker Hill to the south. Dogtown and Lincoln Heights were to the east across the railroad tracks and river, Elysian Park and Toonerville to the north, and Chávez Ravine and Echo Park over the hill to the west.

When all of us guys got off the streetcar, we stuck together as we walked up the hill to the school. Efren joined our group. He asked me how come Tommy wasn't on the streetcar, and I told him I

## Down the Foggy Ruins of Time

didn't know. The two gavachos from Glassell Park were brothers, and the four Chicanos were friends from Divine Saviour Elementary School in Cypress Park. We got there ten minutes before test time, so we joined the growing crowd of guys already gathered on the schoolyard. Tommy was still nowhere in sight when three Christian Brothers came out and put five large cards up on the side of the building. Each card had a range of letters from the alphabet: A to C, D to G, H to M, N to S, and T to Z. Using a megaphone, one of the brothers told us to line up alphabetically by last name. Once we were all lined up, there were five groups of fifty or so. We marched into the classrooms on the ground floor of the main building.

I was already well into the test when I saw Tommy passing in the hall accompanied by a brother who was showing him to the room where all the guys whose names began with R were. That was the last time I saw him outside of school until we graduated from Saint Dominic's, except the couple of times when I ran into him at Margot's house and at Louise's birthday party.

When I finished the test, I went back down to North Broadway to wait for my streetcar. Juan Parra, one of the four guys from Cypress who'd been on the streetcar earlier coming in, had finished the test just ahead of me and was already there waiting. We compared notes and both of us were feeling pretty good about how we'd done. It took a couple of weeks for the results to come in. About ten days before graduation, I got my passing grade and my acceptance to the school.

My time in grammar school was rapidly coming to an end. A week after I got accepted to Cathedral, we started rehearsing for graduation. We lined up at the side doors of the church, girls on one side, boys on the other, and we practiced marching in and taking seats in the first two rows of pews. Then we practiced walking up to the altar to get our diplomas and back to our seats. On the day of the last rehearsal, as we lined up at the side door, Tommy pulled a small jar of India ink and an Exacto knife-blade from his pocket.

"You wan'a tattoo, ese?" he asked.

I'd wanted a tattoo ever since I'd seen the cross on his calf. Antoine had a crude homemade heart with an arrow through it and his initials and a girl's, not Francesca's, tattooed on his left forearm. He also had a little dot just above his left index finger on the back of his hand. That's what I wanted Tommy to give me, a dot just like my dad's. He got some India ink on the tip of the Exacto blade and jabbed it a few times into the back of my hand about three quarters of an inch above the top knuckle of my left index finger. The next day I graduated from elementary school.

# Thirty

On his birthday in May, Antoine bought another new car, a '55 Buick Special, three-holer. In the fifties, Buicks came equipped with little chrome ports in the sides of the front fenders. They were strictly decorative, having no mechanical function whatsoever, and they remained a trademark characteristic of the Buick design until the early nineteen-seventies. They were separate holes, round in '55, teardrop-shaped in '56 and '57, trimmed in chrome, three or four in number depending on the model. The top and middle of the line—Roadmasters, Supers, and Centuries—were four-holers. Our Special was the bottom of the line, and only had three ports, but in those days even the cheapest Buicks had luxuries that the best Chevies and Pontiacs didn't have. It was the first car we owned that had an automatic transmission, power steering and power brakes. It was a big, heavy four-door sedan with a 322 cubic inch V-eight under the hood. A real Detroit iron.

"It don't take your breath away when you floor it like Gilbert's Century, but it's got plenty a' poop to suit me," Antoine said.

Gilbert, Dad's Canadian buddy, had bought a Century two-door hardtop in April, and it had the same engine as our Special, but it was a lot lighter and faster than ours.

"Hell, any Buick you get's a poor man's Caddy, and someday I'm go'n'a own a Caddy, too."

And one day he would.

The car was just a month old when we took another trip to Minneapolis, the last trip we'd all four take together as a family. Frank wouldn't be going on the next one. My graduation from Saint Dominic's was on a Thursday, and we took off on Friday afternoon around five o'clock. Edith stayed at our house for the two weeks we were gone, taking care of Penny, who was pretty much blind and deaf by then. She stood on the front porch holding Penny in her left arm and waving goodbye with her right. As we drove up the hill on Argus, we watched them disappear from view at the first bend in the road.

We passed Victorville at twilight, and we crossed the desert under a diamond sky with a moon that looked like a scoop of vanilla ice cream dipped in marshmallow sauce. We didn't take our usual route this trip: Las Vegas, Salt Lake, Wyoming and the Black Hills of South Dakota. Instead we took a more southerly route so that we could visit Uncle

## Down the Foggy Ruins of Time

Danny at his new parish in Monticello in southern Utah.

We spent our first night in Searchlight, Nevada. Antoine had planned this stop for the express purpose of playing the tables. From several miles away, the neon obelisk on the roof of the motel looked like a solitary beacon. The first thing Dad did after we checked into our rooms was spread the map out on the table, and only then did we see that it was the only building for many miles in any direction on a remote desert crossroads in the middle of nowhere. There was a casino in the building, so Antoine managed to gamble for at least a couple hours. About an hour before daybreak, the roar of an airplane taking off somewhere very close by awakened me.

We got an early start Saturday morning. Breakfast at the motel restaurant, and gas at the Ethyl pump out in front. Then we got onto U.S. Highway 95 south. Frank was behind the wheel. As we pulled away from the crossroads, we passed a landing strip. There was a shack and a pole with a windsock just inside a low chain link fence. A lone tumbleweed had blown up against the fence.

"You kids 'member hearin' a plane take off this mornin' 'fore sunrise?" Antoine said. He was riding shotgun.

"Yeah," Frank and I said in unison. My elbows rested on the back of the front seat between Dad and Frank.

"Well, it took off right here, and it takes gamblers back and forth between here and Los Angeles. They advertise it in the want ads. Got 'em goin' to Hawthorne and Tonopah too. Round-trip flight usually costs ten bucks. Searchlight one's free, I think. Sure a lota' gamblers in that damn casino last night."

We cut across the Colorado River to Kingman, Arizona where we picked up U.S. 66 going east. We got to Flagstaff at eleven o'clock and Antoine took the wheel. Frank was looking at his Cathedral High yearbook, and I fell asleep and didn't wake up until we got to the northern outskirts of Tuba City. That was where the paved highway ended, and I was jarred awake because suddenly we were jolting along on a dirt road. I got up quickly and looked out the rear window and got a receding view of the town through a sheer curtain of beige dust. It was a little town that looked a lot like Eagle Rock Springs Tourist Court because all they seemed to have there were trailers. I didn't see any houses anywhere.

Our new Buick really took a beating from that point on. According to the map, the road from Tuba City to Monticello was supposed to be graded all the way, but it was washboard where it was graded, and where it wasn't, the wheel ruts we were following simply disappeared into gullies and washes and then reappeared on the other side. The car bot-

## Down the Foggy Ruins of Time

tomed out a couple times, once over an especially deep rut, and another time there was a good-size rock in the road. Antoine stopped both times and got out to inspect for damage, and luckily the oil pan was still intact. He moved the boulder off to the side of the road.

It was a slow, tedious trek up through Kayenta and twenty miles beyond where we crossed over from Arizona into Utah. We bumped and bounced our way through Mexican Hat, Bluff and Blanding before finally arriving in Monticello, which was nothing but a dusty little adobe pueblo (probably stucco and red tile). The place looked like what Utah Phillips called the Mormon muddy mission years later in his talkin' blues, "Moose Turd Pie." There were a few Mexicanos and Navajos out strolling around on the only two blocks in town that were paved. The town's main street was in a festive mood. It was like a miniature Cypress Avenue. I liked this little pueblo; I was feeling right at home here.

As we turned onto Uncle Danny's street, I began to feel uneasy about seeing him again. This was going to be our first meeting since he'd bloodied my nose ten months ago. We arrived at his house late in the afternoon. He didn't have his own church yet. They were going to start construction on it soon. He said Mass in the Methodist church weekdays and Saturday mornings at seven-thirty, and at nine o'clock on Sundays. He preached a sermon at the Sunday Mass. He did have a rectory, and it was on one of the dusty, unpaved side streets one block off the main drag. It was a little flat roof stucco house next door to a vacant lot, the site of the future church.

The hundred and fifty miles of bad road had made it a long, hard, hot and dusty trip. Uncle Dan saw how beat and thirsty we all were, so he invited us into the rectory for iced-tea and lemonade. His little house was sparsely furnished. The living room had a couch, chair and coffee table facing a fifteen-inch television set on a wobbly metal cart with casters. A wood desk stood in one corner. A pile of manila folders was stacked next to a blotter on the desktop. There was a chair on casters pushed into the knee well. A crucifix hung on the wall above the desk, and a statue of the Virgin Mary was on a small shelf bracketed to the wall just inside the front door. A table was in the corner next to the kitchen door.

One of the bedrooms was furnished with a small foldout davenport that was already made up into a bed with the blanket turned down. An end table with a lamp on it stood next to the right arm of the couch. The other bedroom was his bedroom, and it looked like a monk's cell. He had an austere-looking twin bed that was really not much more than a cot. An easy chair, the only luxury in the room, stood next to it to the left of the door. A two-tiered

## Down the Foggy Ruins of Time

nightstand with Danny's daily prayer book and Bible stacked next to a table lamp was positioned between the two pieces of furniture. A chest of drawers stood in the corner opposite at the foot of the bed. The crucifix in that room was above it. Lined up on the dresser were three statues of the Virgin Mary—one each of Our Lady of Lourdes, Our Lady of Fatima, and Our Lady of Guadalupe. In the other corner stood a statue of Jesus Christ that was about as tall as I was.

"Take a look," Uncle Dan said, pointing at the statue.

We stepped into the room to get a better look. The easy chair was set up so that when he was sitting in it, he would be looking straight at the statue. Standing by itself in the corner, it was an almost-life-size rendering of the resurrected Jesus Christ with his nail-wounded right hand elevated to about the level of his neck, his thumb and conjoined index and middle fingers pointing heavenward. His ring finger and little finger were bent at the middle knuckle. His left hand, also with a nail wound, was open palm-out at his side in a gesture of greeting. He also had nail wounds in his feet, and there were little cuts, oozing droplets of red paint, around his forehead where the crown of thorns had been. White linen, clean and spotless, done in ceramic as part of the sculpture, was draped over his shoulders and bent-right-arm, covering his torso, loins and legs.

All that was missing was a cave with a stone rolled back from its entrance.

"I sit in the chair and read my daily prayers," Uncle Dan said, "and I have this wonderful feeling of being face to face with the image of my Lord and Savior, Jesus Christ, resurrected from the dead."

We all went back into the living room and drank our cold drinks while Dan explained to us how lucky we were to get through on the road we'd come in on.

"You wouldn't have made it if it had started to rain," he said. "You would've had to go back and circle around and come in from Moab out of the north."

"It was rougher'n a cob as it was," Antoine said. "I need a drink. You got somethin' in your cupboard I could fix me a tasty?"

"Sure," said Danny, getting out of his chair and heading toward the kitchen. He said over his shoulder, "I keep liquor on hand. My buddy, the pastor of the parish up in Price, likes to have a drink when he comes visiting."

Antoine followed him, and I could see them through the door as Danny pulled a fifth-bottle out of the cupboard and handed it to him. I was too far away to read the label. The open kitchen door framed Antoine's silhouetted back, and I heard a bottleneck touch the lip of a glass as he poured him-

## Down the Foggy Ruins of Time

self a stiff shot, neat. He knocked it back, gritted his teeth and exhaled heavily. "Whew." Next I heard the sound of ice cubes clinking as he poured himself another shot, this time on the rocks. He performed the entire ritual with the panache of Kirk Douglas as Doc Holiday in *Gunfight at the O.K. Corral*. The two men returned to the living room, and Antoine took a seat next to Mom on the couch and sipped his second drink. The rest of us were still drinking our lemonade.

Mom started putting together a dinner of chicken and mashed potatoes that Uncle Danny's part-time volunteer housekeeper had picked up before our arrival. After dinner, we lounged around the house and talked. I was relieved that he didn't lecture me or chide me on my bad behavior a year ago. The subject never came up.

At 9:30 he retired to his room to read his daily prayers. We all washed up, brushed our teeth and hit the sack. Mom and Dad slept on the davenport that was made up in the spare bedroom. Frank and I slept in the living room. He got the couch and I got the floor using the back cushions from the couch for a mattress. The temperature had been in the nineties all day long, and it probably never went below eighty through the night. Sometime during the night, I was awakened by lightning, thunder and rain. When I got out of the sack at six o'clock, the sky was clear, the ground was damp, and the fresh smell of the desert in bloom was in the air.

In the morning we went to Danny's nine o'clock Mass. Most of the people in his congregation were Mexicans. This was a cool town, and a cool parish. There was a scattering of native North Americans, Navajos, I guessed. I only saw five other gavachos besides us. The church was about three quarters full for the Mass. Of the four of us, only Antoine went to Communion, and before we got on the road, Uncle Danny lectured and scolded those of us who hadn't gone. He really laid a guilt trip on us, but I didn't care, because there was no way he was ever going to hear my confession. Danny was just too close. Besides, I was getting to a stage where I didn't even want to be going to Confession anymore. I was really losing interest in the doctrines and rituals of Roman Catholicism. It had started last year when I got confirmed, and then just two months later, Uncle Danny slugged me, and that about made my alienation complete. I continued to go to Mass on Sunday through high school only because Francesca was on my case. When I graduated and went into the Navy, I quit doing that, too.

We hung around after Mass and talked with Danny and some of his parishioners in front of the church. We finally got back on the road at around 10:30, and we drove north out of Monticello and east into Colorado. Shortly after we crossed the state

## Down the Foggy Ruins of Time

line, the highway turned into a tortuous mountain road winding its way up through Glenwood Canyon where the Colorado River flowed. What a beautiful ride! We'd come around a sheer cliff on our left, and on our right, hundreds of feet straight down, the river's white-water rapids tumbled away from us.

When we crossed the Continental Divide, we didn't see the actual spot where the river changes directions because we were going through a tunnel, but the next time we caught a view of the river after we came out, it was moving in the same direction as we were. The view going down the eastern slope was breathtaking. We spent the night in a ten-room roadside motel outside Denver.

We got an early start the next morning, and spent the next night in Ames, Iowa. I never saw so much corn in all my life as I saw on the trip from Ames to Albert Lea, Minnesota. We were going north on U.S. 69, passing Emmons and State Line Lake when Antoine sat up in the driver's seat, got a new grip on the wheel, and said:

"Well, Ma, boys, we're back home. Next stop Minneapolis."

We were on the southern outskirts of the Twin Cities by early Tuesday afternoon, and we pulled up in front of the house on Russell Avenue North at around two o'clock. Grandma and Jessie came out onto the front porch as we stepped out of the car and stretched our legs.

# Thirty-one

That first Tuesday afternoon, we hung around with Grandma and Jessie. Since Edith had moved to Los Angeles, Jessie was the only one of Francesca's siblings still living at home. Like Frank she was going to be a junior come September at Saint Anthony's, a Catholic high school for girls in northeast Minneapolis. We left our suitcases in the car for the time being and went up the steps to the front porch where Grandma greeted each of us with a hug. Once we got inside the house, I noticed the television set, new since the last time I was there.

"That's 'Edge of Night,'" Grandma said, indicating the program on the little screen. "I started watchin' it when they quit playing 'Ma Perkins' on the radio."

She turned it off and went into the kitchen to get a pitcher of lemonade from the refrigerator. Francesca got six glasses out of the cupboard and a tray of ice cubes from the freezer and brought them to the dining room table. We drank lemonade and listened as Dad told Grandma about our trip.

## Down the Foggy Ruins of Time

"Father Dan sends his blessing," he said as he looked at a picture of Uncle Danny on the shelf next to where he was sitting.

Mom said, "We would've lit some candles for you and Pa at his church, but they don't have candles in the Methodist church where he said Mass."

"What a sweet thought," Grandma said. "And I've been praying to Saint Christopher for you since last Friday when you left home."

After we finished our lemonade, Antoine and we three teenagers went over to Penn Avenue and took Grandpa's bus to the end of the line and back to Thirty-fourth Avenue. His professionalism hadn't diminished one bit with his shift from street-car conductor to bus driver. They'd already done throughout Minneapolis what they'd be doing in Los Angeles come next January. They'd paved over the tracks, taken the trolley lines down from overhead, and replaced all of the streetcars with diesel-powered buses. This run was Grandpa's last of the day. As we were disembarking, he told Antoine that he'd catch the next bus home after he was relieved and be there within the hour.

When we got back to the house, Grandma and Francesca were busy preparing a big meal. Grandpa got home at around 3:30. We ate early, and at six o'clock Maddy and Josh showed up with their three kids, Juanita, Ted, and their little toddler, Al-ice. Ten minutes behind them, Luke and Jessica arrived on the scene with their boys, Danny and Paul. The oldest one, six-year-old Danny, was a little hellion on wheels. I was surprised by how much Luke put up with from him. I kept expecting him to come down on the little shit, but he never did.

As usual, it wound up being a really fun party. Antoine, Maddy and Luke polished off a fifth of Seagram's Seven Crown. Grandpa scolded Maddy and Luke, but he didn't say a word to Dad, who got just as drunk as they did. He admired Antoine so much, and there was just no way he could find any fault with him.

On Wednesday morning we drove down to Logan Avenue South to visit Uncle Luke and Aunt Megan. Jessie went with us. Luke was a fireman at the main fire station in downtown Minneapolis, and that Wednesday was the first of five straight days off for him. He didn't have to be back on the job until Monday morning, so he got to spend a lot of time with us while we were there.

At noon we four teenagers got into Kenny's '47 Chevy and went downtown to the Pan Theater for a one o'clock showing of Mister Roberts. Kenny and Jessie sat together in the balcony, and Frank and I were downstairs in the middle of the half-empty auditorium. At one point when the theater was illuminated by a bright daylight scene on the screen, one of those scenes out on deck, I looked up at the bal-

## Down the Foggy Ruins of Time

cony and saw the lovebirds smooching. They weren't even watching the damn picture. They looked like Siamese twins joined at the mouth.

Casey had planned a backyard party at his house that afternoon. The adults gave us directions and told us to meet them there after the movie. He lived in Richfield out near the airport, south of Minneapolis. The Chevy he'd bought at Johnny Lail's was parked in front of his house. We pulled up behind it. Our Buick was parked in front of it. As we were getting out of the car, a big four engine commercial airliner took off overhead, making one hell of a racket. With Jessie leading the way, we went in the front screen door and walked through the house to the backyard. So far, the Farots and Bergmans were the only ones at the party. Casey introduced us to his wife, Josie, who was carrying their baby daughter Rosa on her hip. Shortly after our arrival, everybody who'd been at Grandma's the night before showed up at Casey's.

It was another great family gathering, but the Konig boisterousness was somewhat muted for the rest of the afternoon by the noise of the planes taking off and landing. As evening approached and the sun descended to the western horizon, the air traffic decreased, and we got some relief from the noise, but at the same time, clouds started to gather followed by rain, so the party moved from the backyard into the screened back porch and house and

311

went on until after ten o'clock. Antoine, Maddy and Luke got pretty wasted, and once again, Grandpa scolded his own two kids and fretted over their heavy drinking, but he still didn't say a word to Antoine.

Dad let Frank drive us back to Grandma's because he knew he'd had too much to drink himself. Grandma and Grandpa had arrived at the party with Luke and Jessica and their kids. They went home with us. The Bergmans went back to south Minneapolis in Kenny's Chevy.

After spending Thursday morning hanging around with Grandma and Jessie, we Farots went back over to Megan's house, and from there all seven of us went to visit old Wiktor Sadlo in Columbia Heights out northeast. Wiktor was Dad's and Megan's stepfather, and we'd never visited him before on any of our previous trips, nor had we visited Antoine's parents when we were in Minneapolis because they'd both died before I was born. This would be Frank's and my first meeting with Wiktor. I didn't really want to see the guy at all, and I was sure Antoine didn't either. He'd told me plenty of stories about how mean Wiktor was to him and his mom. We only went for Aunt Megan's sake. She'd been trying to talk Dad into going ever since we'd first seen her and Uncle Luke the morning before. She claimed that he'd always been good to her. When she was seventeen, he'd bought her the player

## Down the Foggy Ruins of Time

piano she still had in her living room. That was the same year Antoine clubbed the old bastard with a baseball bat and hopped freight trains to Los Angeles.

I felt no attachment to him; there was no genetic connection between us; and I just didn't like the nasty old coot. Whenever I thought about him, I only had visions of Antoine as a kid smothering gristly fat in maple syrup to make it just bearable enough to get down, eating it only because the old man forced him to. He was a shriveled up little old man, no older than my grandpa, but in a lot worse shape. In his old age he was paying for his bad behavior as a younger man. When we got to his place, I was polite and said hello to him, but that was all I could force myself to do. Frank and Kenny and I only stayed five minutes, and then we split to a small playground around the corner from the old man's house. I guess the adults could only take so much too, because before Kenny could finish his second Chesterfield, the Buick pulled up alongside the curb and the adults told us to get in.

We went back to the Bergmans' house where we spent the rest of the afternoon and stayed overnight. A thunderstorm had started up on the drive back to their place and continued on into the night. We kids stayed up late and watched the light show in the sky from Kenny's attic loft. We saw the dark backyard lawn below the window light up and flicker as jagged bolts of lightning split the black, starless night.

We got up early Friday morning, left Megan at home, and the rest of us headed back to Russell Avenue North. Luke put his Evanrude outboard in the trunk of the Buick. At Grandma's house we got some fishing gear and a couple changes of clothes together, left the women there—Mom, Grandma and Jessie—and headed up to Lake Osakis. Luke Konig took a vacation day and went with us. Casey couldn't do that because he didn't have any vacation days coming from his job, and he'd already taken off early on Wednesday afternoon for his own party, but he did drive up by himself early Saturday morning. We got everybody else in the Buick for the trip to Osakis. I rode in the front seat between Antoine and Luke Konig. Luke Bergman, Kenny and Frank were in the back seat.

When we got there, Paul Konig was already there again in one of the two lake-front cabins they'd all gone in on together, and his Mercury was mounted on the stern of one of the boats down by the shore. Luke started to hook his Evanrude up to the other boat as soon as he got out of the car, and by noon we all had our lazy ikes in the water and were trolling the lake. We fished all the rest of the afternoon, and everybody caught at least a few good-size northern pike, but a lot of the northerns we caught

## Down the Foggy Ruins of Time

were too small and we threw them back. Antoine, Paul and Luke Bergman each caught a walleye.

The next morning I got up early and went down to the lakeshore to watch the sun come up. I was surprised at how different the sunrise was on the lake from what it had been that morning at the beach in Newport. At the beach it had been a long, shimmering candle with a bright platinum flame. At Osakis, after it got above the surrounding hills, it appeared as a smooth gold disk on the lake's flat surface.

That day I went out in Paul's boat with him, Antoine and Luke Konig. We left Luke Bergman and the other two boys behind to wait for Casey to show up. At about 9:30, they came cruising up to us, and the two boats stuck close together for the rest of the day. Our luck wasn't as good that day as it had been the day before, but it was cool because Casey caught himself a nice ten-pound walleye. The rest of us caught our limit of northern pike, so we had a lot of fun reeling in several more under-size ones and throwing them back. Antoine, Paul and Luke Konig did some pretty heavy drinking both nights, but they stayed cool and didn't, as Paul kept suggesting, go down to the tavern in Osakis and get into a brawl. Sunday morning we headed back to the Twin Cities (I rode shotgun in Casey's Chevy; Frank and Kenny were in the back seat) early enough to be able to go to eleven o'clock Mass at Saint Anne's.

*Jerome Arthur*

When we got back to the house on Russell Avenue North, Mom, getting ready for our return trip to Los Angeles, was in the basement doing a load of laundry in Grandma's wringer washer. All the guys who'd gone fishing left their catch and went home. Casey dropped Luke and Kenny off at Logan Avenue South on his way. Grandma started putting together another fish fry, and later on in the afternoon, all of the siblings, Mom's and Dad's alike, came back with their families for one last farewell party before our departure the next morning.

It had been a fun five and a half days, and as the time approached to say goodbye, I started to get that old melancholy feeling. I'd had such a good time, and I just wanted to keep it going for a while longer. The feeling continued through the night and on into the morning when we were pulling away from Minneapolis going west toward Lake Benton. I looked longingly out the rear window of the car at the Foshay Tower as it faded from the landscape. To take my mind off my melancholy, I looked at my baseball cards.

We made Rapid City the first day on the road. The next day was a grueling, grinding trip through the Black Hills, without stops for sightseeing, across the Great Divide Basin and into Evanston, Wyoming on the Utah border. We were back on the road fairly early Wednesday morning, and we

## Down the Foggy Ruins of Time

sped through Salt Lake City without a sidelong glance.

It was just getting dark, as we were coming down out of the Muddy Mountains northeast of Las Vegas. The town looked like a sparkling piece of costume jewelry, the lights all a-glitter on Fremont Street in downtown and along Las Vegas Boulevard almost reaching the edge of town. What used to be a desert highway that brought gamblers in from Southern California was now a busy casino midway called the Strip. All of the biggest, fanciest hotel/casinos were out on the Strip, and new ones were cropping up all the time. We went out there and checked into the Sahara, close to the outskirts of town.

We were now only a half-day's drive from home, and my longing, melancholy feelings for Minneapolis were long gone. Now I was looking forward, with anticipation and expectation, to the new life I was about to enter when I got back to Los Angeles. I was going to go to Cathedral High School, and when I got there, eighty percent of my classmates would be Chicanos. I just knew I would fit right in with them because I'd always fit into those kinds of situations in the past. All my best friends right on down the line—George Nieto, Ramón Sandoval, Ronald Day, Sister Johanna and Tommy Riley—were either American-Mexicans or Chicanos. Up to that point in my life, I'd always

317

thought of myself as a misplaced Mexicano, and now I truly thought of myself as a Chicano. I was confident I would do just fine when I got to Cathedral.

We pulled into our driveway at one o'clock Thursday afternoon, twenty-eight hours shy of two weeks since we'd left. It was early enough in the day for Edith to still be at work, but Penny came up to us and sniffed us out, her little butt swaying back and forth as she struggled to wag her tail.

# Thirty-two

The day after we got home from Minneapolis, I rode the Colt over to Margot's house. The news in her life was that she hadn't seen or talked to Tommy since school got out. She told me she didn't think she'd ever see him again. He hadn't gone to her and made the break official, but somehow she just knew she'd seen the last of him. I told her what he'd said to me when we took the entrance exam at Cathedral. We both agreed that he was a jerk, and we were better off without his friendship.

"'Sides," Margot said. "Priscilla and I are going to Saint Andrew's, so I probably won't ever see him again after September, anyway, or you either for that matter. Pasadena's a long way away from downtown."

"Yeah, I know, but it don't have to be that way. Who knows? Maybe I'll go to one a' your dances, or you might come down to one of ours."

And even as I was saying it, I knew it would never happen, because in my mind, I was already on my way out of Eagle Rock.

*Jerome Arthur*

We hung out together for a while longer, and then I got on my scooter and headed home. The damn thing stalled before I even got to the top of the hill on Argus, but I was close enough that it wasn't hard pushing it the rest of the way up. I coasted down the other side straight into our driveway. And that was the last straw. I'd pretty much had it with the Mustang Colt. It was too much hassle. I made up my mind to get rid of it. When Antoine came home from Topper's, I told him of my decision. He knew a guy at work who wanted to buy it, and the following Wednesday the guy came to the house, gave Dad fifty bucks, loaded it onto his pickup truck and took it away. Thus ended the first phase of my motor-cycle-riding period. Three summers hence, I'd get a regular-size Mustang and begin the second and last phase.

I was seriously anticipating my upcoming exit from Eagle Rock for more favorable digs downtown. I'd been living there for ten years and I was ready for a change. When Frank brought home his freshman yearbook and I saw all those pictures of Mexicanos in it, I wanted to get to that school as quickly as possible. Then Tommy came along and introduced me to some Chicanos from Cypress Park and Lincoln Heights, and in my own mind, I became a Chicano. I'd had enough of bland white bread; I was now looking for something with a little more color and texture. To that end, I spent the whole rest

## Down the Foggy Ruins of Time

of the summer hiding out in our living room watching daytime television. I didn't want to go over to Yosemite playground and hang out with any of the guys I'd played sandlot ball with or gone to school with. I'd made up my mind. The next new person I was going to meet would be from Boyle Heights or Echo Park or Watts, anywhere in the city except Eagle Rock.

Frank and I took the streetcar to Cathedral on the first day of school. As we walked down Yosemite Drive to Eagle Rock Boulevard, we passed the Schwarz twins at the corner of Yosemite and Norwalk. They were on their way to their first day at Eagle Rock High. We were on opposite sides of the street so we didn't stop and talk; we just waved to each other in passing. I didn't want to miss my streetcar, and none of us really would've had much to say to each other, anyway. When Tommy got on at Avenue Forty-five, Frank moved away from me and went and sat with him. I hadn't told Frank what Tommy had said about him back in May. Ignorance is bliss. When we got to Cypress Park, Loro and a whole bunch of other Cathedral guys and Sacred Heart girls got on. At that point Tommy moved off with Loro, and one of Frank's classmates took Tommy's place next to him. Some Nightingale Junior High kids also got on for the short ride down to their school on Figueroa. Juan Parra, the guy I'd met on the day of the test, saw me and sat in the seat next to me.

"So, what homeroom you in?" I asked him.

"105. How 'bout you?"

"107. I got Spanish."

"Me too."

"Cool."

The Sacred Heart girls got off where Broadway forks at the north end of the bridge. Their school was on Mozart Street, down Daly Street not far from the playground I'd gone to last year with Tommy. When our streetcar pulled up to the safety zone at Bishops Road, about fifteen guys got off. A few, including Tommy and Loro, stuck around on the corner in front of Bosso's showroom, smoking cigarettes.

When I saw those guys puffing their frajos, I thought they looked pretty ridiculous, and it really made me glad I wasn't doing it myself. They were probably the main reason I never started smoking in the first place. It was my contrary nature to be a non-conformist, so if my peers were doing it, I wanted no part of it. Besides, the one and only time I tried smoking, that night out in Melo's backyard, I got so sick I could barely walk home.

My parents both had smoking habits for as long as I could remember, and I always knew it wasn't something I wanted to pick up from them. Antoine started smoking at age fifteen when he was

## Down the Foggy Ruins of Time

hopping freight trains during the Depression. He was now up to three packs of Camels a day. Francesca had been doing about half that since she'd met Dad when she was nineteen. All the houses and trailers that we'd lived in over the years were stinky and stale from burned tobacco. God only knows how black my lungs were at age fourteen, or to what degree I was addicted to nicotine. Frank and I both got our share of second-hand smoke growing up in the same house with them. I didn't see any need to pick up the habit when I got older.

Juan and I and the other guys who got off the streetcar, and some other guys from northbound streetcars, walked up to the school and went into the schoolyard through an opening between the two main buildings. There were at least six hundred other guys hanging around out there. Over next to the gym, there was a three-wall handball court, and two guys were playing while a dozen or so others watched the game and waited their turn. There were two basketball courts down on the lower part of the campus between Bosso's used car lot and the school cafeteria. Eight three-man teams were playing half-court. All the other guys were milling around the yard in groups. A group of seniors was hanging around on the Senior Bench next to the Senior Arcade.

Ten minutes after we entered the yard, the bell rang and I went off to room 107. Cathedral High

School consisted of two two-story red brick buildings side by side facing Bishops Road. The brothers' residence, also a two-story red brick building but smaller than the other two, was on the northwestern corner of the property where Bishops Road met the frontage road alongside the Arroyo Seco Parkway. The gym, which looked like a big green stucco barn with a Quonset-hut roof design, was situated so that the main entrance let out onto the frontage road on the backside of the schoolyard. The football field and track were behind the gym. We were called the Phantoms because the field used to be a graveyard. The Annex, where the shop classes were held, was down on North Broadway between Saint Peter's Catholic church and Bosso's used car lot.

The freshman classrooms were on the ground floor of the bigger of the two buildings, the one closest to the brothers' house. 107 was one of the two rooms just across the driveway from the residence. It was actually the same room I took the entrance test in. The office, library and bookstore were also located on that floor. The second floor was all sophomore and junior classrooms on two sides of a locker-lined central hallway. The campus was on a sloping parcel. The Senior Arcade was a covered footbridge with arching Roman viaduct architecture that connected the two buildings at the ground floor of the bigger building and the top floor of the smaller structure. The classrooms that housed the senior

## Down the Foggy Ruins of Time

homerooms were on the upper floor of that smaller building. The cafeteria was on the lower level.

In religion class during first period homeroom, we studied guys like Saint Augustine and Thomas Aquinas, and of course, the patron saint of the school and founder of the Christian Brothers Order, Saint Jean Baptiste De La Salle. We even read some Ignatius Loyola, the guy who founded the Jesuits. I say "we even read," because Loyola High School out on Venice Boulevard was our arch rival, and the Jesuits who taught there were friendly rivals with our Christian Brothers. The rivalry was over who were the Church's best classroom teachers. I always thought the Christian Brothers were the only ones who could truly lay claim to that title, because the Jesuits were really more the intellectuals, philosophers and thinkers in the Church. I think the rivalry has endured and still continues today. The sports rivalry between the two schools was one of the oldest in the city, and I bet those guys read as much De La Salle as we read Loyola.

Brother Clyde, our homeroom teacher, started the class promptly at nine o'clock. The desks were the old-fashioned wooden kind like the ones we had at Saint Dominic's for the first six years, only these were adult-size. Six three-foot-wide aisles across and one along the back of the room separated five rows of desks from each other and the back and side walls. There were forty-seven guys in the room.

Brother Clyde's seating chart was arranged in alphabetical order starting with the row closest to the wall that had the two doors and the two cork bulletin boards. I sat toward the back of that row. Jules Dufresne sat in front of me, and Joaquín Folquenón was in the desk behind me. When Brother Clyde assigned us lockers, Joaquín wound up being my locker partner. He lived on Gillette Street off Brooklyn Avenue and had gone to grammar school at San Antonio de Padua in Boyle Heights. He got the nickname "Bubblegum" after Brother Clyde mispronounced his last name during roll call (Fáll-kwanon). Joaquín corrected Brother's pronunciation up front (each vowel has only one sound in Spanish; the O is always a long O, and Q-U-E is always pronounced keh). He and I were pretty good buddies through freshman year and the remaining three after that, but he never became one of my best friends. That lot fell to two other guys, Carlos Williams and François Rojas who were assigned desks in the two rows by the windows on the other side of the room.

I met them at the lunch hour when Joaquín and I sat at the same table with them in the cafeteria. They were sitting with two Filipino dudes from the class, Craig Cubangbang and Marc Pérez. Craig and François had been friends since first grade. They had graduated together from Saint Vibiana's, the grammar school at the cathedral downtown. They had just met Marc and Carlos that day. Marc sat in the desk

## Down the Foggy Ruins of Time

directly in front of François in the fourth row, and Carlos' desk was across the aisle next to the windows. Marc had graduated from Our Lady of Loretto in the Rampart neighborhood. Carlos had gone to Saint Joe's in Clanton just south of downtown, but he'd grown up in Aliso Village in East Los Angeles and had recently moved to Opal Street in "Varrio Nuevo," one block from Eighth and Lorena. François lived right downtown on Stanford Avenue just off Seventh Street ten short blocks east of Broadway.

The rest of the day after lunch was uneventful, actually not unlike Chuck Berry's "School Day," except we didn't go to the juke joint when school got out. We'd had plenty of that in the cafeteria where a Wurlitzer jukebox blasted out "Eddie My Love," "Don't be Angry," "Ain't It a Shame," and a lot of other cool rock 'n' roll and rhythm and blues tunes.

Last period was physical education, and all Mister Dalrymple did for that class was take roll and march us over to the bookstore so we could buy our purple trunks and gray T-shirt jerseys, the uniform of the day in P.E. class (the school's colors were purple and white). We were in the bookstore a good forty-five minutes, almost the whole period, so there wasn't enough time left to suit up for the class, and Coach dismissed us after we got back to the locker room.

*Jerome Arthur*

I left with the five guys I'd spent the lunch hour with, and we took a walk down to Queens (Our Lady Queen of the Angels, the Catholic girl's school in Chinatown), arriving there just as the girls were getting out at three o'clock. We hung around and talked to some chavalas François and Craig had known from their days at Saint Vibiana's. This was great! I was finally where I thought I truly belonged, living the lifestyle I'd been longing to live for ten years, ever since George Nieto and the west side of Long Beach. Among the six of us guys, Carlos and I were the only gavachos, and both of us thought we were Chicanos. He was actually closer to it than I was. His step-dad's name was Nazareno Gutiérrez, but everybody called him Nash.

We only hung out for a few minutes, and then we walked the girls down to their streetcar on Broadway. Carlos, François, Marc and Joaquín took the same streetcar as the girls and went on home. Craig and I crossed the street and got on the Twenty-five bus and took it up to his house on Ulysses Street in the Mount Washington area about three miles from Eagle Rock. He invited me up to meet his parents so I got off with him. I thought, what the hell? There wouldn't be anybody home at my house at that time, anyway. His mother and father were at least as old as, if not older than, my grandparents. Craig had a brother and a sister, who were both married and had kids. His father, Anselmo, was a little

## Down the Foggy Ruins of Time

old Filipino who spoke both Spanish and English with a Filipino accent; his mother, María, was an equally little Mexicana who also spoke Spanish and English, but with a Mexican accent. I stayed and talked with them for a little while, and then I took off down the hill back to Figueroa to catch the bus home.

As I arrived at the corner, a Twenty-five bus was just pulling away. I didn't think it was any big deal, and I decided on the spur of the moment to walk the two miles up to the corner of Figueroa Street and Avenue Sixty in Highland Park, where Mom had a job winding coils. I could catch a ride home with her from there. It wasn't all that far to walk, a straight shot up Figueroa. I kept a lively pace and it only took me about forty-five minutes, making it to Francesca's work place just before five o'clock quitting time. By ten after five we were cruising into Eagle Rock on Figueroa in Mom's fifty-three Ford. Thus ended my first day at Cathedral High School, but it really wasn't my final exit from Eagle Rock. That wouldn't happen for another eleven months when I got a job downtown at Clifton's cafeteria on Olive Street.

# Thirty-three

I'd taken my first step out of Eagle Rock. There would have to be a few more before my escape would be complete, but I think I finally found the identity I'd been searching for since I was three years old. Most of my best buddies were Latinos of one kind or another—one and a half Chicanos, two Filipinos, one Nicaragüense—and not one of them lived within three miles of Eagle Rock. I wasn't necessarily hanging out in their neighborhoods, but as the school year advanced, I found myself spending more of my waking hours in barrios in the city other than Eagle Rock. During the day I was in school, and when it let out, I hung around campus with the guys, or we'd walk down to Chinatown and hang out at Alpine Rec. Center a block from Queen of Angels and shoot some baskets.

One time François and I took the streetcar down to Seventh and Broadway, which, at the time, was Los Angeles' version of Times Square, and the two of us just hung around there for a couple hours. For me, it was a special experience, but naturally, it was no big deal for François because it wasn't even

## Down the Foggy Ruins of Time

a mile out of his own neighborhood. In fact, he was very familiar with the spot; he changed streetcars on that corner every day on his way to school and back home again. As I was boarding the Five Eagle Rock, a Whittier Boulevard streetcar was just pulling to a stop at the safety zone where he was standing.

Most days after school, I got home right at dinnertime. I never saw anybody from grammar school anymore, not even Tommy. Friday nights after dinner I'd head back down and meet the guys on campus, and we'd hop on the school bus and go to the home football games the Phantoms played at Exposition Park down by the Coliseum. We played there because our field on campus didn't have lights. On the nights when there wasn't a game, we'd go to dances in the gym or at Sacred Heart, Loretto or Queens.

One Friday night early in the month of October, some of the guys and I went to one at Loretto. I took the Five car into downtown and met Carlos, François and Wolfgang Benavides at the corner of Broadway and Temple. Wolf was in room 105. He'd been born in Nicaragua, and like me, had moved to Los Angeles when he was very young. He had the darkest complexion of all my new friends. We took a bus up Temple and got off at Alvarado. Marc was waiting for us on that corner, and the five of us walked the two and a half blocks over to Loretto.

After the dance we went to Tommy's over at Beverly and Rampart. We got in the line that curved out into the parking lot, and it took us ten minutes to get to the counter and order our chiliburgers and sodas. Then at a little after midnight, we walked over the hill on Rampart to Temple and took the bus back down to Broadway. Marcky got off at Alvarado and transferred to a bus that took him out Glendale Boulevard and dropped him off fairly close to his house on Fargo Street. The rest of us continued on and got off at Broadway. Those three guys took the Five car south. Wolf took it straight out to his house in Olympic Park near U.S.C. and the Coliseum. The other two guys transferred to the W car at Seventh Street. I waited by myself at Temple and Broadway until about a quarter to one for the northbound Five Eagle Rock. The motorman and I were the only two people left on the streetcar after Division Street in Cypress Park. Then he was alone for the last four blocks of his run after I got off at Eagle Rock and Yosemite. I was the only one on the street at that hour as I walked the half-mile up to the house.

That was a night I didn't want to end and having to go back to Eagle Rock was a big letdown. I'd had such a good time hanging around with guys who had darker complexions than mine (except Carlos, the only other gavacho in the group, with brown hair and brown eyes enlarged by thick prescription glasses, which prompted us to nickname him Mister

## Down the Foggy Ruins of Time

Magoo) in a colorful section of town with texture to spare. It seemed like such an anti-climax to go back to smooth, pale, monotonous Eagle Rock where they all looked like they'd been delivered by the milkman. I'd lived up to the promise I'd made to myself at the beginning of the summer. All the guys I'd met since I'd sequestered myself in the living room with the television were from every section of the city except Eagle Rock. Suddenly, I had no motivation to hang out there anymore. I'd lost interest in the place. John Lennon's response to the reporter who asked him why the Beatles broke up, "boredom," accurately describes my feelings about Eagle Rock at that time in my life.

On the third Sunday afternoon in October, Carlos, François, Craig and I went to see *Rebel Without a Cause* at the State Theater on the corner of Seventh and Broadway. After the movie we went around the corner on Seventh to the Orange Julius stand, and we talked about James Dean over our drinks. We all thought he was so cool in his red windbreaker with the collar turned up, cruising his customized forty-nine Merc. up to the planetarium in Griffith Park. He got killed in a car wreck just three weeks before we saw the movie. What a blow that was! I couldn't believe he was gone. Suddenly he became the main subject of conversation around campus. One day after school, I joined a group of students and Brother Declan, Wolf's homeroom

333

teacher, outside the bookstore, and we talked about James Dean.

"He doesn't act," Brother Declan said. "He only plays himself in his roles."

I thought that was probably true, but I still liked him and liked his acting in the roles he did play. In fact, I was just then entering the stage of my life when I was starting to identify with the likes of Cal Trask and Jim Stark. James Dean was definitely a cool dude, and just as I was starting to get into his scene, he was gone.

In February I went out for spring training with the J.V. baseball team. I made the team but I wasn't a starter and I didn't play enough innings to earn a J.V. baseball letter, but it was a fun season, and it gave me the necessary experience to be in the starting lineup and to get the letter in sophomore year.

My next step out of Eagle Rock was prompted by an event so awful that I completely removed myself mentally from the town after it happened. I stayed there in body only; my mind was already living downtown. It happened one night in February about two weeks into baseball spring training when I went with Bobby Forest and Frank to Yosemite playground. That night left such a bad taste in my mouth that it was absolutely the last time I had anything to do with Eagle Rock. When we got there, Alan Andrade was hanging around the basket-

## Down the Foggy Ruins of Time

ball court shooting some baskets by himself. A couple guys were playing tennis on the court next to the basketball court. We played some games of half-court, Alan and Frank against Bobby and me until a quarter to nine when the park office closed, and the lights went out on the two courts. The two guys had finished their game of tennis about ten minutes before the lights went out. We started getting ready to go home when six punks from Highland Park came through the front gate and over to where we were hanging. The leader, a guy named Snyder, knew Alan and started asking him all kinds of questions about another guy named Crane.

"Go'n'a kick his ass real good when we catch 'im," Snyder said to Alan, who was suddenly looking kind of shaky.

Then all six of them turned and went back out the way they'd come in. We four started to head that way ourselves, and just as we got to the gate, the six punks confronted us and backed us into the playground.

"Hey, Alan," Snyder said, "we just got'a kick some ass tonight, and we figure these guys're as good for it as Crane."

"Ah come on, Snyder. What do you wan'a go and jump these guys for? They didn't do nothin' to you. 'Sides, they're my pals, man."

"Shut your mouth, Al, or I'll throw you in with 'em."

Then they surrounded us and hustled us over to the lawn area on the other side of the clubhouse and office. The lights were still on in the park director's office, so he must have been inside, but I'm sure he couldn't hear anything and didn't know what was going on outside. As Snyder and Alan stood by and watched, two of Snyder's five weasels grabbed my brother and two others grabbed Bobby. The two punks who had Frank, pummeled him to the ground. He tried to cover his head with his arms, and they started kicking and hitting him with chains with locks on the end. Ditto for Bobby, except he managed to get away from his two jerks and run out the side entrance of the park where he sought and got refuge at someone's front door.

The fifth punk started coming after me swinging a chain with a lock on it in circles over his head. I took off, shouting as loud as I could, hoping somebody would hear me, running straight into an enclosed corner of the lawn area. I was running out of room when I heard Snyder over my shoulder calling out to the punk,

"Hey, leave the little kid alone! We're done here, anyway! Let's get the fuck out a' here!"

The footsteps I heard chasing me moments ago were now retreating. When I turned around, Alan was helping Frank get back to his feet. Bobby and all the Highland Park punks were nowhere to be seen. I joined Alan and helped Frank. He was beat

## Down the Foggy Ruins of Time

up pretty bad. His face was all bruised and cut, and he was holding his sides trying to ease the pain in his ribs. Alan went home from there and I helped my brother get to our house. We were both so scared shitless that the adrenaline was pumping, and we were hyperventilating. When we got home, Mom called Louise Forest and found out that Bobby had made it home, but he was pretty beat up, too.

That was the last bad experience I had in Eagle Rock. It was definitely the last time I went out alone after dark there. After that night the only time I'd show up on the street in Eagle Rock after dark was when I walked from my bus stop to my house and vice versa.

The last good experience I had in the town was a couple weeks after Easter when I went by myself to a Saturday matinee at the Sierra Theater. The movie was *Lust for Life*, and it was one of the last pictures shown there before they closed the place down at the end of May. It was fitting that that movie should be the last one I'd ever go to in Eagle Rock. Like *Rebel Without a Cause*, it made a strong impression on me. I couldn't get over how Van Gogh was so tortured and misunderstood; I could relate because I thought I was misunderstood, too. Kirk Douglas and Anthony Quinn both played exceptional roles, and it motivated me to start checking out Vincent Van Gogh and Paul Gauguin.

337

*Jerome Arthur*

My third and final step out of Eagle Rock came at the end of May at a Friday afternoon sock hop at Sacred Heart. That was when and where I met Lana Guerrero. She'd been named after Lana Turner. Her mother was a domestic worker in Lana Turner's next-door neighbor's house during the time she was pregnant with Lana. She became good friends with Carmen Cruz, the actress' own domestic worker and friend. As a result of that friendship, she got to meet and talk to Lana Turner a few times, and she developed a genuine admiration for her, so when her baby was born, she named her after the actress. Lana was a sophomore, and her brother Nestor was a Cathedral freshman in the same homeroom as Wolf.

Lana gave me her phone number, told me to call her soon and I didn't waste any time. I called her mid-morning Saturday, and she invited me over to her house that afternoon. She lived in a small bungalow on Mott Street off Sixth behind Hollenbeck Junior High. The graffiti on the wall of the Water and Power building on the corner of Sixth and Soto identified the neighborhood as El Hoyo Soto. When I got to her house at one o'clock, only she and her older sister, Rachel, were at home.

We sat on her front stoop for a while, and then her sister came out and suggested that the three of us take a walk to the record store down on Whittier Boulevard. As we went down Mott to Whit-tier, Rachel took the lead, and Lana and I trailed along

338

## Down the Foggy Ruins of Time

about fifteen feet behind. In the record store, Lana picked a copy of the Platters' "My Prayer" out of the record rack. I followed her into one of the sound booths and we listened to it before she paid for it. Rachel stayed out in the store looking through the racks. She wound up buying a copy of Frank Sinatra's *Songs for Young Lovers*. It came in a cool little packet that consisted of two forty-fives inside a cardboard cover. Each disk had four songs, two recorded on each side, and each disk was inside its own paper sleeve with pictures and liner notes.

After they got their records, we continued our walk around the block. We went right on Soto and headed back up to Sixth. Rachel continued to lead the way, giving Lana and me time alone together. As we held hands going up the small hill on Sixth alongside the school, she cocked my arm behind my back and pulled me to her, giving me a long, wet French kiss. Then she relaxed her hold slightly and rested her head on my shoulder.

"Where didt you learn that?" she asked.

I was confused by the question. I didn't think I'd done anything, but I replied, "When I was twelve, I was going with a fifteen-year-old girl and she taught me."

She sighed and kept her head on my shoulder until we got back to her house. I hung around with her and her sister till about four o'clock. We listened to "Ain't it a Shame" and some of her other

*Jerome Arthur*

forty-fives. *Songs for Young Lovers* was playing on the record player as I was leaving. I headed back up over Sixth Street to Soto and down to Whittier to wait for the W car into downtown. I was heading back to Eagle Rock one more time, but it was only my body doing it. In my mind I was already out of there. I was all pie-eyed and goofy with the new life I saw lying before me. All my best camaradas were Chicanos, and now my new girlfriend was a Chicana. I had arrived at my destination, and was now immersed en la cultura chicana. As I sat there on the bench waiting for a streetcar, all I could think and feel was, it doesn't get any better than this. I was now poised and ready for my last step out of Eagle Rock, two and a half months hence when I'd get a job in downtown Los Angeles.

The End

1999-2019

## About the Author

Jerome Arthur grew up in Los Angeles, California. He lived on the beach in Belmont Shore, a neighborhood in Long Beach, California, for nine years in the 1960s. He and his wife Janet moved to Santa Cruz, California in 1969. These three cities are the settings for his ten novels.

Made in the
USA
Lexington, KY

54388322R00209